SEVEN
YEARS
of
BAD
LUCK

❧

J.L. MAC

DEDICATION

*For the flightless bluebird who woke from her long slumber
and sprouted new wings.*

CHAPTER ONE

Favorite coffee cups

I sat up in my bed and glanced over at the too bright, green numbers on the cable box to check the time. I was in a time zone two hours behind my best friend, and it was late on a Sunday night, but I had the sudden urge to call her. As cliché as it sounds, Cheyenne Reed was my best friend, and she would be the only one who could possibly understand the mess I was in. Mess was an understatement. My situation felt more like a catastrophe that had lasted a lifetime. She was in Florida, and according to the time, it was two A.M. for her. I knew she was sleeping, but I grabbed my cell phone anyway. Quickly scrolling through my recent calls, I swiped her name with my thumb and waited for the phone to connect while preparing for the unpleasant chat that awaited me. On the third ring she answered in her not-so-happy, half-awake voice.

"HELLO?" She nearly barked at me. I wondered if she had even checked the ID on her phone to see who was calling so late.

"Hey Chey, it's me," I said calmly.

"Ugh, what time is it? Why are you waking me up in the middle of the freakin' night, Kat? What the hell?" Cheyenne was less than pleased with being woken up in the middle of the night, or at any time for that matter. She was infectiously bubbly, giddy even, but if you woke her from sleep, watch out! I, however, was immune to her wake-up attitude. I was, in fact, completely unaffected by it, something which was great for me and, incidentally, our friendship. Most people would probably offer up a few choice words at the sight of her unprovoked laser eyes every morning, but I didn't mind. If being a grump in the morning was my very best friend's only downfall, then I was more than grateful.

"Sorry, sorry. I know it's late. Well, early. Whatever. Anyway, I have to tell you something important" I stuttered out words like a dodgy car only moments from stalling due to a lack of fuel.

"What's so important that you *had* to wake me up instead up just texting me or something in the morning?" She didn't sound very impressed with me so far.

"I moved his coffee cup." I said the words almost as though they were part of some grand conspiracy and had to be spoken in a hushed voice.

"What?" Now she sounded *really* irritated with a side of confused. I pressed on.

"Then it fell and shattered." Cheyenne huffed into the phone making her displeasure with my late night call all the more evident.

"Kat, are you drunk?"

I made my best effort to explain myself.

"Yesterday morning, when I went to get a cup for my coffee, I opened the cabinet and shuffled some cups around looking for *my* favorite cup, and well, I didn't realize what I had done until after I had done it, but I grabbed *his* favorite coffee cup and shoved it up to the top shelf. Anyway, I came back later, and when I opened the stupid cabinet *his* favorite cup fell off the shelf and shattered on the floor." I knew Cheyenne well enough that I could nearly hear her sit up in bed to take in the meaning of what I was trying to say in my inarticulate manner.

"Oh?" She sounded like she was testing my statement with a questioning "oh," but it wasn't really a question.

"Yeah," I said matter-of-factly. This gesture of putting my husband's favorite coffee cup out of sight since he too was often out of sight would seem ordinary to most people, but the fact is, to me it was one giant symbolic representation of the storm brewing within me for the past seven years. The cup breaking all over the floor, sending skittering pieces of glass everywhere only further confirmed what I felt. Cheyenne recognized the coffee cup incident for what it really was, immediately just as I did. She let out a long sigh, now fully awake and no longer sending beautiful ice-blue laser eyes in my direction across a long distance. She asked another question that wasn't really a question, but more a statement.

"So you're done, then?"

"Yeah, I'm done." Without missing a beat, my closest, friend told me she would make arrangements to take a couple days off to fly out and spend a long weekend with me. Cheyenne's career choice had just one perk: she determined her own schedule. Other than that, she hated being a masseuse. It was a bit of a fallback career. She needed the work once her jerk of an ex,

Matt, had asked for a divorce out of the clear blue. She was qualified, and she was a great masseuse; but she always had bigger plans that had yet to come to fruition. She had a ridiculous clientele base, mostly male, and mostly wealthy. However, her drop-dead beautiful looks greatly influenced that, I was sure.

A few days after I told Cheyenne about the coffee cup incident, I was in my car and on my way to pick her up from the airport. It was a Thursday afternoon in the middle of fall in El Paso, Texas, and I bubbled with excitement and nerves at the sight of the airport parking lot. I parked my little Honda that I loved so much, smacked my lips in the mirror after applying a little lip gloss, then strode across the parking lot as fast as my legs would carry me. I was wearing my favorite jeans which were pool-water blue and had this vintage look to them like they had been worn a least a million times and washed just as much. They also had these really great holes across the knees I had put there on purpose. They now had character, with loose light blue threads hanging down from the fair sized holes that exposed each knee cap hidden below the mess of torn, loose thread. Before, they just looked like jeans that had gone through the wringer. With the tattered knees and especially with me wearing them, those jeans more than looked the part. Every time I slipped them on, I could not suppress the thought that they were very symbolic of my life in general. A tangled mess of worn, damaged threads nested around a hole that barely concealed the flesh and bone peeking out from beneath. I chose my favorite brown leather boots and a simple white knit fitted top that didn't overexpose my figure.

I had been lucky enough when drawing from the gene pool

to inherit full breasts, curvy hips, athletic legs, a fair backside, auburn hair, emerald green eyes, and plump lips. As an adult I felt blessed for having the features and form that I did despite the torment I endured as an overdeveloped young girl.

After entering the front entrance of the airport, I made it to Cheyenne's gate just in time to see her face bounce up and down behind a few people blocking her path.

My best friend was not blessed in the height department. She stood a mere 5'1", but I had to give her credit: she knew how to work every inch of that 5 feet. She beamed her super white, toothpaste commercial smile at me while wiggling past the horde of other passengers.

Cheyenne really was gorgeous. Together, we always commanded the attention of others in a room, and it often created more trouble than we would like. We talked a little too loud, laughed too hard, and always had a great time together. She, too, lucked out in the gene department. Other than being rather short, she was undeniably a knockout. She had natural platinum blonde, baby-soft, straight long hair, flawless alabaster skin, the most crystal blue eyes I had ever seen, a superior smile that could reduce any dentist to tears of joy, a curvy body like mine, and toned muscles for which she worked hard. Many women either secretly envied her or just didn't care to hide it and outwardly spewed their bullshit in her direction, venom which we both got a kick out of. We found it shallow, but incredibly entertaining to see grown women act like teenagers. By my own definition, a grown ass teenager is an adult who is stuck in a perpetual state of adolescent behavior. These types of women are almost always shallow, close-minded, and envious of anyone who is better than them in any way. We had actually become quite skilled at laughing off the verbal assaults and evil eyes sent our direction. These women intended their insults to be hurtful and demeaning, and I imagined they would ooze pleasure from every pore at the sight of a few tears or even one of us bolting for the door. However, when we burst into uncontrollable laughter, they really saw red. We had been called every name in the book and have even been accused of some pretty terrible things. We always laughed it off knowing that they were just words, that both of us have had our fair share of real hurt and real tears, and that any of that crap didn't even merit a watery eye or a second thought.

After hugging, jumping up and down, and talking in sentence fragments over each other, we made our way to my car and headed straight for a place where we could get drinks. Sitting down at the bar I knew what was coming because she got that look on her face that told me she was thinking about something.

"Okay, what? Just come out and say what you want to say," I said, dreading the conversation. The bartender took an awkward three seconds too long stare at the both of us, and we both smiled politely thanking him for our drinks but mentally dismissing him from our conversation at the same time.

Cheyenne drew in a short breath and huffed it right back out. Her elbow was propped on the bar, and she rested her chin in her upturned palm. If her goal was to look annoyed and exasperated, she had accomplished it quite well.

"Okay, fine. Where is Aidan?" she asked flatly.

"Um, he has business in California," I replied with the same tone, and there we were like two tennis players serving up bullshit by the mouthful. I stirred my drink with the tiny red straw and kept my eyes turned away from her.

"Have you spoken to him about... you know... the whole coffee cup thing?"

"No. I didn't really plan on explaining that one. He'll think I'm nuts and give me that crazy stare which just makes me want to kick him in the balls and run." I followed up my statement with a shrug and a slight smile. She gave me the same crazy stare for talking about the crazy stare which made both of us erupt into a huge fit of laughter that caught the attention of everyone else at the bar and won us a few dirty looks from the "grown ass teenagers." After we wiped away our tears from laughing and caught our breath, we continued our conversation and cocktails.

"Seriously, Kat, what is the plan? What is going on? Spill it." I knew those were commands disguised as questions from an irritated Cheyenne.

"Well, it's just... I don't know." My shoulders slumped in defeat. I gestured at the bartender for another round and then clasped my hands together hoping that holding my own hands so tight could help me hold onto my sanity a bit longer. Cheyenne squared her shoulders to face me and crossed her arms over her chest.

"Okay, start talking. What the hell has been going on between you two? Did he screw up again? Because I swear, Kat, if he did, I will kill him myself!"

I laughed at her idle threat. Mostly because Cheyenne was so pretty and petite it was hilarious to see her super pissed. A visual image flit through my brain of Cheyenne going head to head with my husband in a physical altercation. Although she could be quite feisty when she needed to be, there would be no contest unless there was a gun, flame thrower, or explosives involved. My husband, Aiden, towered above both of us at 6'4". He was exceptionally tall and lean with a chiseled body of defined muscle. He boasts an all-American-boy smile which he gladly shared with anyone who looked. He was and probably always will be a diehard flirt. Aidan had beautiful blue-gray eyes and ash brown hair that he kept rather short on the sides but longer on top, and he always styled it to look sloppy. His hair going in no specific direction gave him that distinctive look that he either just walked out of the shower or the bedroom. Either scenario was fine by me and plenty of women who laid eyes on him.

Cheyenne rolled her eyes and clicked her tongue. "What has he done this time to make you move his favorite coffee cup, which caused me to fly across the country to be with you? Also, what is the likelihood of me going to jail for assault?" I nodded and gave her an endearing smile, knowing full well that she was serious about the jail part.

"Well, it's just that with everything that he's done in the past seven years, it feels like I am at the end of my rope." I furrowed my brows thinking aloud about the disaster that had been my marriage. "He has betrayed my trust so many times, it just feels like irreparable damage now. He has done enough to take down three or four marriages. Honestly, I'm not sure how we made it this long. He is just so damned charming; he knows what buttons to press to reel me back in every time. My missing backbone certainly doesn't help." I audibly scoffed at myself, and it came out sounding more like a mixture of a disapproving cluck and a gag. I actually felt repulsed with who I had become and how much time I had wasted at Aidan's side. I took another long sip of my cocktail and absentmindedly spun a napkin around on the bar.

"Well, has he had another affair?"

"Not that I know of, but I haven't been digging. I'm just too tired to deal with it, Chey. I'm not going to snoop around like some private detective all my life." I shrugged and glanced at Cheyenne. She looked at me with sympathetic blue eyes, and I instantly felt the sting of looming tears. The lump in my throat grew exponentially, and it was hard to discern if it was the alcohol or my circumstances that were making me so emotional. A couple of fat tears rolled down my cheeks.

"I don't even know how I got to this point. I'm such an idiot." My voice was weak and quiet. I shook my head slowly from side to side as I looked down. The weight of the shame and embarrassment I felt was crushing.

"Hey. Don't do that to yourself." She reached over and placed her hand on my shoulder as she kept talking.

"You loved him, and you got lost somewhere along the way. That doesn't make you an idiot. It makes you human."

"No, but tossing myself and all my dreams into the trash and staying with him for so long definitely makes me an idiot, Chey." She didn't respond to my self-deprecating dialogue.

"Kat, I only want you to be happy. Is this what you want? Because divorce is ugly and painful, and it's going to leave a nasty scar. Are you ready to walk away?"

I knew I had two options. I could either stay with my husband and just cope with having to share him with God-only-knows how many women and possibly never get myself together or gather what was left of my dignity and walk away from seven years of nothing but bad luck with a little hope. I knew what I had to do. After the coffee cup incident, I found myself doing a body check similar to the motion that a person makes when she is in some type of accident. Except my check was more of an emotional inventory.

Heart? Broken. Brilliant.

Ego? Seriously wounded. Great.

Self-confidence? What's that? Oh joy.

Dignity? Little to none. Excellent.

Self-worth? No habla ingles! Ah shit.

I escaped that thought, and I turned in my seat to square my shoulders with Cheyenne's; then I tossed back some words she once spoke to me.

"It's over. I have to leave him. What choice do I have?"

CHAPTER TWO

Victory lap

My extended weekend with Cheyenne flew by entirely too fast just as I had anticipated. She and I spent the majority of our time in the kitchen and in the living room. We were in our element simply hanging around the countertops of my kitchen, whipping up fine culinary works of art. We sampled each creation that rolled out of the oven and off of the stove and basked in the contentment that our time in the kitchen always brought. We talked about everything and nothing all at once. We confronted demons from the past and hopes for the future. We laid to rest all-consuming regrets and dreamed up new adventures. We laughed uncontrollably at inside jokes that only she and I shared, and we cried while sharing memories of painful times that only she and I were witness to. She was perhaps the only person with whom I had shared all my hopes, secrets, dreams, and nightmares. Our friendship was a valued outlet, an outlet that was dependable and safe. Those two things didn't really exist for me outside of my close bond with her.

I had to give her credit. She was highly skilled in a kitchen. Watching her in her element brought a painful reminder that as far as I knew, my dearest friend had set aside her goal of a self-owned and operated bakery indefinitely. I had fought her tooth and nail over that sacrifice to no avail. Although she did well as a masseuse, I knew it was a far cry from her passion, her dream. I made a mental note that weekend to confront her once again about the bakery.

After driving her to the airport and saying some quick goodbyes, I returned to my dreadfully quiet house. When I met her, quite by accident, I never would have guessed that we would have become such close friends. We were both living in Denver, Colorado at the time. Aidan was in real estate development and had been offered a great position in the mile high city. Cheyenne had been living there with her now ex-husband, Matt, who held a job as an accountant for a major ad firm. I was the 'new neighbor,' and Cheyenne was the accommodating, friendly neighbor. We hit it off immediately, mostly since we were both born and raised in southern states. My being a Texas girl and her a Florida girl, we had more than enough in common, including the Gulf of Mexico. Two years in Colorado came and went, and Cheyenne's marriage came to a sudden halt one day after Matt's request for a divorce. She did not do much to fight him over it. She had too much dignity for that, and I understood her reluctance to fight for a marriage to a man who adamantly refused her. I asked her if she was going through with the divorce, and she spat out the words that I eventually shot back at her years later.

It was months later that we discovered the reason for Matt's request. Her name was Monica, and she was a real piece of work. It was all I could do just to keep Cheyenne from going after the little hussy with a baseball bat. We later heard that Monica cheated on Matt and got knocked up—on accident of course. Matt ditched her, and so did the mystery sperm donor. *Well played, Karma,* I thought to myself. The night we heard the news, we shared the thrill of silent victory over a really great bottle of wine... or two.

We drank and laughed, and I imagined the two of us hauling ass around a professional racetrack for our victory lap. I could see us jumping out of our cars, popping open expensive bottles of champagne, and shaking them obnoxiously. I pictured confetti raining down around us and camera flashes going off wildly like seizure-inducing strobes. Revenge was sinfully sweet on my lips. I thoroughly enjoyed the thought of this Monica woman being miserable as part of some kind of cosmic reparation for hurting my dear friend. I felt guilty about my vengefulness for all of two seconds before the guilt fled and contentment flooded back in. It felt like this wrong in the universe had righted itself. It was a great feeling and I made sure that I lapped up every drop of it while it lasted.

With only a couple of hours alone to gather my thoughts before Aidan would be returning from his business trip, I was scrambling to compose myself. He had always been incredibly determined, ambitious, and clever. If I let him see that I had undergone a grand epiphany with the help of some favorite coffee cup, he would quickly start bringing down my defenses. Even if I put up a fight against his persuasion, he would pull out all the stops when necessary, and according to my track record, I always was terrible at refusing him when he started his charming onslaught.. I was in need of a game plan. I decided that impassive would be my best bet. That routine could buy me some time if I did it right. If Aidan was unable to read my body language and facial expressions, he couldn't manipulate me so easily. He would be hung out to dry and likely just grasp at straws to get back on my good side.

Not working this time, I insisted to myself.

He was so well practiced at this stupid game of battle of the wills. I found it quite repulsive that my life had been reduced to playing head games with the man I called my husband. How lame of a life I must've led. I often reminded myself that cheap used car salesmen often bore some of these same qualities. I couldn't count how many times I had imagined him in a cheap cowboy hat, lousy three piece polyester suit (as cheap as the hat), and crap boots, reeking of a raunchy cologne. I could imagine him in the whole get-up attempting to dupe me into buying some shit car for a rock-bottom price! Aidan was just as bad as a con man. He just made the packaging so damn appealing that it was easy to get haggled into a shit deal built out of a foundation of lies and deceit. He knew how to dress something up to look way better than it actually was. I always wondered if he ever truly felt guilt. Guilt for all the lies. Guilt for all the women. Guilt for dragging me through it all. Mostly I wondered if he had guilt for breaking my spirit or if he even noticed that I had become so different from the woman he fell in love with.

Stupid, I know.

When Aidan pulled his car into our driveway, I immediately felt the butterflies and had a split second of doubt. I heard the slide of the deadbolt on our front door. and I looked up for just a moment. There he was. My husband was standing there in all his boy-next-door glory. His all-American smile spread across his clean-shaven face, his eyes sparkling at me, and his scent. Oh, that man had a scent that could render any women's panties soaked with arousal. I sat on the living room couch doing my best to appear lost in the book I wasn't really reading. I was actually staring at the same line on the page for what felt like hours and cussing myself on the inside for being so easily swayed by his mere presence. He hadn't even uttered a word yet, and I could feel the grip on my determination slipping.

Kathleen Cooper, get a grip on yourself. PRONTO!

I looked up again from my book whose name I could not even remember. He shot a full smile in my direction, a smile which was, of course, a battering ram against my defenses. The reinstated inner voice of reason that had eluded me for years was back in effect.

I have his number; I know his game. I won't give in. I won't give in, I chanted inwardly.

I gave him the phoniest, plastered-on smile I could, and he picked up on it instantly. His eyebrows furrowed only slightly before he quickly smoothed away any telling expressions that would reveal him. He knew my smile was forced, and he sensed the nervous tension pouring out of me.

"Hello, my love. You're a sight for sore eyes." Hearing his voice sent a tingle up my spine.

Shit!

"Hey, how was your trip?" I was going for neutral ground in hopes of derailing any of his plans for the night. I could see that look in his eyes as he gave me an up-and-down gaze that dripped of his intentions. He made no effort to hide it either.

"My flight was fine, and the trip went well. I am sure glad to be home, though." I pressed on with my shield-o-scorned woman in place.

"Want some coffee?"

So far, so good, I thought to myself.

"No, what I want—I already have, and she's sitting right in front of me." I glanced up at him and saw the most mischievous look on his face as he leaned back on the sofa across from me.

Oh, damn—spoke too soon.

"Come sit with me." He gave his thigh a pat with his hand indicating where he wanted me. I scrambled around in my stupid brain for a lifeline and came up with nothing.

Shit, damn, shit!

I hated this man for being so irresistible to me. He easily wielded his pull over me to manipulate my willpower, and it almost always infuriated me as soon as I was able to think straight again.

"Um, my cup is empty, I'm going to grab a refill."

I could tell I was screwed, both figuratively and literally. Aidan smirked, his way of laying his cards on the table and letting me know that he was aware of my pathetic attempt to fight him off and that he was ready to charm his way in. Seeing that smirk also reminded me that Aidan enjoyed the challenge and was looking forward to the hunt to get me into bed and back to following his every command like a sad little puppy. I used to be just as confident as he was. I used to be brazen, strong-willed, and opinionated. I don't even know when the old Kathleen died, much less realized she was on her way out. Had I known what was becoming of me, I think I would have fought; I think the true Kathleen would have refused to be snuffed out. I think I ignored the loss of my true self until recently, and when I realized the horrific truth, I found myself mourning for the death of the person I used to be. I liked who I was. I liked being a strong, determined woman. I was who I was, take it or leave it, and whether a person liked me or not, I slept just fine at night.

Years had passed with Aidan and that Kathleen had long since been replaced with a new me. The Kathleen that I found myself looking at in the mirror was someone that I disliked so very much. I have always felt like a person's self-worth is invaluable, and the sad truth is I not only allowed Aidan to rob me of my self-worth, I practically handed it over, lock, stock and barrel. I became inwardly bitter and resentful towards him, but mostly towards myself for being such a fake. I had dismissed my dreams and aspirations. I had held my tongue when I usually wouldn't have. This Kathleen was not at all me, and I despised the pathetic excuse for a woman I had become. I hated her for being weak. I hated her for caring too much. I hated her for even existing. I felt short-changed, betrayed, not just by Aidan, but also by my own treasonous self for allowing me to become some sacrificial lamb with a slit throat, bleeding out its life source with each passing second. Aidan's betrayals and affairs had hurt, but nothing hurt me more than the realization that I had long ago given up on being myself. I had quit fighting, and worse—I had bought into the bullshit that my life was fine and that I was happy. Aidan didn't do the convincing; he didn't really have to. I did. He simply bid, played his hand, and watched me bluff myself into oblivion.

As I walked back into the living room after getting coffee, I saw Aidan sitting comfortably on the couch with his suit jacket off, tie undone and set aside, and his fresh white dress shirt unbuttoned to halfway down his chest. I made eye contact with him, which was a monumental mistake on my part because his eyes screamed "come hither." He didn't have to utter a word; he had me so under his thumb that my hand set down my coffee mug, much to my brain's protest.

Pathetic zombie lady, I taunted myself inwardly, knowing precisely where the night was going.

I approached him on the couch and shuffled onto his lap. He swept the palm of his hands down my sides sending a shiver through me. "I've missed you." He has always been so good at whispering just the right thing in just the right way into my ear, sending stealthy words slithering right through my ear canal into my brain, turning it into instant pudding. *Security breach* is what I called that. With my defenses down, he knew he was able to make me submit. I was a pliable mass of female hormones who had a one track mind when I was in Aidan's grasp. I was so easily dragged into his web of seduction. Fighting against it would only drive him to continue, and I would be more entangled in his web. I submitted to him as I always did.

I didn't even bother trying to speak. I had learned enough by now that avoiding stuttering and stammering like an incoherent moron was well worth keeping my mouth shut. Trying to argue with his sex appeal was so beyond stupid that even my feeble pudding mush brain knew to just keep quiet. I knew the routine all too well after seven years together. Mouth shut, legs open, brain liquefied, same old song and dance. I kissed him back when he put his hand on the nape of my neck and pulled me to him. My lips touched his and all plans of resisting him flew out of the window. I wiggled on his lap to get more comfortable and then unbuttoned his shirt the rest of the way. I removed his cuff links, set them aside, and leaned into him.

We were chest to chest and face to face. I could smell his scent, and that made my liquefied brain evaporate. Leaning in closer to his neck, I ran my nose across his skin taking in his sensual scent like a drug. We didn't speak. Aidan had both of his hands gripping my hips as he pulled me tightly against him. His lust-filled eyes stayed on me. I could feel his arousal beneath me, and I was fully intoxicated with him. I was so drawn to him physically that he rarely had to do much of anything at all to get me beneath him. We were terrible with our marriage, but we always did intimacy really, really well. It was the medicine that alleviated our ailing commitment.

He sat on the couch with me in his lap watching the magic he conjured work me over on his behalf. I was like a sex zombie, a woman with one need, one desire driving her actions. My desire was currently planted under my undulating hips. Aidan dug his fingers into my hips and rocked our hungry bodies towards each other. He pressed his erection against me through the fabric that separated us. In a frantic daze of need for his body to be on me, in me, and around me, I slid his shirt off his shoulders and tossed it to the side. I leaned forward and peppered his shoulders, neck and chest with soft kisses and gentle nips from my teeth. He groaned as I worked him into a fever pitch. I cupped his head in my hands and kissed him hard then trailed off to his ear lobe. He let out a groan that sent my need for him into overdrive. I slid off his lap while holding his heated gaze. He leaned forward from the couch were he sat, lifted my shirt to my breasts and pressed his lips to my stomach just below my navel.

I stood between his knees while he remained seated. He easily removed my pants while I slipped off my shirt. I stood before him in only my bra and panties while he held a firm grip on my hip with one hand and his other hand softly danced up the inside of my leg, beginning at my calf and ending at the sensitive junction between my thighs. I was all too eager to have him. In a few easy movements, Aidan stripped me of my bra and panties and had me sitting on the edge of the coffee table in front of him. He nudged my legs apart then perched my heels on the couch cushion in front of me. My legs caged him. I couldn't wait any longer. He had me hungry and desperate to have him, shit marriage be damned. He smirked as he lowered himself down on his knees. He kissed the inside of my leg starting at my knee and worked his way up, then back down the other. He came back to my center and ran a long finger through my wet folds, causing me to let out a needy moan.

"Please," I begged of him. He grinned arrogantly at his handy work.

"That's my girl." Before I could beg him any further, his mouth landed on my hot, wet center, and I gasped as I let my head fall back. His tongue slid over my flesh and lazily stroked my sensitive center. His tongue plunged into me over and over, then he turned his attention to my throbbing clitoris. He stroked me there in a circular motion, then slid two long fingers into me. He worked me over for what felt like a minute or two before I shuttered and quivered with his face between my thighs expertly drawing out my orgasm. Aidan sat back on our couch and waited for what he knew I would do next. As soon as I came down from bliss I got down to my knees and made quick work of getting his dress pants off of him, but first I crouched a bit to take off those gleaming Oxfords of his. I took off the left shoe and sock first, then promptly went over to the right. I needed those pants off soon, or I would combust. I could see his chest rising and falling with his rapid breath, his eyes locked onto me watching every move I made. His erection pressed against his pants and boxer briefs, waiting to be freed. I tugged off the right shoe, and he raised his foot slightly to allow me to remove his sock, and that's when something caught my attention. My eyes zeroed in on something stuck to the bottom of his right sock. It was small, shiny and metallic looking. At the sight of it, I felt lightning course through my body, instantly reviving my hibernating brain, and with what felt like a clap of thunder reverberating through my ears, I jerked the sock off his foot. I instantly stood, incriminating sock in hand, leaned forward over him with wide eyes, heart pounding furiously, my stomach dropping when I made eye contact with him. The feeling is eerily similar to being punched hard in the gut and instantly made me want to double over and vomit.

"Should I even entertain any explanation for this shit, or should I just cram the evidence down your throat and let you choke on it?" His eyes grew wide, and his skin instantly paled. Tell-tale signs of a busted cheater. I may have become a hollow, poor excuse for the woman I used to be, but one perk of being married to a man like Aidan was I had become a human lie detector. There was no getting past me. I could read a person with ease. I was forced to hone this skill into a reliable tool over the years.

"What are you talking about Kathleen? If you're looking for a fight tonight, you're going to have to take it elsewhere because I'm exhausted and I'm in no mood to deal with any of your shit!"

I snatched up my clothes from the floor and dressed in a record time. I had to give him credit for the nearly believable attitude he was putting out. Good thing I always dismissed his mouth when I had to confront him, or anytime it was moving really.

"You're a real piece of work, Aidan. So what number is this one? Good job using protection, though. Safety first!" I was a few notches above sarcastic and teetering on full-fledged taunting.

"I mean, seeing part of the foil condom wrapper clinging to bottom of your sock? It's stuck there along with all the other dirt and scum you step in like a nasty little secret. It is so beyond ironic don't you think?" I stood in front of him with his sock in one hand while my other hand moved all about with animated hand gestures. He was temporarily speechless, and I could see his brain working at an explanation and/or a distraction.

"You are so damned determined to catch me doing something wrong! I could have picked that up on my sock anywhere." The moment that poorly formed and rather unbelievable explanation slipped out of his mouth, I could tell he wanted to kick himself for it.

"Wow, you're losing your edge, my dear. For someone who has been extremely successful, thanks to his smarts and killer instincts, you can't seem to be smart enough to avoid getting caught cheating. At any rate it doesn't really matter because I'm done." I tossed the sock at him. Aidan looked at me warily and began gathering the clothes he had shed while I stood before him with my arms crossed casually.

"Let me clue you in, Aidan. You have spent nearly our entire marriage screwing around behind my back, and you have caused me terrible pain. While you were off sampling the female population out in California, I had a small revelation." I whispered the last part of the sentence, feigning shock and awe.

"I realized that I am just as shattered as our marriage, and I can't stand the sight of you because of what you've done, and I can't stand the sight of me because I stuck around and let it happen. I'm done." I stayed put in front of him with my arms crossed, and I made sure to keep up a cool exterior. He cocked his head and narrowed his eyes on me.

"So you can take your dirty socks and get the hell out. I'm done with being the mindless little peon wife living in the shadows." I turned away from him and slipped on my flip flops then turned back to him.

"Oh and Aidan, don't worry about not having me to keep your bed warm, you will always have that huge-ass ego of yours to keep you company."

He sat back down on the couch with his mouth gaping wide in shock at my words, and I didn't even allow him the opportunity to respond before I spun around, snatched my purse, and headed out of our the front door with thoughts of winners' circles, champagne, confetti and Cheyenne on my mind. I couldn't help but think about my seven years with him being nothing but bad luck. Like a curse of sorts. I asked myself what I could have possibly done to deserve this.

Geez Kat! You must have really been a screw up in a past life. I chuckled out loud at that thought and drove away from the home I had made with Aidan—feeling very liberated.

Stressful months had passed and my split from Aidan went ahead full steam, I kept thinking about my less than good fortune in the love department. I came to the conclusion that my crap marriage was likely my own doing. They say if you break a mirror, you will have seven years of bad luck. I don't think I had ever broken an actual mirror, but I definitely peered into a metaphorical mirror and saw myself reflected in true form. I was strong, willful, unbridled. I allowed the person whom I knew as me to be broken, shattered, and forgotten. My heart and soul had been beaten into submission by circumstance and blinding lust. The person whom I saw reflected after that was a distorted, lackluster impostor. My conclusion was that I deserved my bad luck for sacrificing myself.

Way to go Kat.

CHAPTER THREE

Happy birthday

May, 11th, 2013. Day 214 since the dirty sock disaster. I sat down on the living room floor of my new place and allowed my exhausted muscles a moment of rest despite the fact that I really didn't have time for rest. I was in a bit of a rush to get settled. I had job interviews lined up, and Cheyenne would be arriving the following day. Seven months had passed since I marched out of the home that I shared with Aidan. Seven months that brought with them major changes to my life. Less than a month after kicking Aidan to curb, I turned twenty-six. I found it extremely comical that I managed to ruin my own birthday by deciding to dive head-first into a nasty split with Aidan only weeks before my birthday. It was all very fitting, though. Every birthday that I celebrated with him at my side was miserable for one reason or another.

In all my eighteen-year-old wisdom, I had accepted his proposal, much to my parent's disbelief. I was their golden child, though they would never admit to it. I don't think my three older brothers would appreciate the favoritism. I was the youngest of the four children, and I was the only girl. It was a true perk. Being the only girl *and* the baby of the family allowed for a bounty of rule bending. My three older brothers made sure to compensate for that. I was tortured, teased, nagged, coerced, blackmailed, and pushed around on a daily basis. However, having three older brothers did have an upside. If anyone in the neighborhood dared to mess with me, I had my own troop of bodyguards who didn't mind in the slightest scuffing up any other kid on our block. I later realized how ridiculous it was that my brothers could taunt me endlessly, reducing me to seething angry tears, but they were damned if anyone else tried to take pleasure in this favorite pastime of theirs. I would later be very glad for the childhood that thickened my skin. My ability to be tough when I need to be is part of the reason I am not dead.

Birthdays nineteen through twenty-six were all complete shit! My nineteenth birthday, my first as Aidan's wife, was spent alone, since he was away on business. I sat alone to blow out a singular candle on a store-bought cupcake in our scarcely furnished apartment in Chicago, Illinois. I had been married all of four months at that point and was a southern girl living in a big city miles and miles from home. I found myself missing Texas and the Gulf coast where I was raised.

My childhood home had overlooked the bay and allowed for a breathtaking view of the water. I longed for the salty gulf breeze from the water. Every evening when the sun was low in the sky painting the horizon with vibrant hues of purple, pink, yellow, and orange, the sea breeze would pick up. It came from nowhere and was a steady wind that easily kept the hair swept from your neck. It was strong and gentle, cool and warm all at once. In Chicago I was way out of my comfort zone. I was young and alone in a new place with not a single friend to call my own. I didn't even bother singing 'Happy Birthday' to myself that year. I had thought about it for a fraction of a second but instantly felt more depressed at the thought. I settled for a mumbled, "Happy birthday, Kat. Make a wish." I licked the icing off the cupcake, ate half of it, threw the rest in the garbage, showered and went to bed, alone and homesick. That night I had vivid dreams of saltwater and painted skies.

My twentieth birthday was not much different, except for the fact that Aidan and I were at a very bad place in our marriage. He was distant and cold. I overheard him on the phone talking to his mother one day just two weeks before my birthday. I was not sure what the conversation was about until I heard the fateful words that bit at my heart like a wild animal feasting on its prey. He paced the back patio of our townhome, and as I went to open the door to find him, I heard the words. "Mom, I'm just not sure I even love her anymore." My guts had twisted with disgust. My heart's steady pace turned it into an erratic thud, one which reminded me of a pinball machine. My ears had filled with a ringing noise, and the room spun. I never knew words could screw a person up so much. I backed away from the door as if it were moments away from attacking me.

A week passed, and by then, the tension between us was like a third entity living in our home. He finally gained the nerve to inform me that he wanted "a break." I was heartbroken when I called my mom to tell her what was going on. Within an hour of the phone call, I was informed that my oldest brother, Dalton, and my father were flying out to retrieve me.

The very next morning, my dad's and Dalton's rental car pulled into the drive. I greeted them at the front door. My father pushed past me and disappeared into the house. He came back out a moment later with my things in hand. He tossed my things in the trunk, and we were off to the airport, booked for a southbound flight to Texas. My twentieth birthday came and went during my time in Texas. I was with family, but depressed nonetheless. I didn't understand why Aidan had shoved me out of our home. My mom was the one who started digging. She gained access to our cell phone account and printed three month's worth of bills including call logs. It was she who called me to the dining table and slid a highlighter-riddled stack of papers in my direction. After seeing the evidence of Aidan's deception, my depression got worse. I confronted him about it, and that's when I discovered he had been having an affair with a woman I knew and had even invited into my home. After only four weeks in Texas, Aidan convinced me that he was sorry, and he needed me home. I gave in to his request and flew home.

Stupid girl.

My twenty-first birthday had been shit too. We were living in Denver, Colorado by that time. Aidan had taken a job offer that was a huge step up from his position in Chicago. I had only just met Cheyenne, and we had yet to develop a close friendship. I was once again alone in a new place in a new city with no friends or family. Aidan's betrayals had been taking a toll over the two and a half years we had been together. Looking back, I recognized that the real me had already begun slipping away by then. I had decided to keep my family in the dark about my marriage. If I had let on how many times he was fooling around behind my back and how hurt I was, my family would all go postal and demand that I leave him. They certainly would have been disgusted at the knowledge of how I was beginning to lose myself.

Simply put, I chose Aidan over myself. I let Kathleen slip into the dark recesses of my life. I was buried alive in lies and lust with no lifeline in sight. Aidan went on a business trip the day before my twenty-first birthday. He had been gone for four days. My parents offered to fly out for my big day, but I told them not to. I was in no shape for a masquerade. I once again blew out a single candle on a store-bought cupcake. "Happy birthday, Kathleen. Make a wish."

Icing. Half of the cupcake. Garbage. Shower. Bed. Cry. In that order. I no longer dreamed of home. In fact I had stopped dreaming during sleep altogether. I thought it peculiar, but didn't dwell on it.

My twenty-second birthday was sad. Aidan was not on a business trip this time, but my birthday was terrible for entirely different reasons. Over the year between my twenty-first and twenty-second birthday, the Kathleen that I knew myself to be my entire life slid into an abyss. She was gone. I didn't recognize it fully at the time, likely because the thought of the whole tragic scenario was too much to take. Ignorance is bliss more often than not, and I clung to my ignorance like a life raft on turbulent seas.

Aidan's behavior continued, of course. I had school as a distraction from my depressing private life, but I knew I would not be a student forever. Graduation was looming, and I would be done with my bachelor's degree and applying to law school.

I embraced a fake version of myself that was much more suited to the pathetic life I led. I completed college and earned my degree. I scored well on the LSAT and applied to law school. I was accepted, but lacked the ambition to continue. I gave up my dream of becoming a lawyer. So I became a lesser version of what I wished to be: a paralegal. Being a paralegal allowed me to go to work in the field I loved. However, my unfulfilling life was always the first and last thought I had upon waking every morning and before sleeping each night. I was consumed with sadness that I kept secret. Five days before my twenty-second birthday, we received a phone call that informed us that Aidan's younger sister had been involved in a car accident and had died at the scene. We immediately flew out to be with his family. She was laid to rest on my birthday. The entire thing reminded me painfully of my own internal death. She had been put into the ground, and subconsciously I think I laid the true Kathleen to rest that day as well. I didn't even bother to wish myself a happy birthday.

If there is something that Aidan and I have always done well— regardless of circumstances or the condition of our marriage—it was intimacy. We had always been very attracted to each other and enjoyed each other in the bedroom. The only bit of me that always remained was my libido and attraction to him. I knew he used this against me, but I honestly didn't care. I had nothing else. I was hollow and miserable in nearly every aspect of my life. I might as well indulge in the one thing I did enjoy. The August after Aidan's sister passed away I became deathly ill with walking pneumonia. I felt awful and was sick for a solid month. It wasn't until October that I discovered that I had become pregnant. Apparently antibiotics and birth control pills don't mix. I told Aidan over the phone while he was away, yet again. He seemed excited, and I had this sinking feeling of anxiety and panic that this life inside me would be a permanent ball and chain tying me to Aidan. I immediately felt guilty for feeling that way about this little life growing within me. It wasn't my child's fault that I chose to be with a man who shared himself with any female who would have him. I resented Aidan for being the catalyst to these dreadful thoughts. When I told Cheyenne about the pregnancy, she, too, was nervous for me. She put on a good show of being congratulatory and happy, but I could tell she had the same thoughts as I did.

My twenty-third birthday is one I will never forget. I had been seven weeks pregnant and had warmed up considerably to the idea of being a mom. I think I may have even gotten a bit excited. Aidan was away on business, but had decided to come home early from the trip to surprise me. I had actually thought that maybe the birthday curse was over. This birthday felt like it might actually be okay. I was stupid to let my guard down and to be excited about anything that could be stripped from me in one fell swoop.

Aidan's intentions of making my twenty-third birthday a special one were good. Little did he know that his actions didn't make my day special—- they made it a painful memory that I would never forget. He came home a day early and had plans to take me to dinner for my birthday. He greeted me as usual and informed me he had a great surprise for me the following day. After a brief discussion about his business trip, he went off to the master suite to shower. While Aidan was in the bathroom, I heard his cell phone ringing from its spot on the kitchen counter. Normally I wouldn't bother with his phone, but he had told me he was expecting a call from his mom and that if she called, to answer it. I scurried to the kitchen and grabbed his cell without even glancing at the ID. I answered it. That's when I heard a woman on the other end of the line, a woman who was definitely not my mother-in-law. I didn't even have to ask her name because she made a point to be quick about informing me of who the hell she was. Her name was Caroline, and I could practically hear her smug face contort into an evil smile. She went on to inform me that she had been having an affair with my husband for two months, and she intended to make it a much more 'permanent' arrangement, so I should simply bow out gracefully seeing how my marriage was already crap.

My head spun, and my gut churned. I told her to go screw herself and hung up. I had never been verbally accosted by any of Aidan's little hussies. This woman had made my skin crawl with her arrogant tone. Perhaps I had felt threatened by her. Maybe I thought that she could perhaps steal away Aidan from me, leaving me to be a single mother. I saw red at the thought of it. I slammed my fist down on the counter with so much force, my arm shuddered at the vibrating pain that shot up to my shoulder. The next moments of my life are a blur.

I had barged into the bathroom, ripped open the shower curtain and launched Aidan's cell phone at him. He shot evil eyes in my direction and growled obscenities at me. I made sure to explain that Caroline had just called and was more than eager to take my place, to be married to him and all his bullshit. He began making his way from the shower towards me. He grabbed my left arm, and I jerked away from his grasp. I felt pure rage, uninhibited fury. I wanted to attack him, but refrained from such a thing since I would never want to harm my sweet little baby. He was still in the bathroom scrambling for a towel when I bolted out of the front door, keys in hand. I jumped into my car and sped out of the driveway. I was so enraged at Aidan for hurting me so badly and for his piece on the side having the nerve to tell me to 'bow out gracefully' that I never saw it coming. I never even had a chance to react. Even if I could have reacted to the collision, I'm not sure my efforts would have yielded a different result.

I was driving through a green light at an intersection near the interstate. and apparently a drunk driver barreled through his red light and hit my compact car broadside. I was told my car had flipped to its side and skid across the intersection. I don't recall anything but a very loud noise, then darkness. I can vaguely remember a scent. It was a distinct scent. It was a combination of a few elements. I could smell burned rubber, exhaust from a car, smoke that smelled like burned plastic, and the vague scent of blood.

I awoke in the hospital the following day. Everything was blurry, and I was very confused as to what was going on. I saw Aidan sitting beside my bed with his head bowed. I willed my eyelids to open more and blink to clear the fog. I whimpered at the pain that simply blinking caused me. My head felt strangely detached and large, and my brain pulsed loudly in my ears. Aidan must have heard the whimper escape my throat because his head shot up from his hands, and I immediately noticed he looked tired, disheveled.

"Aid—" I couldn't make my mouth form a word. My throat hurt; it felt like I had swallowed sandpaper.

"Hush! Don't talk. Try to relax. I'll get a nurse."

A nurse? Shit! I really am in a hospital. What the hell happened?

The nurse came into my room, followed by Aidan. He stood

in the corner of the room as though he was afraid I would bite him. I couldn't understand the look of fear on his face. The nurse checked my vital signs, then left to find my doctor. Aidan still had a look of trepidation on his face. His body looked rigid. I had never seen him like that. I began to worry, wondering why he was behaving that way. I wondered what was going through that head of his. What did he know that I didn't? He made his way across the room back to my bedside, but his stride was hesitant. This definitely was not the supremely confident man I knew him to be.

"What's wrong?" He barely had a chance to sit before I started in with the inquisition.

"Kathleen, you were in a car accident. Do you remember any of it?"

"Well, I... uh... I'm not sure; my head is so foggy. What happened?" My mind began to reel with blurry flashes that I assumed were memories.

"You just took off, Kathleen! You took off so fast, I didn't have a chance to talk to you about... her." I could tell he was on pins and needles as he spoke to me.

"Oh, yes. I DO remember that!" The snap I put into my tone exerted more energy than I currently had to expend, and it made my head throb fiercely.

"Kathleen, I'm so sorry. I screwed up bad. That woman—"

"Caroline, is THAT woman's name. But surely you already know that, Aidan. You have always been great with names, especially if they are female names. How long have you been screwing her?" My anger momentarily made me forget the pain coursing through my body.

"Yes, Kathleen, I know her damned name. I haven't... I

only... it's been about two months." He hung his head in what looked like shame, but I knew better. That wasn't shame; that was embarrassment for having gotten caught. "Listen, Kathleen, we can discuss that situation later. Right now I want to talk about your accident." He drew in a huge breath of air and expelled it. "Kathleen, you were hurt pretty bad you know? You have a concussion, three broken ribs, a broken ankle, and... Kathleen... you, the baby..." He hung his head again in what appeared to be genuine sadness, guilt even. My heart stopped at the word.

Baby.

In the fog of waking up and trying to figure out what had happened and of course being so damn consumed with Aidan, as usual, I had forgotten about being seven weeks pregnant. I gasped, and tears welled up when I realized that he was trying to tell me something horrible. I began shaking. "No. No! Aidan! Tell me! Tell me now!"

"Kathleen, you lost the baby. The impact of the accident was really rough; your car is totaled; you could have died Kat, and... the... baby, the baby, it was just... the baby is gone." He hung his head again. I felt an immediate sense of emptiness and loss. I felt violated beyond words. My eyes welled and spilled over with unstoppable streams of tears. He tried to touch my hand, and I withdrew faster than I should have because my body made its protest known with sharp, piercing spears of pain.

"This is your fault. Get out." My voice was a monotone whisper.

"Kathleen, please..."

Is this man seriously begging me right now? He robbed me of the most precious thing I have ever been given and he wanted to beg me? For what? More? More of what? I had nothing.

"GET OUT." My clipped tone must have roused his attention because his brows rose in shock, he had tears in his blue eyes, and his mouth hung open as if words failed him for the first time in his life.

"OUT! NOW!" I bit out my demand with a level of seething fury that I didn't know even existed. He let out a sigh of resignation.

"I'm so sorry Kathleen. I will be outside if you need me. I won't leave you here." His shoulders slumped in defeat.

"I did need you, but right now I don't even know if I want you. Go!" I didn't even acknowledge my birthday that year. I went home and allowed my physical wounds to heal. I needed Aidan and Cheyenne, almost around the clock, for everything. If not for my physical wounds, I needed someone to help mend the emotional trauma. I healed— physically.

My twenty-fourth birthday was miserable of course. So was my twenty-fifth birthday. Nothing catastrophic happened, but I celebrated with just Cheyenne and two cupcakes. I was lucky to have a best friend who was willing to come to me no matter where I was, just like I would for her. Aidan magically had to be out of town on my birthday every year after I lost the baby. I think the memory of that day was too much for him to have to face so he tucked tail and ran every year instead. At least this year he didn't have to bother making up some bullshit story about a business trip. I had beaten him to the punch by walking out three weeks before.

CHAPTER FOUR

The book thief

Sunday, May 12th, 2013. Day 215 since Aidan.

Cheyenne had been in Dallas less than twenty-four hours, but you would think she had lived there her entire life. She blended with the locals with ease, and seeing her so happy to be in Dallas was a welcome sight for me. I had been stressed to the max with all the new changes that had taken place in my life. I was relieved of some of my stress when Cheyenne arrived and then relieved of even more when she checked out our new home and absolutely loved it. I was worried that she wouldn't feel at home in the place I had rented for us but of course she loved the place as much as I did. Our new apartment wasn't anything outrageously fancy, but it was undeniably lovely. Our place was a two bedroom and two bathroom apartment on the 3rd floor which gave us a decent view of the people buzzing around the city streets below us from our balcony. The location was extremely convenient for both of us. The rent on our place was a bit high, simply because we were on Main Street, but being so conveniently placed was well worth it. The location put us in decent proximity to just about everything— including the night life.

We both loved our new home, and it felt great for both of us to be starting over in a new city. I had lined up three interviews for the following week, giving me just enough time to hop on my flight back to El Paso to meet up with Aidan and our lawyers to tie up loose ends. We had decided to sell our home and split the profit, but of course I was required to be in town to sign my name a million different times on a million different legal documents to finalize our divorce and finish up the sale of our home. I was not looking forward to being in the same room with Aidan or the same county for that matter, but I really didn't have much choice. Seeing him and taking the final steps to sever my life from his was necessary. I was scheduled to be in town to finalize my divorce for three days which gave me plenty of time to accomplish everything, including stopping by the tattoo parlor to pick up my sketches. I had called Fred weeks before and asked him to help me out with a tattoo I was planning. He wouldn't be the one doing the work, but as my friend he was more than happy to draw up what I asked for. I would have to locate an excellent artist once I was back in Dallas to whom to take my sketche. This particular tattoo was very important to me, and I would not settle for just any artist.

My flight out was that night, Sunday, May 12th, day 215 since Aidan. I felt it was shit timing having to leave Cheyenne alone when she had only just arrived, but there was no avoiding it. I would be returning Wednesday to prepare for the interviews I had scheduled. I had applied for a paralegal position at three different law firms here in Dallas, and I was very excited to start work again. I needed the structure and routine that holding a job required. I had been managing my emotions quite well over the past seven months, but a new job would ensure that I was busy week to week. As a paralegal I was always on the run at work. I was great at my chosen career and aimed to impress my employer. In the past my employers didn't relish handing out loads of 'atta girls' or pats on the back for a job well done, but I worked hard and efficiently nonetheless. I had yet to do any research whatsoever on the three firms to which I had sent my resume. I would just have to scramble to get it all done in time. My first and second interviews were both on the following Monday.

I set out towards the airport. While I was on the road, my cell phone chimed alerting me to an incoming text message. I stopped to fill my car with gas and opened the text while I refueled. *'Hey babygirl! Need yall's address, so I can send Chey's birthday flowers. It's a surprise; don't tell her.'* The text was from Emma Rae Walker, Cheyenne's mom, who was also known as Mama Rae to just about everyone who was young enough to have been her kid. After reading the text, I kicked myself for forgetting about Cheyenne's birthday only a few days away. I couldn't believe I could forget her twenty-eighth birthday.

Shit!! I'm such a jerk! Crap, what am I going to get her?

I texted Mama Rae back and glanced at the clock on the dash. I realized I had a little time to spare before I had to be at the airport, so I pulled into a book store knowing just the thing she would love. I was a woman on a mission. The book store was small and quaint which made me worry that they might not have what I was looking for. I hopped out of my Honda after I whipped into a parking space haphazardly. I liked the store. The place was called Book Ends, and it smelled like new books, cookies, and coffee, the last two I discovered were complimentary refreshments for patrons.

How nice.

I scanned the small store for the section I needed and found it. The cookbook section was small, but promising nonetheless. I knew Cheyenne would love to have *Mastering the Art of French Cooking, 50th Anniversary Edition* by Julia Child. I would not have time to order the book online, nor would I even if I did have the time because Cheyenne might be tempted to open any packages sent to our apartment. This way I would have her gift with me, ensuring that she would not ruin the surprise. I quickly scanned the section for the book and spotted it. I nearly jumped for joy with the prospect of diverting a birthday disaster by forgetting to get my very best friend a great gift. If I had screwed up and not gotten her a gift, she would forgive me, of course, but I wouldn't forgive myself. I darted towards the book and noted that it was the only one left.

I'm a lucky lady today!

I snatched the book off the shelf and like the graceful swan that I am, I juggled it around like a moron before it fell to the floor with a thud.

Ugh! Geez butter fingers!

I went to stoop down to pick up my prize when I noticed a large, masculine, hand complete with long, graceful-looking fingers swiftly snatch it off of the floor.

I guess there are gentlemen around these days. Pretty fingers? That's odd.

I stood up from my crouched position and nearly fell back on my ass. The hand, pretty fingers and all, belonged to an equally gorgeous man. I mean really gorgeous! Scratch that. He was smokin' hot.

"I'm sorry. I'm all butter-fingers today, I guess," I muttered and felt my cheeks begin to burn so bright they felt sunburned.

"No need to thank me. Thank you for practically tossing this book at me. I have been looking for it." His voice was a perfect match to his appearance, remarkably sexy. His voice was low and deep, and words seemed to slip out of his mouth like satin.

Ugh! Shit! Do I have extra panties readily available in my bag? I may need them thanks to Mr. Sex-on-legs.

"Oh, um... you have?"

"Yes as a matter of fact it's a gift for someone special." His sex appeal and charming personality suddenly took a nose dive for me.

"Oh no. I am buying that book. I only just dropped it. It's a gift for *my* someone special. Thanks for picking it up for me, but I will take that back now. I really have to get going. I'm in a hurry." I held out my right hand palm up expecting no dispute about the book. He simply gave me a once over, and then a slow-moving, arrogant smirk eased across his impossibly handsome face.

"Well, lady, you dropped the book. It was no longer in your possession, I picked it up, thereby taking possession of it, so... I'll be buying this book today. Thanks again for being so... instrumental in finding it for me." The heated moisture that was mounting in my panties instantly evaporated like water in the Sahara, and I narrowed my eyes on his turning body.

"No way, mister! Hand it over! I had it first. What kind of

person practically steals merchandise from other shopper's hands? Besides, as you can see, it is the last copy on the shelf, and I don't have time to order another one on the internet. Surely you understand. Right?" He had his back to me at that point, but stopped in his tracks and turned back to face me.

"What I understand is possession is nine-tenths on the law, and I have this book in my possession. Surely you can understand *that*." He stood before me with the damned book in his hand smirking at me like he was enjoying this little argument we were having, and I just wanted to punch him square in his stunning face for being such an ass. I would have to game plan on the fly.

Okay, fine, chief. You want to be like that? Time to try my hand at charming female persuasion. This could work. It needs to work.

I stifled my unpleasant mood and plastered the best smile I could muster up on my face. "Listen, um..."

He crossed his arms across his clearly muscular chest with the book safely tucked under his left arm.

"Ben." His tone indicated that he was less than impressed with my ploy and clearly saw right through what I was working at. I proceeded anyway.

"Okay. Ben. My name is Kat..."

"As in the animal?" He interjected.

"Um, no. As in Kathleen, *Ben*." Now he had a smug look on his face like he was thoroughly pleased with the banter between us.

Alright, jerk-wad. Keep it up, and I'm going to snatch that book from under your arm and bolt for the cashier.

I held out my hand to him to shake. He looked down at my

extended hand before him and quirked an eyebrow to go along with his smug grin. He waited a moment too long to extend his own hand, an omission which I assume was meant to add insult to injury.

Nice! This guy just oozes chivalry.

"Nice to meet you, Ben. Like I was saying, my name is Kat. Surely I can convince you to hand over that book. I really need it. It's kind of an emergency." He crossed his arms over his chest again and leaned one muscle-capped shoulder against the wall with ankles crossed. Clearly he was getting comfortable for the show I was putting on.

Asshole!

"It's highly doubtful that purchasing a book is some kind of emergency, Kathleen."

"No. It's just Kat. K.A.T!!" I said impatiently.

"My apologies, Kathleen" was his response to my clarification of my preferred name followed by a simple arrogant smirk and nod. He was positively infuriating and purely male flawlessness

What the fuck, guy?

"I'm sorry to say you're going to have to do better than that since I, too, need this book."

You have GOT to be kidding me!

"Well, Ben, I don't know what to tell you. It's my best friend's birthday soon, and I am to be out of town for a few days and won't have time to comb the city for this particular book, and as I said before, I won't have time to order one; with shipping and all, it would take days. I would appreciate your understanding."

He scoffed at my plea. An audible, rude as hell, scoff.

Oh this just keeps getting better and if I keep dancing in circles with this tool bag, I'm going to miss my flight. Just what I need.

"Hey! Don't act like that! I am new to this city, and I don't know my way around enough to be stopping by one bookstore after another."

To hell with my female persuasion. I'm going to let this joker have a piece of my mind. I may not get to buy the damned book, but verbally assaulting this guy will definitely make me feel better.

He stood there unmoved and still leaning against the wall as casual as can be. A glimpse of my old self peeked through the veil and made her presence known, and I was happy to feel that way.

"You know what? Take the damn book! You're practically a thief. Have a shit day, jerk!" I waltzed past him, making sure to shoulder swipe him as I went.

"Pleasure meeting you, Kathleen." He tossed over his shoulder at me while I stomped away at a steady pace.

"Piss off, Ben!" I tossed back, earning me a few stares. I heard him chuckle, clearly pleased with himself.

Shit! What now?

I stomped out of the store and continued on my way to the airport, empty-handed. I parked my car in the lot that charges you an ungodly amount per day and trudged into the airport. I made it in the nick of time and scurried to my gate. Once I was on board I plopped down in my seat and couldn't get Ben out of my head.

What a total arrogant ass, but boy, was he incredibly handsome. The last thing I needed was another arrogant, smug, uber-handsome man in my life! I just offloaded one of those, and he did a crack job at screwing up my life. Perhaps I should just date moderately handsome men.

I chuckled at myself for that bright idea.

News flash Kat! Jackasses come in all shapes, sizes, and varying degrees of attractiveness. I must be the most self-destructive person I know. Do I have a sign on my back that says 'hey come screw with my head and mess things up for me... I love that shit.'

Still, after scolding myself for swooning over Ben's looks, I couldn't help but think about him. I squirmed in my seat a bit while I mentally catalogued his features head to toe. He had on jeans that had a great worn look to them like I usually buy. A snug fitting gray V-neck tee which also looked vintage, or maybe he has simply worn it a lot. He had black boots on his feet. I got an up close look at those when I was crouched on the damn floor trying to pick up the book. He smelled great, too, although we were not exactly close enough for me to get a great big whiff of him.

I know he was a couple inches over six feet tall simply because I am 5'4", and he towered over me like Aidan used to; I know for a fact that Aidan is 6'4". His hair was a chocolate brown and shiny. It reminded me of hot fudge. His hair was about finger length I guess and wavy. It had no particular style to it.

I bet he just runs his hands through it to 'style it.' Bet he doesn't even own a comb.

I snickered a bit at my preposterous assumption about his not owning a comb. Everyone owns at least some type of comb or brush unless that person is bald or something.

Just then I got a visual of the exact opposite. I pictured Mr. Arrogant sitting in front of a girly vanity combing his beautiful locks of wavy finger length hair over and over like a lady. I let out a full laugh at the ridiculous thought. It earned me a few perplexed looks from a couple of other passengers. One was from a "grown ass teenager," of course.

I shot the lady a huge smile that was saturated with pure cattiness to which her response was an eye roll and a quick turn away from me.

Yeah, that's right lady; keep your butt planted in your floatation device in case of an unexpected water landing.

I chuckled again. My thoughts came back to Ben. I found myself pressing my thighs together and squirming a bit.

I needed to get laid soon. Getting all hot and bothered over some random guy who turned out to be a total tool bag was unacceptable. *Sex. Yes, sex would remedy this problem. With whom, though? Hmmm. I'll come back to that one, though to be honest, I would give a lot to see what's under Ben's clothes.*

I could tell by looking at him that he had a great body. I was sure of it. Even through clothes, that was obvious. His arms were muscular. Very muscular. So were his legs. His jeans fit somewhat snugly across his thighs, so of course, that meant he had great legs.

Washboard abs are a given, then.

His lips were full, and what I saw of his teeth through that smug smile of his were beautiful, straight, and white. Clearly the product of excellent dental care. He had a bit of a facial hair. I assumed it was due to simply not shaving for a day or two. It looked great on him, though. His nose was proportionate to the rest of his features. The best part, though, the best part was his eyes. He had stunning eyes. They were a sort of blue-green hue rimmed with a deep sapphire blue. Simply stunning.

No wonder I'm squirming in my seat! Oh well, thanks for the daydream, Ben, you book thief!

CHAPTER FIVE

A thrill and a half

꒷꒦ꙮ꒦꒷

The following day, after arriving in El Paso, I met with Aidan and our lawyers. Monday, May 13th, 2013. Day 216 since Aidan. The last time I had laid eyes on him, he looked miserable. I felt a bit sympathetic for him. He had single-handedly dismantled our relationship. We had so much potential, and we were happy and in love at one point. Then, he became his own worst enemy. I know he will never forgive himself for the role he played in my car accident. I blamed him pretty ruthlessly right away. I felt his behavior was the catalyst that had caused me to drive away from our home that night and straight into life-altering tragedy. We don't speak about the child we lost. In fact, the entire incident was swept under the rug and ignored by both of us. Some things were simply too painful to confront.

I had wept for the loss of our child. Tears didn't come initially, only anger. I swallowed it down like the foulest thing I had ever experienced the taste of. I choked it down whole and it had hit the bottom of my stomach with a crippling, explosive crash. It resided there from then on. The pain and heartbreak lived deep within me, festering and eating away at me like a cancerous growth. I always thought that perhaps one day I could be purged of my ailment. I thought, maybe even hoped, that I would heal emotionally. My mother always said that in order to heal, I would have to be willing to let it go. Clearly, I had not yet gotten to that point. I wasn't sure that I would ever be to that point where grief and grudges escape a person's death grip and leaves her standing as only half the person she was before, but leaves her, nonetheless. As for me, right then, it was just me and my anger and grief in the throes of a tumultuous dance to a sad ballad on an endless loop.

Much to my surprise, when I saw Aidan, he didn't look all that miserable. In fact, he looked like he was coping with our split rather well. Of course there was likely a woman or two to thank for that. When I walked into the conference room at my lawyers office, Aidan and his lawyer were already seated and waiting for the festivities to begin.

Oh joy. This should be a thrill and a half.

I seated myself beside my lawyer, and we were in and out in less than thirty minutes. Aidan and I didn't speak to each other the entire time, and I made sure not to make eye contact with him. It was a highly uncomfortable and awkward situation. Once all of it was done, I shook my lawyer's hand and quickly made my way from the building to my rental car. Aidan was still discussing some things with his lawyer. I sped from the place like it would explode violently at any second. That's when Aidan came jogging across the parking lot towards me.

Ah, crap. Should have known. That meeting was too easy. I didn't have any such luck.

I rolled my eyes while my head was turned away, and I was busy digging through my purse for keys. Aidan came right up to me, bringing his scent with him; and just like an animal, I caught a whiff of him, and all my senses came to life.

Jesus, Kat! What the hell are you,, a dog in heat or something?

"Hello Aidan. How are you?" I did my best to sound civil and friendly.

"Kathleen. I... um... I'm alright, I guess." He looked down at his feet and crinkled his brow a bit as if he were searching for words to say something and came up with nothing.

He was clearly not doing just fine. *Great! Don't feel guilty, Kat. You have no reason to feel guilty.*

I tried my hand at playing dumb.

"That's good Aidan. I am glad to see that you're alright."

Keys, car, vroom, vroom. Walk away now!

"You are?" His voice sounded almost relieved and unsure, which had me puzzled because the Aidan Cooper I knew was in love with himself and was confident in everything he said or did.

You had better recover quickly, Kat. Squash whatever ideas he has churning in that head of his. This is over.

"Well, yeah, I guess. Even though we're over, we should still be civil to each other, and I don't take pleasure in anyone being upset. So yeah, I guess I'm glad you're fine." I shrugged casually for good measure.

There, that ought to do it.

"Oh. Yes, I guess you're right." He still hung his head, only making eye contact with me for a second or two at a time. He kept his hands in his pockets and shuffled his weight from one foot to the other.

He was nervous. *That is really bizarre!*

I was now looking at him like he was some type of riddle in the form of a human being.

"Kathleen, listen..."

Oh crap, here it comes.

"Kathleen, I um... I miss you a lot, you know? I haven't seen you in months, and I... dammit..." He pulled his hands out of his pockets and ran both hands through his hair, clasping his fingers together at the nape of his neck. He then turned away from me and let out a defeated sigh. He turned back to me and continued:

"I'm sorry. Please forgive me. God knows, I will never forgive myself. I still love you. I can't get you out of my head. I'm so lonely without you. I can't sleep. I can't function. I messed up, and I know that. But God, I would do anything for another shot!"

And there it was. Great!

He then came closer to me and tugged my hand from my side and drew me into his arms. He exhaled the breath he was obviously holding. I felt him smell my hair as he squeezed me tightly in his arms. I allowed him the embrace. He held me there for a long moment then I gently pulled away from him.

"I'm working on forgiveness, all right? I'm not mad at you anymore, but I have so much to sort out with myself okay. I'll get there one day."

"Do you still love me?"

"I think I will always have a place for you in my heart. We spent seven years as husband and wife and made a child together. Even though that child is not here with us, it was still something special between us. I will always have that with you. But if you're asking if I'm in love with you, the answer is no. Too much has happened. We had something great, and whatever it was, it's been gone for years." I suddenly felt like the biggest jerk on the planet, even though none of this was my fault. It was really difficult to keep looking at his face. He had tears swimming in his eyes, and it hurt a bit to see my ex-husband reduced to tears.

"Okay, I understand. But before you walk away, let me just tell you that I hope you will understand that I still love you, I still want you, and I don't see myself just giving it all up. You're my wife. I want you back. I want *us* back."

"You don't have a choice in the matter. It's done and that's okay. You will be okay. I'll be okay. But, we won't be okay together. I'm sorry." I lay my hand on his bicep, gave it a reassuring squeeze, and turned to get into my car.

"Goodbye, Aidan." I was getting teary-eyed just then and was glad to be facing away from him.

His voice came back in a choked whisper. "I meant what I said. I won't give up on winning you back. I love you."

I didn't risk looking at him. I just got into the rental car and drove away with him in my rearview mirror, for once, looking like a broken man. I went back to my hotel room and spent the rest of the day and night crying for Aidan, for our failed marriage, and for the tragic debacle that had been the past seven years of my life.

After picking up the sketches from Fred and saying my goodbyes, I made my way back to the hotel and decided to get back to Dallas sooner rather than later. My flight was scheduled for the next day, but I was eager to start my search for the artist I would need to do my tattoo. I packed up my belongings, and I was off to the airport again to hop on the next flight out.

CHAPTER SIX

Rookie mistake

I managed to get to the airport and check in just in time for the next flight out which was scheduled for 11:45 A.M. After I boarded the plane, I took one last look out of my window from my seat and felt at peace. I felt like I had some bit of closure. I would not be returning to this city or to Aidan. It was final. I buckled myself into my seat, and I was off to Dallas, again. My flight was uneventful, and the plane was scarcely occupied by other passengers. I had the entire row to myself.

I was startled awake by the sound of the captain over the speaker system and quickly realized that I must have fallen asleep. It shocked me that I had fallen asleep during my flight home. I didn't sleep much in general, but I most certainly never slept in cars, boats, trains, or planes.

I blinked away the sleep and heard what sounded like the captain's final remarks about 'making our descent.' I straightened my clothing and sat up in my seat to brace for the landing. While I was getting readjusted, I realized that I must have been sleeping awfully hard because my entire right side from my shoulder down to my toes was tingly and asleep. My right arm and leg were useless with the odd sensation of a million needle pricks under my skin. It was dreadful. I made my best effort to bring the blood flow back to my extremities, but by the time I had to get up and exit the plane, my right side was still rather useless and numb. I decided to attempt walking normally.

Well, I can't feel a damn thing, but I'm walking. One foot in front of the other. This works.

I was rather pleased with myself for walking so well in my favorite jeans and new high-heeled leather boots, even though I couldn't feel one bit of my right side. I made my way down the terminal with my leather messenger bag hanging off my shoulder and the portfolio with my sketches firmly gripped in both my hands. I held my sketches to my chest to make doubly sure that none of them would be lost. I was beginning to second guess my choice of footwear when I realized that the combination of being partially numb and wearing new boots made me less than steady on my feet. I'm sure that perhaps I even looked intoxicated.

Great, Kat! That's what you need. Get tossed out of the airport for being an alleged drunk!

I did my best to keep my stride steady and even, but the boots on my feet were very slick on the bottom. Like a true genius, I had not taken the time to scuff up the bottoms on pavement to ensure they would have some traction.

Rookie mistake Boss! Try not to make a total fool of yourself in front of all these passengers.

I inwardly chided myself.

Excellent. Now you look like a drunk, physically handicapped child walking around an airport with zero grace, except you're a twenty-six-year-old, unemployed divorcee who was dumb enough to wear brand new, high-heeled boots through two airports today.

I wasn't sure which one of those descriptions was more flattering, and my self-esteem shrank even further as my deprecating private thoughts ran amok. My private reprimand was partially muttered to myself, and I could see other travelers staring at me from beneath my double-coated mascaraed lashes. I did my best to keep walking, but the feeling in my right arm and leg was dreadfully slow to return. I stared down at my feet willing them to keep steady and straight. I was just about to walk past a set of bathrooms when a man came speed walking from behind me and crossed in front of my path, effectively cutting my unsteady self off.

I attempted to halt my walk abruptly to avoid a collision but in doing so, I staggered forward. I had wide eyes as I spun around while stumbling backward like a small child ice skating for the first time. As I stumbled back a few steps doing my best to gain control over my body, I tripped over and tangled up in a yellow 'Caution Wet Floor' sign and fell backward with great force. My arms flew up and fluttered like a flightless bird attempting to defy destiny, and the last thing I saw was colorful art sketches floating through the air, raining down around me in slow motion. My head hit the floor with a thud and subtly bounced like a half-inflated basketball. Then I saw... nothing.

What seemed like hours later, I began to wake up from the darkness that had swallowed me. I attempted to convince my eyes to open, but they refused my pleas. Suddenly I felt a swift jerk beneath my sprawled, limp body, and my hair swished and tickled around my neck.

Ouch! Oh no, no, no. Crap, my head! Wait, someone just picked me up. How embarrassing! Snap out of it, Kat!

I was lifted off the cold hard floor. I still couldn't open my eyes, and my head began thrumming and pulsating with pain and rushing blood. I couldn't tell who or what had picked me up off of the floor, but I could smell something.

Mmmmm, smells nice.

I could smell something, or rather someone, and that person smelled heavenly. With my eyes welded shut, my nose was as keen as the snout on a bloodhound.

Something smelled like the woods and body soap and fresh laundry and... man.

My hearing was muffled, but I could make out multiple different voices around me before he spoke. I felt him speak more than I heard him. Whatever came out of his mouth sounded unclear, but I could tell he had a deep voice. His words escaped my ears and reverberated as a tactile sensation, vibrating through his chest and into my incapacitated body as I was held close to him. The feeling was surprisingly soothing. I tried to make out what was being said while I battled with my own body to cooperate. My hearing began to clear, and only a low-pitch ringing remained to hinder my ability to listen. Even through the ringing in my ears and the pulse in my brain, I could make out the words that he was speaking to me. His mouth was right up against my left ear, and I could feel the warmth from his breath against my ear. I could feel his lips brush against my skin, and my wretched body went bat-shit crazy with the sensation that the stroke of his lips against my ear elicited.

"Are you with me, Kathleen?" That voice was one I knew, but couldn't immediately place.

Who the hell is this? He knows my name. I know this person. Wake up, dummy!

Realization hit me like a bullet in the chest, and if I could have gasped, screamed and gone running in the opposite direction at that moment, I was sure I would have.

Oh. My. God! Please God, deliver me from this hell. It was him. 'Him' was Ben. Ben was 'him.' *No! God, no. Not the highly arrogant, super handsome, Mr. Sex-on-egs, BEN, from the bookstore!*

It was him. Mr. Rude-as-hell Book Thief himself, in the flesh. I couldn't believe it. I was searching my brain for answers.

Why is he carrying me? Where are we going? What if he is a murderer? Open your eyes, Kat!

At that point of realization, I began having a panic attack along with a pounding head and a generous side of complete humiliation. The adrenaline from my self-induced panic attack was a perk, since it helped me convince my heavy eyelids to open, allowing my green eyes to peep out. As soon as my eyes focused, I was able to confirm my suspicion. It was strong, handsome, arrogant Ben the Book Thief carrying me against his chest. I nearly fainted again once I saw him, but instead my mouth spoke on its own volition.

"Put me down now!"

Way to sound appreciative, Kat.

The moment I spoke, his eyes shot down to mine, and he half smiled at me.

"Oh. Good. You are with me," he said in a relaxed manner while I was sure that I was moments from suffering a massive coronary.

"Please put me down. I can walk," I pleaded.

"Well, sorry Kathleen, but you took a nasty fall back there. I'm taking you to my car, and we are going to the hospital." He didn't even look at me while he dictated what I would be doing.

"We will be doing no such thing. I'm fine. I fell, no big deal. The only part of me that is wounded is my ego, and you only wound me further by carrying me through an airport like I'm a child! Shit! Where are my things?" He kept on walking without even acknowledging my demands to release me.

"There is a nice gentlemen walking behind me that has all of your belongings. I assure you they have not disappeared. I am taking you to the hospital. You lost consciousness, which means you should be seen by a doctor. Have you ever had a head injury?" I was taken aback by his sudden interest in my medical history.

"Uh, yeah, I, um... had a concussion few years ago. Why the hell does that matter?"

"All the more reason to be seen by a doctor."

"For God sakes Ben, will you please put me down?"

"Okay, fine! Here." He abruptly dropped me to my feet rather roughly, making his distaste for my demands clear. I stumbled and got light-headed again.

Dammit! After making his point that I was still unsteady on my feet, he grabbed me around my waist and held me firm against him as we made our way out of the airport.

"See? You're not well. You need to see a doctor. Come with me and stop fighting over it. It's pointless. I don't negotiate, but

I believe you are aware of this." Just then, for effect he winked at me and grinned, nearly turning me into a simpering idiot.

Oh boy! He's really beautiful.

I couldn't help but notice that Ben was not even remotely winded from carrying me. He was unruffled. I knew I was in deep trouble.

"What about my car? It's in parking."

"Give me your keys. I will have it delivered to your home."

"I will do no such thing! I don't even know you. I will concede to the point that I may need to see a doctor, but you are not going to have access to my car or knowledge of my home address!" Raising my voice at him was rather dumb because the effort it took made my head throb harder. I leaned in against his firm muscles. My head lolled against his pectorals—nothing to complain about. "My head," I groaned.

"Come on." I was in no condition to argue with his demand, so when a black Cadillac Escalade appeared before us curbside, I allowed him to usher me into his car, and he belted me in. He took the keys from the valet and got behind the wheel.

"My car." My eyes were shut, but I could smell him beside me, and I could feel him looking at me. I could feel his arm resting against mine on the console between our seats. The contact between us was initiating a lightning storm of nerves deep in my stomach. It felt like butterflies on steroids.

"I'll take care of it."

"My sketches?" I began to worry at the thought of my beautiful sketches being scattered and lost in the large airport corridor.

"I have them."

Man of many words.

"Do you take care of random strangers all the time?"

"No, just you."

I had asked the question with intent to be sarcastic, but he seemed to answer with sincerity.

"Are you an artist? Did you do these?" I peeked through a cracked eyelid to see Ben shuffling through the many sketches while we waited at a red light.

"Hey, give me those, and no, I'm no artist, but those are mine. My friend is an artist, and this is his work." I had both eyes open, and the sun was much too bright to keep them that way for long. I snapped my sensitive eyes shut.

"My apologies. I didn't mean to intrude, but can I just say that these are beautiful? What will you do with them if you don't mind my asking?" I cracked my eyes open again to attempt a fitting answer. He looked at me quizzically, and I couldn't help but admire those beautiful blue-green eyes of his.

"I, uh, I will have them... permanently." It was a highly vague response, and I expected him to push for a more specific answer, but he didn't. He just nodded his head and focused back on the traffic around us.

"So, if you are not the artist, then who is?"

"His name is Fred."

"Your boyfriend, I assume."

"No. Not my boyfriend. Fred is a friend of mine. He lives back home in El Paso." Even in profile, I could see Ben's face grow serious, and his brows bunched together.

"I thought you said you lived here when we met in *Book Ends*."

I felt the need to reassure him. "Well, yes. I only just moved to Dallas from El Paso. I had business to attend to in El Paso;

that's where I've come from today." I put my fingers to my temples and began rubbing at the unforgiving pain there.

"I see."

We arrived at the hospital a short while later. Ben sat beside me in the waiting area and did a good job of distracting me from the awful pounding headache I had.

"God, I hope this doesn't take all night. You know you can leave. I appreciate your help and all, but really I'm fine, and I can call my friend to come get me."

He turned his intense gaze on me. "I won't leave you alone here." The moment he spoke those words, I felt my face drop, and my heart clenched in my chest. I couldn't help but remember that the last time I was in a hospital, someone else spoke those exact words to me but for far different reasons. I felt the threat of tears coming, and I did my best to battle them away. Ben noticed the shift in my expression.

"Hey, are you all right?" He leaned in close to me when he spoke and placed his warm hand on my knee. I could feel his breath against my skin again, and it had the same effect on me as it did earlier in the airport. It was warm and coaxing against my body. I felt the urge to wrap my arms around him, but ignored it.

"Yeah, I'm okay." My voice sounded unconvincing.

"You don't look okay." I was getting uncomfortable and worried that if he kept pushing, I would start crying, adding to my humiliation.

"Really, I'm fine. Why are you even here? I don't need a sitter." My words came out more clipped than I had intended, and I felt a little guilt for it the moment I said it.

"Well, I beg to differ. As far as I can tell, you are perhaps the clumsiest person I have ever seen. If I leave you to your own devices, you're likely to injure yourself further. Who knows, you could get run over by a city bus or something while juggling your lipstick around like you did that book." With the mention of the book, my indignation began brewing again. I was glad to feel any other emotion beside sadness.

"I am *not* clumsy. I have a lot going on lately, and I'm... distracted. Besides, I don't wear lipstick. I wear tinted gloss, thank you very much, you Book Thief!" He clutched his hand to his stomach, tossed his head back, and laughed uproariously. I was tempted to join in the laughing with him, but fought against the urge to enjoy the moment. His laugh was infectious and quite sexy. I felt a stirring between my thighs.

Kat, seriously? You're a joke! This man has just insulted you, and you can't seem to get a hold of your sexually deprived self?

"Do I amuse you? Am I some sort of joke to you? A comedian?"

He slowly gathered himself and came down from the moment. "No, I don't think you're a joke, though you are entertaining." He shrugged his shoulders.

"Go to hell, Ben." I said flatly.

"They won't have me," he mumbled.

"What did you say?" I swiftly jolted from my relaxed position in my seat to look him in the face.

"Nothing," he mumbled again and ran his large hands through his ridiculously beautiful chocolate brown, wavy locks.

Oh, back to being a man of many words.

When I relaxed my arm on the arm rest between the two of us, I noticed Ben glance down at the hospital bracelet on my wrist. He scrunched his brows together and looked confused.

"You know you shouldn't do that to your face. You'll get wrinkles prematurely." He looked up at me and relaxed his face into a charming smile; his eyes were sparkling at me with something unspoken in them.

"Why, Miss Kathleen Cooper, are you worried about my appearance?"

My eyes went wide at the sound of my full name rolling off his tongue. "How do you know my name? I never gave you my full name." His eyes glanced downward to the bracelet on my wrist which held enough information for any proper thief to steal a person's identity.

"Oh, I see. I should have caught that. Are you planning on murdering me or something? Because only stalkers or murders pay attention to things like that." I lifted my wrist with the bracelet and waved it at him. "Oh, and why were you at the airport?" He beamed another panty- dropping smile in my direction, one that made the butterflies in my stomach flutter at Mach speed.

"No, Kathleen Cooper, I am none of those things. I assure you I am a law-abiding citizen, and I was at the airport for the same reasons you were. You know, to fly to and from a predetermined destination. I had just returned from a business trip when I saw you trip and fall."

Smartass! "So what do you do?"

He paused for a moment and returned his amused look to meet mine. "I'm a lawyer." The minute that bit of information passed over his lips I let out a dull chuckle. He looked at me with confusion riddled across his features. "Does my occupation amuse you?"

"No not at all. I just find it... fitting that you're a lawyer. I could have guessed that one." He playfully narrowed his eyes on me, and then he, too, laughed.

Ben never inquired about my occupation, so I didn't reveal any details. He grinned at me and patted the bracelet on my wrist. We didn't speak much more while I waited to be seen. After seeing the doctor and undergoing a few tests to make sure that I had no serious head injury, I was released from the hospital with the diagnosis of a monster headache.

"Well, Ben, thank you kindly for your help, but I can take it from here."

He looked down at me while we stood in front of each other at the hospital entrance. I had my hand outstretched to shake his, but he made no attempt to shake my hand.

Well, Kat, don't you feel like a blooming idiot in spring.

"I will take you to your home. You shouldn't be alone."

I shook my head subtly to avoid more pain. "I am quite capable of getting myself back to my apartment Ben. I will be sure to avoid the city buses." I shot him a half-grin at which he chuckled in response.

"Fair enough. Would you like me to return you to your car?" I smiled at him while I privately reveled in my small victory over Mr. Pretentious Sex-on-Legs.

"Yes, please. Thanks." Once we arrived back at the airport parking lot, I said adieu to Ben after expressing my thanks to him once again. He scribbled down his phone number on a piece of paper and gave it to me with instructions to call him if I needed anything. I didn't give him my phone number, nor did he ask for it.

CHAPTER SEVEN

'Get out of jail card'

❦

Wednesday, May 15, 2013. Day 218 since Aidan. I slept like the dead after returning from El Paso. I was both physically and emotionally exhausted, and sleep came easily for once. Cheyenne was still in bed shortly after 8 am when I heard a knock on our apartment door. I abandoned my coffee on the kitchen counter and crept to the door.

I opened the door to a delivery man who held out a clipboard and pen to me.

"Kathleen Cooper?"

"Yes, that's me. What's this?" I quickly signed for the delivery, which was a rectangular package about the size of a shoe box.

"Ma'am, do I look like a psychic?" The delivery man drawled in a southern accent.

I glanced up at the irritating oaf and shook my head. The old me drew back her metaphorical privacy curtain and let loose on the jerk. I cocked my head to the side and quirked up one eyebrow.

"No I don't suppose you are psychic, pal. Just talking out loud." With that, I slammed the door on the delivery man.

Who the hell would be sending me a package? No one has this address yet.

I opened the package and removed the tissue paper to discover what the box encased.

The book.

I was a bit speechless when I removed the cookbook Ben and I verbally tussled over. There was a handwritten note in the bottom of the box as well.

'Kathleen, for your someone special.
—Ben, the Book Thief.'

I couldn't believe that Ben the Book Thief and supremely arrogant lawyer would be so... nice.

He probably just took pity on your pathetic self. There was no return address or information about the sender on the package. Just a simple label addressed to me and the note from Ben inside. I did, however, have his name and number scribbled on a piece of paper. I entertained the idea of calling him for a moment before I decided against it. I was relieved to have gotten the book in the end for Cheyenne's birthday, but had no intentions of seeing or talking to Ben ever again. I would need to stay as far away from him as I could. The last thing I needed was another Aidan in my life. Ben had trouble written all over him, and I knew to stay as far away from trouble as possible, at least for the time being.

I quickly repackaged the gift and hid it beneath my bed. Cheyenne's twenty-eighth birthday was in four days. I made a note to myself to start planning what we would do for her day. I chose not to tell Cheyenne anything about my encounter with the handsome book thief. She would only ask questions that would surely lead to spoiling her birthday surprise.

We spent the majority of our Wednesday hanging out and talking, while both of us sat in front of our own laptops in the living room. Cheyenne was busy looking for employment and I was aimlessly browsing the internet for birthday celebration ideas. I didn't even get to research the three firms I had applied to.

Thursday and Friday came and went, and I didn't accomplish much at all. I had Ben on my mind. I was undeniably attracted to the man, but couldn't understand how he could be so smug yet still kind enough to attend to me at the hospital and send me the book I wanted for Cheyenne. I had to remind myself that he was a lawyer, which in my opinion, made him as sneaky as a snake.

Saturday, May 18th, 2013. Day 221 since Aidan. Cheyenne and I decided to venture out of our comfy little apartment and take part in some bar hopping with the locals. We both agreed that it would be better to celebrate her birthday a day early since her actual birthday fell on a Sunday. We both primped and pampered ourselves before heading out on the town. Cheyenne looked hot in her curve hugging, champagne sequined mini dress and impeccable makeup. I had Cheyenne look through my wardrobe for something suitable for me to wear.

"Seriously, Kat! This is not even worthy of being called a wardrobe!" She waved her hand toward my closet door with an exasperated expression marring her pretty face.

"What? I don't think it's all that bad. Maybe a little outdated, and I might have far too many boring work clothes, but... you know... I just don't shop much." I shrugged my shoulders and huffed.

"Don't shop much? By the looks of these clothes of yours, you don't shop at all! We are so fixing this problem tomorrow. How do you expect to get a man with nothing decent to wear?" Cheyenne threw her hands up and held them there while she waited for whatever sad excuse I was attempting to formulate.

"I don't need a man, Chey. I am all about going to get some new clothes, but not with the intention of reeling in some schmuck."

"Okay, fine! Clothes, tomorrow! Now, shall we go raid my closet for something fantastic to put on you?" Her beaming white smile was the signal that the subject was dropped and we were on our way to happier topics.

"Let's!" I cried with enthusiasm to please Cheyenne.

She ended up choosing an incredibly revealing little black mini dress. It was completely backless except for one wide black satin band that crossed over the top of my back, only concealing a vertebrate or two. The dress barely concealed my backside from prying eyes. The bottom of the dress rested high on my upper thighs and was hemmed with a wide black satin band which matched the same black satin band that held the dress across my upper back. It had tiny little cap sleeves and was a body contouring fit. It was purely scandalous and put me in serious danger of exposing my goods to a lucky onlooker or two. I made a mental note to not drink too much or drop anything on the floor.

Cheyenne looked very pleased when she shoved me in front of her full-length mirror. She had me wearing a great pair of long dangle earrings that reminded me of a disco ball the way they glittered. She also slid a cuff bracelet onto my wrist and demanded that I replace my simple diamond pendant necklace with the choker she had chosen for me. As for the shoes, she browbeat me into wearing a peep-toe, studded heel, leather, zip back pumps. The only feature on these shoes that I loved was the wide cuff that enclosed each ankle. They were obscenely high and uncomfortable of course but I had to admit they were very flattering. In short, my best friend dressed me up like a high-priced hooker, but I was glad to feel sexy for the night. Cheyenne completed my mini makeover by fixing my long auburn hair into a loose up-do, applying smoky eye makeup that she insisted suited my green eyes, my tinted lip gloss, and topped it all off with a spray of perfume.

We chose to go to a popular club as our second destination of the night. The first place we went to was too low key for Cheyenne's taste so we gulped down our drinks and headed on to the next place. The second club was packed with people dancing and drinking. We went directly to the bar keeping up with tradition by quickly downing a lemon drop each then ordering our cocktails.

We sat at the bar and chatted each other up. I saw Cheyenne motion over my shoulder with her eyes, and reading my best friend, I gave a nod signaling my understanding. I waited a three-second count and then casually turned my body a bit to eavesdrop on the two ladies who stood at the bar beside us. That's when things got interesting. I heard one of the ladies chatting not so quietly to her friend.

"I guess this place is just full of street walkers tonight." Her friend giggled annoyingly at her snide comment, then followed up with one of her own.

"You see these two?" She motioned her head in our direction.

"I bet these two have slept with at least a half a dozen of the guys in here tonight." They both laughed like school girls, and I could no longer control myself. In a clear voice I dove head long into a verbal spat with the two grown-ass teenagers.

And cue former self!

The old me peeped through my exterior for the second time in a very short period, and I was tickled with the development. I smiled broadly and let loose.

"Hey Chey, do you hear that? We're street walkers?" She gave me a wink indicating that she was prepared to play along.

"Oh! See, I thought we were prostitutes. Is there a difference other than the job title?" I smiled wide when I saw the two women gaping at the show we were putting on.

"No, not really much difference, Chey. But listen, these two over here seem to think we are terrible street walkers. They only gave us credit for a half a dozen men in here!" I took a casual sip of my cocktail. Cheyenne was Oscar-worthy in her role playing mode.

"NO!" She mocked a look of being aghast. Her eyes were wide and her mouth formed into an O.

"We have banged at least thirty or forty of the penises

walking around in this joint!" Her instigating joke only further pissed off the two.

"Exactly my thoughts, Chey." We both turned and smiled cattily at the two ladies who stood beside us with a look of shock and anger on their snotty faces. I leaned toward them, lowered my voice, and threw out my next card.

"But don't worry ladies; if you plan on picking up a guy here tonight, just give us a heads up as to who the unlucky bastards are; that way when they tries to walk away from you two for us, we will send him back your direction... *unfucked*." Cheyenne now stood beside me shaking with laughter, and the two women were ready to combust. The one woman who apparently thought that her abundant frame could squeeze into a supermodel size zero decided to put her plump finger in my face.

"You two are skanks!" Things got even sketchier.

"I suggest you remove your hand from my face, or we are gonna have problems." At that point Cheyenne stood slightly behind my outstretched left arm that held her back from pouncing on the bigger one.

"Fuck you, whore! You think you can just walk in here dressed like that, actin' all fancy and talk like that to me?" She sent a fine mist of saliva flying out of her mouth when she spoke, and it made my blood boil.

"I dress how I please, and it is not any fault of mine that you two behave like high school freshmen out of jealousy that another woman can be attractive. God forbid, right? Now, put your fucking finger away!" My voice was teetering on becoming a shout. I still held Cheyenne back.

Suddenly, some drunken guy came barreling towards me from behind and crashed into both Cheyenne and me. We were both launched forward at the two women. They immediately started slapping, pulling, punching and scratching at us. We had not meant to start a fight, but with the help of the drunken man who sent us charging forward, we were indeed in a fight in a bar.

Brilliant, Kat! Check 'bar brawl' off the bucket list.

Out of nowhere a large, handsome man with dirty blonde hair and tattoos stepped into the scuffle and peeled all of us apart. Cheyenne was still trying to charge at the two women like a bull when the handsome stranger scooped her up by the waist and dragged her outside over his bulky shoulder. I followed willingly while the other two women hung back at the bar screaming obscenities at us. The police arrived, and all of us, including the handsome stranger, were toted off to the police station to sort out who did what. Luckily for us, when we were given an opportunity to make a phone call, I remembered shoving Ben's scrap of paper with his phone number into my purse.

I guess I just might see Ben again after all.

If I were being truthful with myself, I didn't mind seeing Ben again in the slightest. The whole disaster was a huge misunderstanding, and I was hoping that Ben would help make sure that we didn't face any charges.

"Cheyenne, I have a friend who is a lawyer, I think I should call him."

She looked at me astounded. "You have a friend?"

I rolled my eyes and let out a sigh. "Yes, Chey. I know it must be hard to believe, but yeah, I met this guy the other day. He gave me his number, and he happens to be a lawyer. I should call him. Don't you think?"

"You met a guy the other day?"

I was getting impatient. "Oh my God Chey! Seriously? We are going to do this right now? Can we discuss this later? Can I call him to help us or not?" She smiled at me and nodded her head. The officer who was babysitting us allowed me to make the call. I dialed Ben's number and I felt myself turn crimson. The phone rang twice and he picked up, much to my relief.

"Uh, Ben?"

"Kathleen?" I inhaled deeply and braced myself for the utter embarrassment that was to follow.

"Ah, yeah, this is Kat from the book store and from the airport." He chuckled into the phone.

"How are you?"

"Uh, listen Ben, I'm alright I guess, but I'd be better if I was not sitting at the police station giving a statement and waiting to potentially be charged with a crime. Please say you know someone who can help us."

"Us?"

"Um, yeah, me and my someone special, and some guy who accidentally got thrown into this whole mess."

"I see." I was beginning to worry when he didn't say much. There was a long pause, then he finally spoke.

"Okay, let me see what I can do."

"Oh, thank you Be—" He hung up before I could say anything more.

Oh God, please put me out of my misery already! So humiliating. I'm not a criminal. I swear I will never go to another club for as long as I live!

All three of us were cuffed and sitting in chairs in front of an officer's desk when Ben himself arrived. He was speaking with the police while we waited. I had assumed that he would make some calls and send someone to help us, but he showed up instead.

Oh, this is rich! It just keeps getting better!

Cheyenne was less concerned about our predicament and just sat there smirking at me with her hands cuffed.

"So much for a great birthday Cheyenne. I'm sorry. I shouldn't have instigated those women." She frowned at my apology.

"Are you kidding?! This is the most excellent birthday ever! I got some fancy new bracelets." She leaned forward and jiggled her handcuffs and laughed. Ben approached us, and I immediately wanted to hide under the nearest rock... forever. He looked incredible and casual, of course, which made the blush on my cheeks deepen to the nth degree. He approached Cheyenne first.

"Hello. You must be Kathleen's someone special."

Maybe if I try to escape, the officer will shoot me and end this nightmare.

"Yes, Ben. This is my best friend Cheyenne Reed. Cheyenne, this is Ben." After introducing them, I realized I had no idea what Ben's full name was, even though he knew not only my full name, but my address, too. I sat in my chair with my head down, only peeking up through my eyelashes to see him lay his hand on her bare shoulder, causing jealousy to rear its ugly head.

What the fuck is that? I have no reason to be jealous.

Cheyenne looked at me, puzzled, as an 'oh my god he is gorgeous' grin spread across her face. I simply smirked and gave her a slight nod confirming that I, too, thought he was beyond gorgeous with his wavy brown hair, golden skin, blue-green eyes, tall, muscular frame and to-die-for scent.

"It's a pleasure to meet you." Ben turned to the officer and demanded that the hand cuffs be removed from his clients immediately unless we were being charged and arrested and made it clear that none of us were drunk and didn't pose a threat to ourselves or others. After a moment of arguing, the officer removed the cuffs. Once we were free to go, Cheyenne and I piled into Ben's black Cadillac, and he drove across town to our apartment. The tattooed man had not uttered a word the entire time. He just walked out of the police station and didn't look back. Cheyenne and I didn't think too much of it. We dismissed his behavior as a bad attitude since we had accomplished dragging him into our mess, and he found himself cuffed at the police station. I watched him as he walked down the sidewalk and disappeared around a corner. I wondered who that man was and why was he so reluctant to speak. Ben seemed to know exactly where we lived, which caused Cheyenne to quirk a questioning eyebrow at me. I waved her off with my hand, and she once again smiled from ear to ear, exposing every pearly white tooth. Ben parked, and Cheyenne quickly gave her thanks and made a bee line for our apartment. Before I could stop her, she disappeared behind the doors. Ben slipped out of the driver's seat and began walking towards the entrance with me in tow.

"You know where I live. How?"

"Your hospital bracelet gave me your full name. A person can find just about anything on the internet with a very little information to start. Like a full name." He smiled down at me, and I half smiled back at him.

"Yes, I guess that is true. But that's a tad creeper-ish, don't you think, Ben?" He didn't respond except for smirking at me while we stepped into the elevator. I had to admit that his lack of interest in me was very frustrating. I was incredibly attracted to him, but it seemed that the feeling was not mutual.

"What floor?"

"What? You mean you don't already know that it's the third floor?"

He playfully narrowed his eyes at me in response to my sarcastic question. When the elevator stopped, we both stepped out and began walking to my apartment door. He wrapped his strong hand around my wrist bringing both of us to a halt, and my heart began to speed.

"This dress looks beautiful on you. Your exposed back is breathtaking." His voice was low and throaty, making my insides stir gloriously. A blistering blush scorched my cheeks.

Oh my! This man may be an arrogant ass and a book thief who subsequently returned said book, but geez he is great to look at.

I glanced down and ran my hands across the tiny bit of material that dared to be called a dress, smoothing invisible wrinkles. That dress couldn't have a wrinkle if it wanted to, as tightly as it hugged my curves. "Oh, um, this isn't even my dress. I don't own anything like this. My clothes are boring, really. This is Cheyenne's dress." He eyed me closely and nodded his head.

"Well, you wear it well."

"Thank you for coming to get us. This whole thing was just a big misunderstanding. We didn't mean to get into a bar brawl, but those women just came up to us looking for trouble and then—" He stopped me from speaking any further by placing his hand just beneath my jaw and tilting my head back until I was forced to look him in the face.

"When you speak to me, you should look at me in the face, Kathleen."

And here's Mr. I'm-so-damn-cocky-and-full-of-myself!

I quickly moved to a different subject as he lightly stroked his thumb across my chin before his hand fell away, and I felt a tiny ache at the loss. His mesmerizing blue-green eyes stayed locked on mine in a way that made me feel naked and exposed before him. "Why do you call me Kathleen? Everyone calls me Kat. Only one person calls me Kathleen." It was out of my mouth before I could stop it.

"It's your given name. I'll call you by it. Who is the one person who shares my opinion about this subject?"

Oh, you two share a lot more than just an opinion about my name.

I could tell these two men were exactly the same. Handsome, successful, arrogant, self-absorbed jerks who probably went through more women in one month than a gynecologist. I glanced down again, staring at the nail polish covered toe nails that barely stuck out of the front of my peep toe heels. Ben immediately grasped my chin again, tilting my head back up to look him in the face. "I told you Kathleen that you should always look me in the eye." His voice was lower this time and held a menacing undertone. I jerked my jaw from his grasp and scowled.

"And what if I choose not to do as you say? Would you just boss me around some more? What are you really going to do?"

A chuckle rumbled low in his chest. Then in less time it takes to blink, he had my back to the wall. He caged me in with his amazing body. My breathing caught in my throat when I realized that his body was pinning my lower half. He rolled his hips into mine, and a current shot through my body, ending in my groin, where my steadily building arousal was in full swing. My body was humming with need. He gazed at me for a moment with a wild look in his eyes. His nose was just a hair's breadth from mine. I was panting and wanton in his grip. His lips appeared so full and soft. I wanted his mouth on me more than I wanted anything else. He broke our silent stare-down and leaned forward, placing his lips just slightly against my ear and whispered. "You won't want to find out. Goodnight." He stepped back, releasing me from the wall, slipped his hands into his pockets, and walked casually back to the elevator into which he disappeared.

Holy shit!

When I made it inside my apartment, I was still reeling over the things Ben had said and done and slightly pissed off that he walked away from me when I so clearly wanted more. I somehow managed to sidestep Cheyenne's barrage of questions by giving her the gift that I safely stowed beneath my bed and telling her the short version of my story about Ben. She loved the book, but she loved my story more. She sat and listened, never wiping the smirk off of her face once. I couldn't blame her. We both enjoyed a glass of wine and toasted to get-out-of-jail-free cards, overly handsome strangers and memorable birthdays. I went to bed with thoughts of the gorgeous, bossy book thief swirling in my head.

CHAPTER EIGHT

Someone Special

I woke sometime in the early morning after our night out of starting fights and going to jail. I was panting heavily, and my body was covered in a thin sheen of sweat. My legs quivered, my heart was racing, and my clit was pulsing ferociously, demanding attention. After catching my breath, I huffed and flopped back down on my pillows and did my best to silence my eager body's demands for sex... with Ben.

Is this what it's come to? Wet dreams starring Ben?

Monday, May 20th, 2013. Day 223 since Aidan. I woke early to prepare myself for my interviews. The first interview was that morning, and the second one was in the afternoon, so I would have a couple of hours to burn between the two. I decided to stop by a few tattoo parlors in my spare time, so I made sure to bring my sketches along with me. I wore a navy pencil skirt that rested at the knee, coupled with an ivory-colored, cap-sleeved blouse that flared at the hip and a pair of new taupe-colored high heels. The heels were torture devices, but Cheyenne insisted that they completed the look; her words. I wore pearl stud earrings, and my matching pearl pendant necklace. My fingers were bare of any rings, which reminded me of my single status. All that remained of my wedding band was a faint tan line, and I wondered when it would finally disappear.

My first interview went fine, I suppose, but I was less than impressed with the pay and benefits they were offering. Not to mention the lawyer who interviewed me gave me the creeps. I decided that if they called me back I would decline the offer. I had time to burn after the interview with the creepy lawyer, so I made my way to the nearby coffee shop and decided to use my laptop to gather information about local tattoo artists and parlors. If there was one thing I was very good at, it was research and gathering information. It was why I was quite good at my job. I sat outside of the coffee shop at a small table and accessed their internet connection to begin my search. I was caught off guard when an attractive black man began talking to me. I had seen him when I took a seat at my own table. He sat at the table behind me and had a clear view of my computer screen.

"Looking for a tattoo artist?" His deep voice caused me to jerk, and I swiftly turned to face him.

"It's rude to snoop on people, you know? But yes I am looking for the best artist this town has to offer. Do you have any recommendations?"

The man smiled at me before he spoke again. "Well I know

who the best is. It's Tuck." He spoke as if I would know who this Tuck person was.

"Excuse me?"

He shrugged. "Tucker Barrett. He is the best. May I?" The man motioned his hand towards the empty seat at my table, and I nodded, giving my permission to join me. He sat at my table and began unbuttoning his dress shirt.

"What are you doing?" I squeaked out while my eyes flitted around us to see how many onlookers were staring at our table.

"I'm showing you the best." Just then the man opened his shirt allowing me to view his tattoo. "This is Tuck's work. He is the best, but he stays booked months out, and being the best, he charges a pretty penny."

"Wow. That's beautiful," I mumbled. I gazed at the man's tattoo and admired the exquisite work. It covered half of his chest and wrapped over his should and extended down his bicep and forearm. It was an intricate tribal design. There was no denying whoever this Tucker person was his work was indeed the best. The man gave me the name and address where I could find the artist, and I thanked him before he left the coffee shop. I continued sipping on my latte and decided to Google this Tucker person, but before I could clear the search and start a new one I heard a familiar voice from behind me.

"I wouldn't picture you as being the tattooed type Kathleen." I spun around and placed my hand above my brows to shield my eyes from the sun while I stared up at Ben from my seat. He was dressed in an outfit very similar to the one he wore when I first saw him at Book Ends. He looked good enough to eat.

"You know, Ben, I am beginning to think this town is not as big as I thought." He smiled while he made his way around me and sat at my table without bothering to ask.

"Why sure, Ben, please, do sit." I rolled my eyes at his presumptive rudeness. I mentally noted that the old me was making appearances more and more often. I loved it.

"I come here for coffee often. May I remind you that you are the new kid in town? It's not my fault you chose to come to the same coffee shop that I frequent." I groaned at his taunting words.

"So, tattoos?"

"No Ben, I was only doing some research... for a friend."

"A friend? I see."

"Well, I would love to sit and entertain you, but I have to get going. I have an interview in a while."

"Oh?"

"Yes, I have to get a job at some point. I had an interview this morning, I have one this afternoon, and I have another tomorrow." He smiled at me and slightly nodded his head while he sat across from me with his arms folded comfortably across his muscular chest. I couldn't help wonder why he had a look in his eyes that told me he was refraining from saying something. I had no clue what it might be and quite frankly didn't really care... much. I stood and began walking away from him, then froze when my curiosity got the best of me.

"Oh, Ben, one more thing; who was your someone special? Who were you buying the book for?" His features went completely serious, and I instantly regretted asking him.

Stupid curiosity!

"I'm looking at her. I gave you the book didn't I? I saw you. I wanted to talk to you. The opportunity presented itself. I went with it." He shrugged, then stood up and walked towards where

I stood with a stunned expression on my face. He grasped my chin between his thumb and index finger and tilted my head until my eyes met his smoldering blue-green gaze. His thumb stroked a slow path across my bottom lip while I got lost in his all-consuming eyes.

"Someone special." He whispered for just me to hear. His hand brushed down my arm then fell away as he walked casually away from me. I stood there dazed and utterly shocked for a long moment before I was able to gather myself enough to finally leave.

Well, Kat, at least you now know where to find Ben, the disgustingly-sexy-and-seriously-lacking-fundamental-manners book thief... just in case you get a wild hair and decide to act out one of those dreams.

I had to shake my head at my private thoughts.

I walked into the tattoo parlor, which was called 'The Ink Well,' and began looking around. It had a very vintage feel to it and reminded me of Fred's shop. The floors were waxed to a high-gloss shine and were checkered black and white. There were a few red patent leather and chrome chairs near the entrance. There were six work stations, each of which had a pendant light fixture with a red shade hanging down. Only one tattoo artist was sitting at his station, concentrating on his task which appeared to be some sort of sketch.

Without looking up from his work he spoke to me. "Can I help you?" His head stayed bowed, concentrating on his art.

"Um, yes, I'm looking for an artist named Tucker." The man suddenly stopped what he was doing and lifted his head to look at me.

"I'm sure you are lady," he scoffed at me and returned his eyes to his work.

"Pardon me? What's that supposed to mean? I was told he is the best around so I'm here to speak with him." I crossed my arms over my chest and kicked out one foot with attitude. The man once again lifted his head from his work and looked at me with a cynical look on his face.

"Lady, listen, you don't really look like someone who is here for a tat from Tuck, so what is it you want?" I was becoming impatient with this man.

"Listen, man, you don't know me from Adam, and you're only judging me based on my clothing. I am, in fact, here to see about getting a tattoo, and I was told he is the best. The work I want done will only be done by the best or not at all. I won't settle for less. This shit is permanent, you know!" The man quirked an eyebrow at me and grinned, then let out a body-shuddering laugh as he leaned forward clutching his stomach.

"What the hell is so funny?" I shouted. The man was still laughing at me when I saw someone walk into the shop from the back, out of the corner of my eye. The man halted as soon as he saw me, and my jaw hit the floor. The man who was laughing at me slowly stopped and swiped at his eyes to clear out the tears of laughter.

"Hey, Tuck. This lady here wants to talk to you about some ink. Can you believe that?" The man erupted into more laughter while I stood and stared at the man he called 'Tuck.' Tucker was the handsome stranger from the bar who stopped our fight and dragged Cheyenne out of the place.

"You!" I said pointing a finger at him. He looked back at me and spoke for the first time.

"Me." His voice was gravelly and low. The artist who had again stopped laughing at me glanced at Tucker, then to me, then back to Tucker.

"You know this chick, Tuck?"

I glared at him. "I am not a chick. My name is Kat, and I would appreciate it if you would use it. Do you treat all of your customers with this much hospitality?"

He smirked at me then returned a look to Tucker.

"Yeah, I know her" Tucker said to the man prompting him to return his attention to the work in front of him.

"So, Tucker huh?"

"Yep, that's me, but everyone calls me Tuck. You want some ink done, huh?"

"Yes. I was told you are the best in town, and I need the right artist to tattoo me."

He nodded his head and motioned for me to follow him to the back of the parlor. I followed him into a small office. I sat in a chair in front of his desk, and he took his seat behind it. Tucker was attractive. He had slightly long, shaggy dirty blonde hair that rested on the nape of his neck and draped slightly past his ears. His body looked defined and I guessed he was around six feet tall. He had a short sleeve plain white tee shirt on paired with jeans that did a wonderful job of flattering his body. His forearms and biceps were exposed and he had incredible tattoos covering the expanse of his muscular arms and no doubt the rest of him. They were all tribal designs that seemed to swirl and sway across his skin. I admired his arms and the art that decorated them. After a moment of silently ogling, I pulled myself out of the appraising gaze that I had indulged in. I slid the art portfolio that held the sketches onto his desk. He didn't say anything; he only picked them up and began looking at them.

"Who sketched these?" He asked.

"My friend, Fred, back in El Paso."

"So why didn't Fred do the work?"

"Because I left town. We just moved here."

"We?" He looked up at me with raised eyebrows.

"Yes. My best friend, Cheyenne. We're roommates. Remember the petite blonde you dragged out of the bar the other night?" He smiled a genuine smile, and I was surprised to see any expression of emotion from him.

"Yes, I remember her."

"So will you tattoo me?" My question brought his attention back to the sketches. He stared at them a moment longer, then he looked up to me.

"I don't usually do this, but I will make you a deal." He closed the portfolio and set it on his desk to the side and continued speaking.

"I will do this work for you under one condition."

"Okay. What is it?"

"This tattoo is going to require two sessions, minimum. I'll fit you into my schedule and do the work, if you tell me all about Cheyenne. And if she agrees to go on a date with me, I won't charge you a dime for the work. Free. You can tell her I'd like a date, but she can't know about our little trade. Got it?"

I smiled at him after hearing his proposition and extended my hand to shake on it. "It's a deal. But Tuck, why wouldn't you just ask her yourself?"

"Simple. She's out of my league. She doesn't look like the type who dates my type."

Wow! Guess he is smitten with Chey. This was going to be interesting.

After shaking on our little deal, Tuck said he would call me later to let me know when he could fit in my first session. I was ecstatic to get started. I had just enough time to get over to the second interview of the day, and after it was said and done, I wished I hadn't even wasted the gas to drive myself there. The position that was being offered was a bit beneath me salary-wise. I had been a paralegal for four years and had an outstanding resume working for highly successful firms, but this firm was only willing to pay a salary that was more suitable for a paralegal with less than two year's experience. I was beginning to worry that finding a job was going to be more difficult than I had anticipated. The thought of having to settle for a lower paying job than what I had left was frustrating. I could only hope that the interview I had the following day would be more promising. Luckily, the sale of the home I shared with Aidan had made for a hefty deposit into my savings account. I didn't like the thought of having to use that money for my regular expenses, but if I had no other choice, I would do just that.

CHAPTER NINE

Such a... lawyer

❦

Tuesday, May 21st, 2013. Day 224 since Aidan. I resented the alarm in the mornings. I firmly detested them actually. On occasion, I fantasized about taking the damned thing outside and smashing it with a hammer, melting down all the pieces, allowing them to cool into a solid form, and then smashing the stupid thing all over again. I reluctantly rolled out of bed after a less than great night of sleep and shuffled to the bathroom to get ready for the day.

I was ill-prepared for my interview that day. I never got around to researching the firm I was to be visiting that day. I knew only two facts about the firm. 1- The address, 2- The name, Chase and Associates. I recruited Cheyenne's help to pick out an appropriate outfit for the day. I personally chose a pant suit that I thought was sensible and gave me a very professional appearance. Cheyenne practically tossed the suit into the trash while she muttered something about grandmas and something to the effect of 'wearing that will make instant cob webs form on your vag.' Cheyenne's choice was much more aesthetically pleasing. She chose another pencil skirt, but this one was a really pretty graphite gray and came to just above my knee. She paired the skirt with a simple fitted white dress shirt with three quarter length French cuff sleeves. She completed my outfit with a pair of gray suede stilettos from her own closet. I allowed my long auburn hair to rest freely down my back, and I wore a pair of simple diamond stud earrings and my diamond pendant necklace. I wasn't too concerned with makeup, so I applied my usual everyday amount. Blush to my cheeks, eyeliner to emphasize my green eyes, a double coat of mascara for my lashes, rose tinted lip gloss on my lips, and I was ready to tackle my interview at Chase and Associates.

I drove to the massive high rise building known as Kennedy Plaza. The magnificent forty-five story building was the home of Chase and Associates. I walked inside and miraculously didn't falter once in my ridiculously high heels. I was nervous about the interview and was hoping it would be just what I was looking for.

Third time is the charm Kat. Don't sweat it. Even if it isn't the ideal position, you're going to take it! You can't live on savings forever.

I let out an exhausted huff as I made my way to the bank of elevators to be whisked upward to the forty-second floor. After exiting the elevator, I walked down a wide corridor to a large pristine lobby. My heels clicked against the glossy granite floor. An older woman at a desk in the lobby greeted me warmly with a smile when I approached her.

"Hello. You're here for the interview. You must be Kathleen

Cooper." I was somewhat taken aback by her knowledge of who I was, as if I had one of those name tag stickers stuck to my blouse. I glanced around a bit and suddenly felt very dumb.

You look like a blithering idiot, Kat. Of course she is talking to you. Talk!

"Oh, yes. That's me," I blurted. The woman nodded and kept talking.

"I'm Joyce. I will let Mr. Chase's secretary know that you're here." The woman picked up her phone and spoke to a another woman named Olivia, and a moment after she hung up the phone, the woman I assumed was Olivia walked out from another small waiting area off of the lobby. She gestured for me to follow her, and I entered into the smaller vestibule area. There were two long plush couches placed in the shape of an L. At the front of the room, nearest another large doorway was Olivia's desk. She motioned for me to have a seat as she retreated behind her desk.

"Mr. Chase will be with you shortly," she said in a pleasant voice. The phone on Olivia's desk rang only a minute or two after I had seated myself on the comfortable couches, and she spoke into the phone quietly then hung up. "Mr. Chase is ready to see you." Olivia got up from her seat and waved me over to the large door in the vestibule. She patted me on my shoulder and opened the door wide for me to pass through.

Upon entering the office of Mr. Chase, I immediately noticed the three large floor-to-ceiling windows that provided a breathtaking view of the city. I imagined how all the twinkling lights must look at night. Once the door closed behind me, I turned my attention to the far end of the room where, from my peripheral vision, I could see someone seated at a large desk. I turned my shoulders and was about to make my way to the man when I froze.

Oh. My. God. Someone shoot me.

My feet stayed anchored to the floor beneath my heels. My eyes were wide in shock, and my jaw shamelessly hung agape. I could not believe the sight before me. It took me a moment to even register thoughts.

You look like a giant moron! Do something! Say something! Anything!

Turns out, "anything" was a bad idea. My inner Kathleen should have been more specific.

"You!" I said accusingly, far more high pitched and squeaky sounding than I wished it had been.

The man I knew as Ben, the Book Thief smiled wide without ever exposing a single tooth and arched his brows as if saying "surprise". He looked like a wet dream waiting to happen in his expensive black suit with a simple white shirt and dark blue silk tie. My mouth watered from simply looking at him. I stayed put at the far end of the room away from his desk still in utter shock and trying desperately to come up with something intelligent to say. Then he spoke.

"Kathleen, come in. Sit." He waved a hand towards the leather chair in front of his oversized, cherry wood desk. I stood where I was for a moment longer, then on shaky legs, I slowly walked to the chair before him and sat. I smoothed the front of my skirt and angled my legs from the knee down as I crossed my ankles.

Yeah, you better sit lady-like. No more naughty dreams about Ben. He might be the new boss.

I pushed aside my thoughts and waited for him to speak.

"It's nice to see you again Kathleen." His voice came out so sultry and smooth that my stomach clenched.

"You act as if you haven't seen me in ages, Mr. Chase." I sounded a bit shaky, but my emphasis on his last name caused a wolfish grin to slip across his face, and he leaned back in his chair with steepled fingers.

"Yes, well, nonetheless I am glad to see you in my office."

"Well, something tells me that you aren't nearly as surprised as I am. When did you make the connection that it was me interviewing for the position?"

"Ah, you're quick, Kathleen."

Impatience stirred inside me quickly snuffing out the flame of arousal that was building in me just a moment before.

"Come on Ben, don't patronize me. When did you know?"

"At the emergency room."

"The bracelet," I said on a whisper.

"When I read your full name on the bracelet, I remembered having read it on something else just before my business trip, and I realized it was the name on a resume I had received from someone applying for the paralegal position at my firm," he said coolly.

"So were you going to inform me of this odd coincidence?" I was becoming highly irritated at how manipulative he had been since he discovered my identity.

"I didn't see the point in it. I knew you would obviously find out when you arrived for the interview, so why even tell you? Besides, you may have decided not to show if you knew who I was."

"I would have come," I blurted almost involuntarily. Ben's smiled widened, weakening me further.

Pathetic.

"Soon enough," he whispered just loud enough for me to make out.

"Wait a second... the book. You sent it to my apartment. You already knew my address from the information on my resume. You never got my address from the internet! You lied to me. You are unbelievable, really!" Ben seemed to enjoy my obvious irritation, which only infuriated me more.

"Correction, Kathleen." He smoothed his tie down his chest effortlessly distracting me from even breathing.

Ah, fuck my life.

I inwardly groaned. Ben held up a finger to make a point.

"Yes, I gained the information I needed from your resume, but I did, in fact, confirm your information by using the internet."

"Such a... lawyer!" I bit out. Ben chuckled at my lack of insult.

"Yes. I am indeed a lawyer and a good one at that."

Arrogant! I scoffed at his self-absorbed remark.

"So, when can you start, Kathleen?"

"How do you even know that I still want the position? I don't even know the details of the position. Salary? Benefits?" He sat straight in his chair and with wickedly serious eyes and a stone cold face. He seemed to stare right through me, leaving me short of breath and aroused all over again.

I could feel a tingling down below my hips that told me clearly that working alongside the incredibly handsome Ben would be next to impossible. This, after all, was the same man who seductively stroked his thumb across my jaw, pinned me to a wall with his hips, and whispered in my ear in my apartment building. The feel of his breath on my skin and the silkiness of his voice caressing the heat raging just beneath my skin would be enough to make any woman insane with need. The thought of having to be the woman who was already hot for him and also, at the same time, his employee made me internally hyperventilate.

I could be professional around this guy without jumping his bones. Hell yes, I could be professional. I am not the weak, submissive, accommodating Kat anymore. No bullshit from assholes ever again!

His stern voice roused me from my private pep talk. "Kathleen, my firm is highly successful and offers excellent pay and benefits to employees. I assure you that you won't find better. You want the job." The double entendre of "won't find better" did not escape me. He stood from his chair and made his way around his desk. My heart thumped rapidly when he came to a stop in front of the chair where I sat. His fingers came to my face and made a slow path along the line of my jaw. His thumb went to my bottom lip and made one sweep across my parted lips. "You want it," he rumbled deeply.

Hell yes I do! If the amount of pure sex that drips off of you is any indication... I'm positive I couldn't find better.

I could feel the heat spreading across my face due to my own naughty thoughts, and it made me want to hide from him. He noticed my blush, and a smug smile curled up the corners of his mouth.

"If you are offering the job, I will take it, but only because the other two firms I applied to were not what I was looking for," I said while doing my best to sound confident.

"Oh I'm sure they definitely were not what you were looking for Kathleen."

Gotta get out of here!

"Uh, um... w-when do you want me, I mean need me..." *Jesus!* "When should I start?"

If the look on his face was any indication of how thoroughly adolescent I sounded, I was positive that he was amused with my obvious unease.

"You will come in tomorrow and complete paper work with the HR department and then come to my office and we will sort out your office." He rounded his desk and sat back down in his leather chair.

"Fine, Mr. Chase. I will see you tomorrow then."

I practically ran from Ben's office in a panic about all the feelings this man was capable of eliciting from me. I got into my little Honda and cranked up music from my iPod

My cell phone rang just before I was about to park and escape to my apartment. I answered it and put it on speaker. It was Tucker informing me that he had a client cancel on him, and he could start on the outline of my tattoo this afternoon. With the excitement of getting my tattoo started, I quickly forgot all about my new job and my new boss.

CHAPTER TEN

Story time at the Ink Well

❧⟋⟍❧

I arrived at Tucker's shop with a few minutes to spare and waited nervously to begin the session. No one knew the motivation behind the tattoo I so desperately wanted. I was beginning to wonder if Tucker would inquire about it, and if he didn't, should I spill the beans so he would know exactly how important it was? In the back of my mind, I also wondered how much information about Cheyenne I should give Tucker. I didn't even really know the guy, and although he seemed nice enough and I didn't get a creepy vibe off of him, he was still a stranger, for all intents and purposes. Besides, Cheyenne's business was her own. Who was I to dish on her to someone else?

But I had already made the deal, and I was a woman of my word. I would just have to be careful about what I said so that Cheyenne wouldn't feel betrayed or overexposed. I would never intentionally hurt my friend, and I knew there were parts of her life she simply didn't like to talk about; I respected that.

"I'm ready when you are," Tucker said as I settled across the leather upholstered table face-down, only my arms concealing my bare breasts before the table shielded me. Luckily, Tucker was nice enough to pull a privacy screen in front of his work station at the rear of the parlor. It successfully provided me with protection from prying eyes.

"Okay, let's do this." My breath was thick with trepidation as it sputtered in and out of my lungs unevenly.

Don't back out, Kat. This is important. You promised yourself.

Tucker must have noticed my uneasiness, because he paused to reassure my nerves while he prepared his tray of supplies.

"Don't worry. You're going to love it once it's done. We're only doing the outline today, then we'll let your skin heal before we do another session." His voice was reassuring, and it did the trick to calm my nerves.

Well, Kat, this is your first one. You chose a hell of a tattoo. Go big or go home, right?

I made myself comfortable and tried to relax. Tucker sat beside the table, and with one quick flick of his foot, he pressed down on the pedal that operated the tattoo machine. It buzzed so loudly that it startled me at first, but the vibrating noise enveloped my ears and my body. A sense of fulfillment and atonement filled me all at once with the precise thrust of the needle penetrating my skin at a rapid pace.

The burning sensation that raced across my flesh was painful, and it reminded me of the pain I had endured over the past seven years. The pain I felt from the tattoo machine that was humming steadily in my ear was a discomfort that I embraced wholly and held tightly to.

With each passing stroke that drew blood and permanently marked my flesh with ink, I was reminded that I was alive and free to finally reclaim my heart and soul from the icy grips of despair and loss. Drastic measures to feel alive? Perhaps. Was it necessary? Absolutely.

Knowing that the ink on my skin would be there forever would provide me with a permanent reminder of what I had done to myself and what I had allowed someone else to do to me. I hoped that having it there would keep me away from ever repeating that history. Above the lower portion of the tattoo that represented my past would be the part that represented my future and what I had hoped to be.

"Gonna tell me the story behind this?" I could tell Tucker was curious about the unique design that he was skillfully applying to my skin. It spread top to bottom from my shoulders down to just barely above my waistband. The entire thing was massive, yet unique and intriguing.

"I don't mind telling you the story."

He sat silent while steadily creating the masterpiece on my back. "I was married once before. So was Cheyenne. We both managed to pick real winners in the men we willingly devoted so much of ourselves to. They never deserved anything from either of us." I took in a deep breath while willing myself to keep talking. I told him about all the terrible things that I had seen and dealt with during my seven year marriage to Aidan- everything from the child I had lost, to the lonely birthdays, to the painful infidelity. I explained to him who I used to be and who I had ended up being. "So, the silhouetted woman on the lower half of my back is me. Was me, still somewhat is me. She has empty eyes to show her sadness. Her skin is dull and lifeless. Her hair is stringy and unkempt. Her wrists are bound in front of her to show how she is a prisoner of sorts. The mirror in her hand represents the reflection of herself that was broken. The biomechanical scene all around the woman symbolizes the mechanical and robotic aspect of the life she used to lead. The ropes that tangle and trail up my spine represent the bonds that kept her, me really, immobile, the seven overhand knots ascending the rope are for each of the seven years that I spent living like that. Lastly, but most importantly, the large blue bird with wings fully spread is the best picture of myself that I could think up." I sighed, careful not to move too much.

"What about the little red rose blossom?" Tucker asked, and my heart squeezed while I remembered the baby that never came to be.

"The child that I lost was due to be born in the month of June, and the small red rose blossom is the reminder that even though my baby never made it to this world, he or she existed and will always be my first child. I wanted the rose tucked under the left wing of the bluebird, flush against the bird's body because I'll never get to hold my first child flush to my body. I guess it's a way to hold her... or him. It's the closest I'll ever get." Tears spilled over the rim of my eyes, and I let them fall freely while remembering the utter heartbreak that losing my child caused.

"The tattoo will make it impossible for me to forget everything."

"I'm so sorry. Sounds like you were dealt a bad hand," was Tucker's response to my story. Once he had finished the entire outline of my tattoo he carefully wiped away excess ink and applied a liberal amount of ointment to my skin. He directed me to a large mirror so that could see it. My heart skipped a beat when I saw the tattoo perfectly outlined on my back. It was stunning and precisely what I had envisioned it to be. There was no doubt about it; Tucker was a skilled tattoo artist.

After covering the area with a light bandage, I gave my thanks to Tucker and left. When I got home that evening, Cheyenne was waiting for me in the kitchen where she was cooking something that smelled amazing.

"Hey Chey. Whatever you are making over there smells like it could send me to heaven at warp speed!"She smiled shyly and shrugged her petite shoulders. "Aww thanks. It's nothing special really. Thought you might want something good to eat after your interview today. Speaking of, how'd it go?"

I took in a deep breath and readied myself for the story that was about to pour from my mouth. "So I went to the interview, and it turns out Mr. Chase of Chase and Associates is Ben. Ben is Mr. Chase; Mr. Chase is Ben. They are one and the same."

Cheyenne's eyes grew as wide as the cooking pan she was standing in front of. "Get out! Are you joking? What did you do? Did you get the job? Wow, Kat what are the odds?" I shrugged my shoulders in bewilderment.

"I took the job. I start tomorrow. I'm not sure getting the outline of this tattoo done the day before I begin a new job was the smartest thing I have done in recent history."

Cheyenne's eyes grew even wider at my admission. "Oh my God! Let me see." I turned away from her and lifted my shirt to expose my back. She carefully peeled away the bandages and retreated a step to get a good look. I glanced at her over my shoulder. She gasped and covered her open mouth with her hand once she took in the sight of Tuckers talent. I didn't say anything. I waited for Cheyenne to speak.

"Kat," she whispered. "It's... it's so beautiful and huge! Geez, Kat, I know you said you were getting this tattoo, but you never said how big it was going to be, and you still haven't told me what it's all about. Spill it." Cheyenne put the bandages back in place, and I straightened my top then began explaining. She didn't have much to say, just gave the occasional head nod. After I was done, she hugged me with care, managing to avoid the tender flesh of my back. "It's incredible, really. I love it, and it means a lot to you. I can't wait to see it once it's finished."

Speaking of the tattoo.

"You will never guess who the tattoo artist is. Tucker Barrett, better known to us as Mr. Bar Brawl diffuser." I pursed my lips together and closed my eyes while slowly nodding my head.

"The hot tattooed guy? No freakin way, Kat! How—"

I cut her off before she could continue. "I was looking for the best artist around, and some good-looking guy at that coffee shop I told you about approached me and gave me Tucker's information. The guy said he was the best, so I checked up on it and sure enough, the guy is talented. You should come with me to my next session. Tucker is supposed to be filling in the tattoo. He said he wants to take you on a date."

She clapped her hands in front of her chest and did a little jump.

"Yes! That would be awesome. Hey, maybe I could get a tattoo from Mr. Sexy tattoo guy himself." She smiled broadly.

Oh, Chey, I am positive that Tucker would love nothing

more than to spend some alone time with his tattoo machine and your bare skin.

I spent most of that night attempting to get comfortable in my bed. I failed miserably. Between the new tattoo and my shot nerves over having to see Ben the next day, sleep remained elusive nearly all night. I finally fell asleep in the early morning hours and was close to being violent at the first sound from my alarm clock.

Wednesday, May, 22nd, 2013. Day 225 since Aidan.

Oh no. No. No. No. Shut the hell up noise maker! Please don't be time to get up already!

I reluctantly flipped back my plush down comforter and rolled out of my warm bed, complaining to no one all the way to the bathroom. I knew Cheyenne would not be up yet, so it would be up to me to get to the coffee pot and whip up some liquid motivation. After my trip to the bathroom, I sluggishly trudged into the kitchen and started the coffee pot.

I returned to the bathroom and got into the shower. I got myself all cleaned up and got dressed in the outfit I had laid out the night before. I stepped into the deep plum purple sheath dress and successfully zipped it myself. The dress had a nice scoop neck but did not plunge low enough to reveal cleavage. The darted seams and delicate belted waist of the dress was very flattering for my curvy figure. I slipped on camel colored pumps to match the thin belt around my waist and checked the whole outfit in my full length mirror.

Okay. Not too shabby, Kat.

I gave myself a nod of approval, then I applied a fair amount of makeup to combat the fatigue that had created bags beneath my eyes. I did nothing with my hair other than semi dry it into a thick, damp mass and pull it up into a slick bun.

Good. Professional looking. Now, off to conquer the world.

I snickered inwardly at my absurd private banter. *Good thing no one can hear your thoughts, Kat. Otherwise, you would already be committed into some 'special' hospital for being mental. Said Hospital comes with cushy accommodations including room service, plush padded walls, very modern minimalist décor, oh, and last but not least... a free jacket! Talking to yourself in the third person tends to make folks question a person's mental stability. Oh, well. Note to self: Self, keep insane third person chatting under wraps.*

I rummaged through our little kitchen in search of my favorite travel mug and came up empty handed. There were still a few boxes lingering around waiting to be unpacked, and I was sure that with my having zero luck with everything in life, my mug was likely buried near the bottom of a box.

No time for this crap, Kat! Awesome. Cheap disposable coffee cup it is.

I searched the kitchen yet again for one of the disposable cups Cheyenne had bought and found the cup, but there was not a lidded one in sight. So like any reasonably intelligent person, I decided to wing it, sans coffee cup lid.

Seriously Kat, what's the worst that could happen? Work. Go. Now.

I stood in the doorway of our apartment staring into the lid-less mug. I was contemplating a whole host of possible mishaps, but shook my head to wipe away my irrational thoughts and verbally scolded myself for wasting time that would be much better used commuting to work.

I really AM mental! Don't walk, run. Can't be late.

On the drive to my first day of work at Chase and Associates, I made sure to listen to the right music to get me excited for my first day. I was usually pretty good at scrolling through my impressive playlists on my iPod. I could even do it without out looking much at all. I knew how much flick from my thumb would put me at or near the artist that I happened to be seeking. However, on that day apparently I was shit at this carefully developed iPod enthusiast skill because I could not make anything work in my favor. When I first got into my car I was content with listening to an excellent selection of songs by John Mayer.

Yeah, that will do the trick.

However, I was ready to skip to the next song about sixty seconds into the first song which happened to be about someone's body being a wonderland, and someone who either took the afternoon off from work to bang said wonderland or was clearly unemployed. This concept simply irritated me mostly because I was jealous of this 'wonderland' person, if she even existed. For my sake, I hoped she didn't. So with that summary of the song flitting through my head it was on to the next song. Flick. Next. The next song that filled the cabin of my car was equally as frustrating as the first song. This song was all about doom, gloom, failure in relationships and metaphorically dancing in burning rooms to prove it all.

Oh, hell no, the newly divorced Kathleen Cooper will NOT be listening to this right now, thanks!

With that, I made my move to scoop up my iPod from its precarious perch atop my center console which also served as an armrest. I fumbled with it for a moment while still driving my car, perhaps a little less fluidly. That's when my front right tire encountered the most foreboding, gargantuan pothole I had ever seen. With a huge thunk-thunk noise, both my tires on the right side careened through the crater. My thumb was poised, ready for iPod flick action when the impact and noise jarred my body and startled me. Upon impact, the iPod was instantly vaulted straight up into the air between my seat and the passenger seat. It landed perfectly, I mean, Olympic-Gymnast perfectly into my lid-less piping hot coffee. The auxiliary cord remained plugged into the damned thing in vain of course because the moment the molten lava enveloped my prized possession, all music about doom, gloom, failed relationships and metaphorically dancing in burning rooms... ceased, and ironically enough, the damn thing maybe even sizzled a bit. I pulled over the first chance I got to survey whatever damage had been done.

Gah! Shit! Damn that highly fucking hazardous crater-sized pothole and stupid missing lid!

I got out of my car and walked around to the front, then along the passenger side to the rear. I could not see any obvious signs of damage but then again a rock would be more knowledgeable about auto mechanics than I. Once I was satisfied that nothing major was wrong with my only source of transportation, I checked on myself.

Yep Kat, definitely jazzed up with adrenaline now!

I checked my clothing and made note of the fact that a few fat droplets of coffee successfully sloshed across my dress. My deep purple dress now had a not-so-lovely array of dark splotches scattered across my lap. There would be no time to return to my apartment and change. I was cutting it close as it was. I returned to the driver's seat and resumed my drive to work, which really did not take long since our apartment was relatively close to Kennedy Plaza. When I arrived and hunted down a parking space, I noted the time on the clock in my car.

Five minutes to get your ass to the forty-second floor Kat!

I didn't want my half-full coffee cup to sit in my sweltering car, in May, in Texas, all day, so I grabbed my purse and my pathetic excuse for a coffee cup and made a bee line for the entrance. I narrowly slid between the closing doors of an already full elevator and waited as it ascended smoothly to my floor. I got a few questioning stares from the people around me in the elevator. *Geez, lady stop staring at me like that. You look like a witless Neanderthal who happens to be generously doused in the most offensive scent I have ever had the displeasure of smelling. Yeah lady, it's a fucking iPod in my coffee cup. What's your excuse for smelling like moth balls, cigarettes, grape soda, cat piss and a stuffy basement?! Sweet Jesus, deliver me!*

I had the raging urge to scream at her for having no manners. Staring is rude as hell and so is going around smelling awful. Everyone knows this. The unsatisfied grunt that I fought to keep tucked away safely in my repressed thoughts nearly escaped my mouth, and I had to fight with more effort to appear unaffected. I didn't want to be completely tacky by covering my mouth and nose in a desperate attempt to spare my senses from the onslaught. The iPod remained in its now cold coffee bath, auxiliary cord and all. I had no napkins to take care of the mess, so I decided to deal with it once I was in the office. When the elevator eased to a stop on the forty-second floor and the doors parted, I stumbled over my own feet as I scampered out into the corridor.

Oh thank Jesus! She didn't get off on my floor! Ah, shit, she was right next to me in that sardine can. Did any of that stink rub off on me?

I stood motionless in the corridor while people milled all around me. I was doing my best to discreetly determine if I was stench free or if a tomato juice bath was in order. I couldn't tell one way or another. It seemed like my olfactory perception had said screw this job, resigned, and skipped town, leaving me one sense short of the status: 'fully functioning'. Dramatic as it seemed, my reaction really was completely warranted.

CHAPTER ELEVEN

Tit for tat

I grumpily walked towards Ben's office. I had already had a morning full of unwelcome difficulties, and I just needed to cross one thing off my list of frustrations before one more problem bombarded me and sent my patience toppling over the edge. The problem I needed to sort was Ben. At times, he seemed interested in me at least in a very basic animal instinct, physical kind of way.

Wishful thinking, Kat, especially from a woman who is desperate to get laid. Preferably by Mr. Sex- on-legs.

I couldn't afford for what was going on between us to turn into anything. I needed the new job. I needed stability and routine. I needed to focus on getting myself together. Ben was a distraction from those tasks, and he spelled trouble in capital letters. He was quiet one moment, then firm and authoritative the next. He had me so confused and disoriented that I could not tell up from down. I had a suspicion that maybe Ben enjoyed this taunting mind fuck game of his. I had my panties in a twist since the interview.

Sort this out before your head explodes. No more mixed signals, gray areas, or unclear boundaries. Handle it!

I walked right past Olivia who said nothing to me. She only stared at me with shock and confusion written across her face. I hesitated for a moment, trying to think better of what I was doing. My repressed inner Kat would have been far more useful in this situation. If I could have just wrangled in my inner self, I wouldn't even hesitate. I would have walked with confidence right into his personal office showing not an iota of worry. I would be able to don a poker face lightning quick, one that was capable of bluffing anyone, or flip a switch to turn on irresistible feminine charm. Both were tools that I once used and knew exactly how and when to employ them. I would be able to tamp down all inconvenient emotion and withstand a vicious verbal assault without so much as a flinch or frown. I would have demanded respect and courtesy from everyone around me on the merits of competence and smarts alone. Anyone who tested me would quickly be made fully aware of my no-nonsense approach and lack of patience. Simply put, I would not have taken any shit from anyone.

Not even Mr. Sex-on-legs, Benjamin Chase. In fact I would likely meet him head to head in every way. Having three older brothers to deal with while growing up proved to be extensive training on how to manage in a 'man's world.' Those no-good brothers of mine unknowingly taught me everything I would ever need to know in order succeed and be a competitive force to reckon with. Kathleen Cooper in true form is, strangely enough, a female version of Benjamin Chase. The person that planned on stomping into Ben's office was a spineless, lowly paralegal. A 'glorified gopher,' as one lousy excuse for a lawyer once called me. He had always been rude as hell, making jokes at my expense and ordering me around to essentially do everything for him short of wiping his incompetent, sloth ass. One day he decided to demote me from an educated, grown woman to a subterranean-dwelling mover of dirt. I said nothing to him to defend myself or confront his serious lack of professionalism. I had blushed bright red like an embarrassed child and widened my eyes in shock to which he had beamed a satisfied smile. I had trembled as I turned away to walk to the ladies room and tried my best to be quiet while I cried in a cold bathroom stall.

I remained his over-bullied, 'glorified gopher' until he took a position at another firm. I wished things could be just like before. Before my spirit was backed into a dark corner and locked away to be forgotten.

I gave Ben's office door a halfhearted knock before just walking right in. *Oh, very ballsy Kat* is what the brave part of me cheered in my head. Ben stood before one of the three windows holding a coffee cup in his hand, staring out at the city below. When he heard the door to his office open, interrupting his private moment, he turned to face the intruder, me. I stood for a moment not saying anything to him. I was scowling and breathing rapidly courtesy of the adrenaline rush I had been riding for the past fifteen minutes. We locked eyes, and his surprised expression smoothed into... was that... delight?

This guy is getting a kick out of seeing me pissed after I barge into his office uninvited, on my first day working for him no less?

Just seeing that smug expression that was a mix of pleased

and amused only angered me further. I broke the silence first while still wishing that just for a moment I could conjure my former self to handle Ben. In a sarcastic voice I asked Ben a question that came out sounding more like a desperate plea.

"Please tell me that it is illegal somewhere for a person who smells so badly to walk around offending others' nostrils with their weapon of choice" I stared across the room at him and waited impatiently for a response.

"Good morning, Kathleen. Please, do come in."

No head games today!

I decided that maybe I could give him a taste of his own medicine. Maybe that would teach him about playing his hot and cold game. Maybe I could affect his rational thinking by jumbling his brain with thoughts of me. Then he would be the one who couldn't think clearly, or sleep, or doing anything for that matter without having to deal with distracting thoughts. If this worked out and I saw that my plot to arouse had been successful, I would simply flip the switch back to professional and feign ignorance. If my little ploy to arouse him didn't work, it could seriously backfire. I wondered for a moment if maybe the intrusive scent in the elevator somehow soaked into my own clothing due to my proximity to the woman.

Ah, screw it!

With my inner self on board and cheering me on, my courage was re-enforced and I marched directly across the room and stepped right into Ben's personal space. I was facing the windows, and Ben was now standing with his back to the city below. I stood slightly off center in front of him looking straight ahead. If I had leaned forward, I could rest my head on his right pectoral. It was a tantalizing thought that I quickly pushed aside, so I could focus on ridding myself of the amateurish crushing girl nonsense. I needed my level head back and needed to stop with the wet dreams starring Ben. If I could not manage to set a clear boundary, being his employee would not have a chance in hell at working. Despite his being an overly confident, self-absorbed, pushy lawyer, I couldn't resist the attraction to him. It seemed to be beyond my control. It was animal instinct at its finest.

Female seeks alpha male, even if he does bite.

I kept my eyes fixed straight ahead of me and did a damn good job of acting all kinds of confident and unaffected by my close proximity to Ben's handsome, hard body. A moment after I stepped into his personal space, my nose was inundated with Ben's masculine, panty dissolving scent, effectively ridding me of the leftover scent from the elevator.

Thank Jesus! Oh, he smells perfect.

It suddenly became a bit harder to keep my eyes straight ahead and my impassive façade intact. My knees weakened, and arousal began gathering between my trembling thighs. I could see Ben in my peripheral vision, and I knew he was openly looking at my face. Chill bumps spread like a fierce wildfire across the surface of my skin. I couldn't tell if Ben noticed or not. I hoped that he didn't. He leaned slightly to his left and deposited his coffee cup onto an end table. Then it was his turn to break our intense silence, and boy, he didn't just break the silence, he shattered it into a million pieces along with my stupid ploy and formerly bolstered, but newly absent, courage. Apparently, once Ben spoke, my smart-mouthed inner Kat disappeared in a hurry. His voice came out low and rough; each syllable that rolled off his tongue seemed to stroke me internally, causing my stomach to flip and flutter wildly.

"Kathleen, am I the one to thank for these chill bumps, all over your skin or did something else do this for you?" As he spoke to me, he lifted his right hand and lightly brushed the backs of his long fingers down my right upper arm then swirled a light circle around my elbow and continued down the sensitive inner skin of my forearm, skating across my flesh with barely-there strokes from his nimble fingers.

I kept my eyes cast away from his. I seemed incapable of looking directly into his eyes. I felt as if looking straight into those glowing depths of vivid blue would cause me to be swallowed up whole and pulled beneath the surface to blissfully drown in him. The fierce sexual energy that permeated the air around Ben made it difficult to breathe, and it intimidated me. I chose not to answer him. Or perhaps I couldn't answer him.

"Kathleen, look at me." His commanding tone and presence was hard to challenge even from a distance and far more grueling a task within such close quarters. I could smell him, I could feel the warmth from his body radiating outward, and I could clearly hear each breath he drew from the space between us and pulled down to fill his lungs. I felt a powerful crimson, heated blush roll through my veins. It coursed throughout my body leaving evidence of my arousal in its wake. My skin heated, and my neck and cheeks flushed into a hot red. I realized that I was helplessly adrift in a sea of desire and arousal and that battling the current would be useless. I could either embrace the journey along the formidable pull of the current, or I could fight in vain against Mother Nature, knowing that undoubtedly I would lose.

"Look at me. Answer my question." I lifted my eyes from the

floor, but still avoided his stare.

He extended his long index finger and placed the pad of it beneath my chin and encouraged my head to tilt back, forcing my eyes to meet his. The moment we locked eyes, my breathing halted , and I felt my stomach flip and flutter all over again with a heightened need that exceeded any feeling I had experienced before it, ever. I battled against myself for composure so that I could finally answer him. I had not the faintest idea of what I would say, but I knew I needed to say something. My eyes darted around a bit, and he released my jaw, giving me an opportunity to speak.

Tit for tat, I thought.

"You never answered my own question, Mr. *Chase*." I made a point to emphasize his name in hopes that sounding more like his employee would bring a halt to his request for an answer. I was hoping we could end this torturous little tango that had me tied up in knots.

No, Kat. You wish Ben had you tied up. He hasn't done it yet.

And with that sarcastic little jab to my sex life (or lack thereof), the inner Kat sauntered back into my head as if she had merely stepped away for a moment, but didn't go too far.

CHAPTER TWELVE

And cue crazy

❧

My eyes slid directly back to Ben's looking for a reaction. I certainly didn't expect him to attempt to answer the ridiculous question I had begun this little meeting with. I was high on adrenaline and extremely agitated with my morning when I barged in spouting off at the mouth.

Ben narrowed his eyes slightly as soon as he heard the embellished way I called him by his last name. Then his eyes focused on my left hand. Quite unbelievably, my left hand still held tightly to the damned lidless coffee cup that held half coffee, half of an eighty gig iPod.

I followed his eyes and half glanced at my own hand which didn't feel like it belonged to me. Actually, my whole body was out of sorts thanks to Ben. I was a combination of heat, blush, numbness, tingling, and excited flutters. I stepped back from him and made my best effort to appear calm and collected. He arched an eyebrow and motioned his right hand outward, pointing lazily at the stupid cup in my hand. He opened his mouth to speak, but I beat him to it.

"No lid!" I nearly shouted at him.

Talk first.

I spoke first, a whole two words that came out in a clipped half shout. The moment I heard myself, I looked down at the carpet and made my best effort to stifle the embarrassed feeling that flooded me.

"How did an iPod end up in your cup? More importantly why are you still holding the cup? Plan on drinking the coffee still?" Ben began chuckling halfway through his last question.

I peeked up at him just a fraction, and he had repositioned his stance. He casually stuffed his hands into the pockets of what I could easily identify as Armani dress pants, thanks to Aidan's own collection of expensive Armani suits.

What the hell was it with successful men and Armani?

Evidently he was getting more comfortable for the show I was providing the exact way he did at Book Ends.

I knew he would act like this, I thought, while I tried to allow myself a moment to plan what I should say. My neck tightened, and I whipped my head into its rightful place, high above my tense shoulders.

"I said, no lid. I couldn't find my travel mug, so I used this disposable one but couldn't find the lid to this one either, and, well... there was this crater in the street, and my iPod went flying right into the cup. I didn't have any napkins to clean up this mess, so I just brought it with me." I glanced up at him sheepishly. I was utterly embarrassed with my loony sounding explanation and ridiculous intrusion into his office. He stood before me with his head cocked slightly to the side and a vague glimmer of sympathy in his intense eyes. I continued to explain my insane outburst. "Then there was that woman. In the elevator. I never... I mean, the smell! Maybe I'm neurotic due to sleep deprivation. I apologize, Mr. Chase. I don't know what my problem is today."

The problem is my extreme attraction to you and your hot, then cold head games.

I slumped my shoulders in shame and nibbled on my lip nervously. I peered at Ben who remained in the same position: his hands in his pockets and his head slightly cocked to the side as if he were trying to see past my words right into my brain. He straightened his shoulders and righted his posture before he spoke.

"You met Louise. That's her name. She has worked in this building for a long time. And yes, she has an odd perfume, but I don't think anyone has the nerve to say anything to her because she is too nice to everyone." I was relieved that it wasn't just me imagining things in the elevator.

"Well, she wasn't pleasant with me. She stared at me with this perplexed look. It was awkward and just... bad manners! I was flustered and breathing fast because I was so rushed and that crater I ran my car through. It was just a coffee cup that happens to have an iPod in it, and as for my dress, it's a few coffee stains. No big deal. She didn't have to openly gawk at me the entire way up here." After I stopped rambling, I placed my right hand on my hip and observed Ben looking me over, head to toe. His gaze lingered for a long moment when his eyes arrived at the skirt of my dress where the dark coffee stains were.

"Come here." His voice was husky and dominating. Much to

my surprise, my legs carried me closer to him immediately. I was agitated at my treasonous body. My brain shouted 'hell no.' My body purred 'yes please.' His eyes burned through me. His warm hand slid across my forearm and took the cup I was still clutching. He placed it on the table with his abandoned coffee cup and turned back to me. My body was on fire and in need. Desperate need. I had not had sex in months and had been teased by Ben since we met. He was a delicious temptation that dangled in front of me tempting me to indulge. Heat gathered in my core, and I shifted my thighs to alleviate the ache that was steadily growing there. His muscular arm wrapped around my waist and swiftly jerked my body to him.

I collided with the firm wall of his muscular body and gasped. Goosebumps once again spread across my skin. Ben lowered his head to mine. His clean shaven jaw rubbed lightly against my cheek.

"I give you chills. You respond to me like I respond to you." As he whispered in my ear, he ground his hips into mine, making the rock solid bulge in his pants known. I clamped my lips together to hold back the moan that nearly slipped out. Before I knew what was happening, Ben had spun me around and backed me up to his desk. He lifted me easily and sat me on the edge of the cool dark wood.

Oh please!

I struggled for words but couldn't decide what my inner plea was for. More? To stop? Ben was panting with need just as I was. He nudged my legs open with his thigh, and I opened to welcome him. He gripped me hard around my waist and pressed my pulsing center against his bulging erection. The cloth between us was unwelcome, and Ben quickly hiked my dress up around my waist. His voice cut through my defenses leaving only my need for him. My breath stalled in my throat. My heart pounded in my chest. Ben dug his fingers into the slick bun I had styled my hair into. His fingers tangled into my auburn hair, and he tugged my head back to give him access. His mouth attacked my neck hungrily. His soft lips kissed and drifted across my neck up to the sensitive spot behind my ear.

"Oh Ben," I mumbled. He released an approving growl and feasted on my neck with vigor. The arm around my waist fell away, and his hot hand slid up my inner thigh to my needy center. I moaned and didn't bother trying to hide it. His hand cupped me through my drenched panties. My arousal became unbearable. I writhed in his grip silently begging for more. His hand between my thighs slid up and down my center teasingly, while his mouth remained at my neck, kissing and licking my skin hungrily. His other hand stayed tangled in my hair keeping me immobile. One deft finger slid under the small bit of cloth cloaking my ready opening.

"You're so wet," he growled into my ear. His mouth left my neck, and his eyes landed back on mine. He was watching the effect he had on me play out. His fingers worked expertly over my pulsing clitoris, and my eyes shut and rolled back as a desperate pleading moan tore from my throat.

Please!

"Open them," he demanded, and I complied like the perfect little submissive. My vacant channel clenched at nothing and ached to be filled. Ben slid two fingers into my begging body and began working me to climax. His eyes stayed on me. He watched every move I made. He took in every reaction I had to him. I bucked beneath him. My hips rolled towards his, wanting more of him. My pleading went unacknowledged while he remained in place using his fingers to work me over with the utmost finesse and skill. A delicious tightening clenched in my stomach and my breathing became even more erratic.

"Oh, Ben," I whimpered again as my eyes slid closed.

"Look at me," he rumbled. When my eyes came back to his, I blew apart under his grip as a painfully exquisite orgasm surged through my body. I quaked and trembled and reveled in the euphoria that overtook me. Ben withdrew his fingers from my body and raised them to his lips. I watched with a twinge of horror, but also wild desire, as he licked one finger clean. A gratifying sigh emanated from low in his chest.

"You taste perfect." Without further hesitation, Ben plunged the second finger into my mouth. "See, Kathleen?" I latched onto his finger and swirled my tongue around it savoring the moment we were sharing. His finger in my mouth was erotic, and I suddenly longed to kneel before him with his erection invading my mouth. The whole scene between us was a grand display of his sexual prowess, and I wanted more. A lot more.

He withdrew his finger from my mouth and leaned in to kiss me when the intercom on his desk came to life. Olivia's voice echoed out of the small speaker and jarred my brain.

Ben dismissed the interruption and told Olivia that he was not to be disturbed for the time being. The intercom disconnected, and I panicked.

"Oh, shit. Ben, I can't. I shouldn't have. Damn." I pushed my way off his desk and free of his formidable frame. His brows furrowed in confusion, marring his beautiful face. I wanted to melt when a look of rejection glinted in his eyes.

Please don't make me feel worse.

I stood on wobbly legs in front of his desk with him standing between me and the exit. He was allowing me the minimum amount of space to right myself. I straightened my clothing and smoothed my hair while trying to avoid eye contact.

"You want this. I know you do. You've wanted this since we met in the book store." He pointed a stern finger at me while reminding me of exactly how much I wanted him. I dismissed the tug in my groin at hearing the truth.

"No. I can't. I-I have... too much to sort out. My life is screwed up. You don't want to bother with me. Trust me." I shook my head while I spoke, but continued avoiding eye contact.

"That's for me to decide."

I paused in my nervous fidgeting and looked up into his disarming blue-green irises. I couldn't discern if his statement was a promise or a threat, but either way it was heady and intriguing.

Fine, I thought to myself. I shuffled nervously on my feet, and Ben stepped out of my personal space immediately easing my shuffling. I felt embarrassed and naked, and I decided to segue into safer territory.

"So..." I softly clapped my hands in front of me and rocked back in my heels to bring his attention back from wherever it was. I needed to get out of his office, pronto. I continued to speak when his attention returned to my face. "Where will I be working? I can put my things away and get over to the HR department."

Ben only nodded his head, motioned me to the door, and he followed beside me. He began giving me basic details of who, when, where, why and how as we walked through his office and back out into the corridor. He guided me to what would be my little office, all the while rattling out information at a dizzying pace in an all-business tone. It made me feel cold and used. I wanted the low-toned rumbling Ben who had been out of breath with need only moments before.

Stupid girl!

I chastised myself for wanting exactly what I just shoved away. His hand was warm and firm where it was pressed against my lower back, but the moment he placed it there, I winced and sucked in a breath through gritted teeth. Ben stopped walking and quirked an eyebrow, signaling me to explain my reaction. I only shook my head dismissively and gave a halfhearted excuse about having pulled a back muscle while working out. It wasn't even close to believable. I wanted to kick myself as I heard the poorly formed excuse stutter out of my mouth. Ben dropped his hand from my terribly tender, freshly tattooed back and smirked while shaking his head. He took the lead and walked ahead of me into the office space I would be using. It was small but well-equipped for doing research and case prep work, drafting legal documents, and writing reports. It was certainly the best office I had been assigned to yet.

Before he left me to settle in, he turned his smoldering eyes on me. "You won't refuse me forever."

Ah. Another threat/promise, I mused, only slightly shocked. The only response I gave was a tiny gasp through parted lips. He marched away, leaving me with only my thoughts, memories of being in his grip, and damp panties.

Once Ben retreated to his plush office down the hall, I put away my purse and went to the bathroom to clean up evidence from my earlier, coffee catastrophe. By the time I finished up with Human Resources, it was a few minutes until my lunch hour began. I occupied the last few minutes before lunch by getting familiar with the office phone that sat on my desk. It was way more high tech than I was used to. The contraption had a larger than normal color screen with icons on it, and more buttons than I knew what to do with. My curiosity got the best of me when I decided to figure the thing out myself. One button. Nothing.

Hmm.

Another three buttons and nothing special happened.

Really? How hard could it be?

I scrunched my eyebrows together and kept at it. Determined to gain some sign of functionality, I pressed another button, and I heard a pulsing beep coming from the phone. Beep-beeeep, Beep-beeeep.

"Uh-oh," I muttered aloud. I stood and immediately began jabbing buttons to make it shut up when a voice replaced the beeping.

"Yes?"

Shit! Ben!

Instead of saying something, I froze and decided to just unplug the cords connected to the back. The screen went dark, and I stood frozen, staring at it and hoping that I didn't make any distinguishing noises that would identify the accidental prank caller as me.

Well played, Kat. Fuck!

I rolled my eyes and looked at the clock which, to my relief, read 12:00. I began to gather my things when my office door swung open, and Ben walked right in. I froze in place, of course. "You called?"

Well, of course, he would know it was me who called and said nothing, then hung up like a nitwit.

"I, uh, I was trying to figure out this phone. It's complicated. I must have called you on accident. I didn't really need to talk to you, or um, I didn't want, I mean, I didn't need anything-Sorry."

Go ahead and show your cards, Kat. Lay em' out so he knows you want AND need plenty from him.

My private thoughts had my heart racing as I stood there praying for an out.

A boulder falling from the sky and dropping on your head ought to do it.

Ben's eyebrows rose, and his lips shifted slightly. He was clearly amused with my explanation yet again. "I see. Well, it's lunch. Let's go eat, and I will get you up to speed on things around here."

Yay for painfully awkward, sexually tense lunch breaks with bosses who star in nightly, erotic dreams and who started my work day with an explosive orgasm!

"Right. Um, okay; let's go." A slightly relieved expression took over his face for a fraction of second before he corrected himself. I followed behind Ben as he walked with graceful, long strides through the corridor and back into his office. He held his hand up beside him at eye level, and without even looking over his shoulder, two fingers extended and flicked forward motioning for me to continue following him into his office. We sat at a comfortable sitting area that was just as inviting as a living room in a person's house. There were two large cushy chairs, a matching sofa, a large glossy, wooden coffee table and coordinating end tables. Ben noticed my puzzled look, and he explained that he always ate lunch in his office.

Once our Chinese take-out arrived, we ate and talked. Ben filled me in on the basics and 'got me up to speed.' Aside from a few lingering looks, Ben acted as if our actions that morning had never happened. I was relieved and a little disappointed at the same time. He seemed to brush it off quite easily, whereas I had been the exact opposite throughout the day.

Once lunch was over, he wanted to introduce me to Trevor Whitmore, another attorney at the firm. We paused at the entry to Trevor Whitmore's sitting area. Ben placed his left hand on my right elbow and wrapped his fingers lightly around it. His fingers were warm, and they were clasped possessively, rousing a gentle blush to my cheeks. He leaned in toward my ear as he held my elbow. His lips brushed my ear as he spoke quietly. I stared blankly ahead at Trevor's secretary while Ben spoke.

"Stay here. I need to speak to Trev. I'll come get you in a sec. Won't be long." The secretary sat behind a desk exactly like Olivia's. She was staring at us with an unreadable look on her face.

Jealousy? Curiosity?

I wondered. She must've noticed the delicate blush that spread across my cheeks when Ben spoke in my ear because just then, I saw her jaw tense, and a muscle in her cheek twitched.

Yep. Jealousy. She must have a crush.

After Ben released my elbow, he strode right past Trevor's secretary without so much as a glance in her direction. However, she gawked at Ben shamelessly. Once he disappeared behind Trevor's office door and shut it, her head dropped, and her shoulders slumped.

Someone has it bad for Ben.

I felt a bit sympathetic for the woman. I walked to her desk and extended my hand to introduce myself. Once the woman noticed me walking toward her, she looked directly at me, and her previous unreadable expression replaced the disappointment written on her face.

Great, another person just dying to be friends!

"Hello, I'm Kathleen Cooper. Nice to meet you."

"Janis Harper." She made no effort to disguise her opinion of me. The moment my hand fell back to my side, Ben reappeared from Trevor's office to bring me in. I gave Janis a half-hearted smile before Ben walked me into Trevor's office. Ben introduced me to Trevor, and he smiled wide before he looked between Ben and I.

We carried on casual conversation for a few minutes then decided it was time to get back to real work. Trevor clapped Ben on the back before we exited and shook his head with an amused grin across his face.

What the hell? Did I miss something?

I wondered what they talked about while I waited with Janis. Ben lifted his hand and waved it in front of us, motioning for me to go ahead of him. As I shouldered past him, he placed a guiding hand on my lower back for just a moment, then it fell away. I felt a pull of disappointment when the warmth of his touch left my back. I wanted to feel it again. I wanted to feel much, much, more. I didn't bother to acknowledge Janis. I didn't have to look to know that she had probably turned an unflattering shade of green.

The rest of my first day went by in a blur. Ben had me busy playing catch-up on all the work that had accumulated since his last paralegal quit. I was relieved to be working again and was determined to prove how invaluable I could be to him. If I were being honest with myself, I wanted to impress Ben more than just professionally. When I came home that evening, I told Cheyenne all about my day, and she told me about landing a position at some high-end spa. I could tell she was glad to get back to work, too, even if it was not what she truly loved. I reminded myself over dinner that night that I had to figure out a way to convince Cheyenne to pursue her dreams of opening a bakery.

CHAPTER THIRTEEN

Making plans

Thursday, June, 27th, 2013. Day 36 since I began working at the firm. Working alongside Ben proved to be challenging in all the right ways. He was a magnificent attorney who was intimidating in the courtroom. He was thorough and efficient and refused to accept anything less from his team and colleagues at the firm. Unlike the putz I had worked for previously, Ben was all too willing to do time-consuming, tedious work alongside me. I told him many times that I could handle whatever he threw at me, but many times he would insist on doing things himself. I was beginning to wonder if he doubted my intelligence or competence. I thought that perhaps he was making an excuse for us to spend more time in the same room together. I had secretly hoped it was the latter, but just to be sure, I was determined that I would work hard to prove myself. I arrived at work in a rather great mood. I'd slept well the night before, and restful nights like that had been few and far between for far too long. I was enjoying my new-found ability to sleep.

Since I had begun working at the firm, Ben and I ate lunch together nearly every day, and that day was no different. I strolled into Ben's office at noon. He was on the phone when I walked in and glanced up at me while flashing that mischievous grin that I had become so fond of during the month I had been working at the firm. Though I was still a nervous idiot in his presence, I managed to control myself by focusing on work. Ben, of course, still made me hot and bothered on a regular basis. Heated glances, slight touches, sexual innuendos, and breathy whispers were just a part of being around him. I was becoming accustomed to it all.

Ben placed the phone in its cradle and silently stared at me while reclining in his desk chair. He was free of his suit jacket and tugged the knot of his silk tie loose before he interlaced his fingers at the nape of his neck.

"Kathleen, have a seat. Lunch will be here shortly. In the meantime, I have to talk to you about something." I fidgeted my fingers anxiously.

"Okay. What about?" Ben appeared simply delicious behind his desk in a relaxed, confident state. I found it difficult to focus on much more than the gorgeous specimen in front of me.

"There is a charity function I have to attend tomorrow evening, and I would like you to come with me."

Confident and demanding as ever.

"Mr. Chase, I don't know if I can." He cocked his head to the side and looked a bit confused.

"And why wouldn't you?" My eyes darted about the room hoping to come up with a decent excuse. I came up with nothing, so I did the next best thing. I answered a question with a question.

"What type of charity is it?"

His smirk returned. I could tell he saw right through me as always. It was quite uncomfortable when he made me feel so transparent.

"It's an annual black-tie ball that raises money for an inner-city children's mentor program. I go every year."

Come up with something, Kat.

"I see. Well, I think that's great, and I'm sure it would be fun, but I can't go because I, um, I don't have anything formal in my closet, and neither does Cheyenne." With that lame excuse, I could almost see my inner self looking down, arms crossed, shaking her head in disappointment with my lack of originality.

"You're right. It is a fun event, and the good news for you is you will get to find out for yourself since you do have a formal dress."

"Uh, Mr. Chase, I don—"

He interrupted me, of course. He held up one finger, signaling in his bossy way for me to shut my lips. I complied.

"I have arranged for a suitable dress to be delivered to your apartment tomorrow. Also, you have an appointment tomorrow at the best spa in town. A car will pick you up at eleven am. I'll pick you up at six for the ball." My mouth hung open in shock.

"Indulgence?" If he was sending me to the best in town, I knew it had to be there. He was already standing to move to the sitting area where we always ate lunch.

"What?" he questioned, appearing confused.

"The spa. Indulgence? Cheyenne works there." I inched behind him, following in his path like a dumb struck puppy. His head cocked to the side, and his brows rose for a second before he shrugged casually.

"Yes, that's the one."

"But that's pretty high-end. I don't know if I can afford that, and what about work?" He let out a long, exasperated breath, and I feared I was irritating him.

Why the hell should I care so much?

I battled against my frustrating train of thought and tried to focus on the conversation with Ben.

"Kathleen, it's all paid for, and you have the day off tomorrow." I stopped inching towards him and just walked to the sitting area to join him.

"Oh. I still don't know if it's a good idea. I have tons to get done tomorrow," I lied.

"Honestly, you would be doing me a favor by being my date. I despise going to these types of events alone. Please." He huffed and absentmindedly rubbed two fingers against his temple.

He is getting frustrated for sure. Or nervous? His date?

"Well, if it helps you out, I guess I can go." There was no way I could refuse his pleading eyes and the mixed expression written across his face. If I were being completely honest with myself, I wanted to go. He smiled triumphantly and visibly relaxed after I agreed.

"So it's settled then," he said with a grin and a wink.

And there's Mr. Cocky.

Friday, June, 28th, 2013. Day 37 since starting work at the firm. I was a bundle of nerves while I waited for the car Ben was sending for me. I didn't even think to ask him what I was getting done at the spa. I wasn't sure if he just expected me to know what I was having done to prepare for the ball or if he already spoke to the staff about what to do with me. Knowing Ben, he would have covered his bases and spoken to the staff. When the car arrived as scheduled, I was taken directly to Indulgence. After I arrived, I was immediately given a Mimosa and fresh fruit. I had already told Cheyenne about the ball and my appointment at the spa, so seeing her there was no surprise. The moment she saw me, she practically ran to my side.

"Hey gorgeous! So, guess what I heard this morning?" Cheyenne waggled her eyebrows while smiling ear to ear. She leaned in and spoke in a whisper like a high school girl sharing juicy gossip with her 'BFF.' I bugged my eyes out, gasped dramatically for effect, and made sure to speak in my shocked soap-opera voice.

"O-M-G, Chey, *do* tell!" Cheyenne rolled her eyes at my little show of drama while I laughed.

"Ha. Ha. Very cute. Okay, cut the crap. I'm serious."

"Okay, Okay. What did you hear, Chey?"

"The word on the street is that some hot shot called to make an appointment last week for his 'friend,'" Cheyenne used air quotes with her fingers.

"And he demanded the full treatment, head to toe. He said to provide whatever his 'friend' aka, you, wanted. The girls at the front desk said he made a big fuss over you. Do you know how pricey the works is?"

I shrugged.

"It's damn expensive, Kat! Ben must seriously have a thing for you if he is willing to do all this. Have you seen the dress yet?" She was talking a million miles per hour and being her typical giddy self. It was hard to keep up.

"Cheyenne, you're getting excited over nothing. He may be flirtatious, but there is nothing going on between us. Besides, he's probably asking the staff to give me a full make over so that I don't publicly embarrass him." Cheyenne rolled her eyes and guffawed.

"You must be deaf, dumb, blind, or all of the above, Kat! She held up two French-tipped fingers, then jabbed them at my chest. "First, have you looked in the mirror? You're a smoking' hot babe! And second, news flash, no one goes to all this trouble for someone they are not interested in." I swatted her hand away.

"That's debatable, but we'll see, I suppose."

"Come on. Give yourself some credit here. Does Ben know about law school? Does he know about you acing the LSAT?" I narrowed my eyes on Cheyenne.

"Nope. Does Tuck know that you are a culinary genius who refuses to pursue her dream?"

Cheyenne glared at me. "*Touché*," she grumbled. I gave her a pat on the back and swallowed hard.

"No need to relive the past, right? Gotta run. I'll see you tonight at home." Cheyenne just sighed and nodded her head as I followed my masseuse away from the spa's lounge.

Two weeks prior, I went to Tucker's shop to complete my tattoo, and Cheyenne came along. I had managed to give Tucker just enough information about Cheyenne to appease him, and it was easy work convincing Cheyenne of how great he was. She jumped at the opportunity to go on a date with him. They seemed to be getting along great and spending plenty of time together. I had hope that he would be good for my best friend, and so far, he was far exceeding my expectations.

Despite my reluctance to go, I had to admit that the spa day was amazing. I was pampered, polished, massaged, waxed, soaked in essential oils, manicured, and pedicured. The stylist shampooed and styled my long auburn locks into loose waves that hung down my back. The makeup artist applied my makeup for the ball, and it was perfect. My green eyes have a burst of amber jutting outward from the center of my irises, and the makeup artist accentuated the emerald green and amber flawlessly. My eyes were a light smoky gray around the edges with bronze fading into a metallic copper colored shadow across my eyelids.

I paced around in the apartment looking ready to impress except I had no dress. I was wearing a ratty bath robe over my polished skin. I had become nervous with only a half an hour before Ben would be arriving and still no dress. I was digging through my closet for formal wear when at last, the dress he bought for me was delivered. I unzipped the wardrobe bag and stared blankly at what he sent for me. It was a jade green Grecian-style designer gown.

Holy shit!

It was positively breathtaking. I had to admit, Ben had great taste. I slipped on the dress, and Cheyenne came bounding into the room and froze.

"Kat! My God, you look... incredible!" She leapt at me, grabbed my shoulders to spin me for a full view.

"Thanks. But it does seem a little scandalous. Yes? No?"

"Are you joking? Hell no, it's not scandalous. It's beautiful, and you wear it like it was made for you." The coloring of the gown made my green eyes vibrant. The dress was chiffon and silk. It had a halter V-neck line that plunged between my breasts. The base of the plunging V had a crystal beaded ornate bronze embellishment. The straps clasped behind my neck, and the front of the gown had draped chiffon that streamed across and over every curve. It exaggerated my hips, my breasts and the contour of my waist, creating an hour glass figure like none I had ever seen. The gown had a plunging back that rested at the small of my back and barely covered my rear from being exposed. It had a thigh high slit, and the hem just barely grazed the floor in the front and a little more in the back. I looked like I had been skillfully wrapped in an expensive bed sheet. He also sent a box that held a beautiful, strappy pair of pricey designer heels that matched the embellishment on the gown perfectly, and a metallic fold-over clutch. All in all, I was sure that the total cost of this ensemble was likely worth more than my car. I had Cheyenne snap a photo of me with my cell phone, then I uploaded it to my social network. It was just too enticing not to share.

Ben arrived right on time as I knew he would. I grabbed my tinted lip gloss, cell phone, compact mirror, and a little cash, stuffed all of it into my clutch and walked out the front door where he stood with his back to the door. His hands were in his pockets, and he spun to see me once I exited my apartment. He took his hands from his pockets and swallowed hard. I blushed slightly when I saw his eyes skate over me appraisingly.

"You're radiant, Kathleen Cooper."

"Thank you..." I wasn't sure what I should call him.

"Please, it's just Ben to you."

To me? What's that supposed to mean?

Ben extended his arm. "Shall we?"

I slipped my arm into the crook of his elbow, and he led us to the waiting car. The driver opened the door to the car, and Ben nudged me ahead of him to slip into the back. When I stepped ahead of him, his hand landed on my lower back, and the skin-to-skin contact sent my senses ablaze. My stomach turned over and felt leaden; a thin sheen of sweat blossomed from my pores and heat pulsed through my core. I hesitated for a moment with his hand on me, and I heard him take in a sharp breath. I slid across the leather upholstery and glanced back at Ben. He stood beside the open door of the car with a curious look on his face; then he shook his head and slid into the car next to me. Our thighs were only inches from touching. I was longing to touch him, to be touched by him. My heart was pounding in my chest, and I felt Ben staring at me.

"What?" I said in a whisper. Ben glanced toward my shoulder, and suddenly I realized what had him so stupefied outside the car.

Holy shit! The tattoo!

I was so consumed with the beautiful outfit that Ben had sent over for me that I didn't even think about the ink that covered the full span of my back. I was sure that he did not expect such a tattoo on a person like me.

Crap! He is going to be embarrassed by me in front of all these high class people. Should I explain? I can't explain this to him, nor do I want to. Should I back out and ask to be taken home? I don't want to insult him. Shit!

I decided to just do my best to let my long, styled wavy locks conceal my tattooed flesh as much as possible. We rode to the Rosewood Mansion on Turtle Creek in silence, but there was more than plenty of communication between the two of us. The sexual tension was palpable, even if ignored. When we arrived, the driver opened the door to let us out, and the arousal that assailed me at my apartment was replaced with sheer nervous terror. I definitely didn't belong in that circle of people. Ben would be just fine there, even though he didn't really seem to be that hoity-toity when I met him in his faded tee and rugged vintage jeans. Although standing before me with his hand extended to help me out of the car, he looked amazing and every bit high class in his flawless, tailored tux.

The stone circle drive was surrounded by large trees that twinkled and gleamed with thousands of tiny white lights. There was a magnificent awning extending from the entry to the hotel. The place looked like a tawny-colored castle, boasting white-trimmed terraces and balconies. The roof was terracotta tile; the windows were massive and arched. The grounds were immaculately manicured, and there was ornate wrought iron everywhere. The hotel was two-story, and at one point was a private home, but that was eventually transformed into a premiere resort with lush accommodations and amenities. In short, the place was old, expensive, and absolutely enchanting. I felt very out of place. The men and women I saw milling around were well-dressed and obviously the upper class of the Dallas area. In an effort to assuage my faltering confidence, Ben leaned into my ear and wrapped his arm around my waist possessively. I relaxed in his grip.

"Kathleen, you are stunning. I hope you like the dress. I do."

I felt like such an idiot. I was so consumed with my thoughts in the car I didn't even think to thank him for the gown, heels, and clutch. "I love it, Ben. Thank you for everything." I smiled just as sweetly as I could manage through my anxiety. Looking at my handsome date made everything much easier to take in. Ben winked and removed his arm from my waist, and we were once again arm in arm. The disappointment I felt when he freed me was disconcerting.

What's my problem?

The ballroom was equal in beauty to the mansion. Large round tables with beautiful floral and candle centerpieces littered the room. The walls were an earthy truffle color. They contrasted well with the crisp white linen everywhere throughout the room. There was a large dance floor in the center with a dimly lit glistening chandelier above it. Wide draping streamers drooped and jutted outward from the chandelier in the center of the ceiling. Near the front of the room was a DJ and a fifteen piece big band. We found our table, and he gave me the details about the charity and told me what the evening would entail. There was a silent auction, dinner, dancing, and mingling on the agenda. I expect the mingling part was important to most everyone there. Rich well-to-do people love other rich well-to-do people. I was introduced to the other guests at our table, and Ben made conversation easily, while I people watched and sat silently with my thoughts.

Geez, Ben must be seriously loaded. More than I had thought.

I didn't think he was the ridiculously rich type. He seemed so normal at the book store. Well, mostly normal, I guess. He sat forward in his seat while engaging in conversation with the others at our table then leaned back when the conversation waned. He lifted his arm and rested it across the back of my chair while sipping on some amber colored alcohol. He appeared far more comfortable than I was.

"Thanks again for asking me to come with you tonight. This must have been so expensive." I made sure to whisper my appreciation discreetly. My fidgeting with my hair persisted. I absentmindedly swept it from my back to rest across my shoulder, down the front of my chest. Ben smiled and winked, then his hand moved to my back, and his thumb made slow sweeping passes back and forth across my shoulder blade. I remembered my tattoo and panicked. I made a move to sweep my hair back off my shoulder to tumble down my back in an effort to conceal some of the ink. Ben caught my wrist with his free hand and leaned in close to my face. So close I could smell the liquor on his breath, and could tell that he was drinking scotch.

"Don't." He placed my trapped hand back into my lap, and I leaned back fractionally to look at him better.

"I... I don't want, I mean, people will look. I don't want to embarrass you. Or myself for that matter."

His eyes narrowed, but his thumb continued stroking my back. "You are not an embarrassment, Kathleen. I don't want to hear you say that again. It doesn't matter what others say; I like it. I'm just glad that I chose a dress that showcases it so well. As far as the money goes? Don't worry about it. I have far more money than I could ever need or use. Do you understand?"

I nodded slowly feeling like a chastised child.

"Say you understand, Kathleen."

Why does he call me Kathleen? Aidan called me that. He knows I prefer to be called Kat.

"I understand."

He nodded and looked out to the dance floor filling with couples while the DJ began to play.

Please don't ask. Please don't ask. Please don't ask.

Ben grabbed my hand in his and pinned me with his fierce smoldering blue-green eyes. "Come dance."

I guess he didn't ask. He demanded... of course.

He dragged me from the table. Once we stepped out onto the floor, he swept me wide from him and swiftly jerked me back into his body. I was pressed against him, face to face. Memories of my first day at the firm flooded my mind. I knew I should resist, but I wanted him so badly. I wanted all of him. I was drawn to the man on a primal level. There was no fighting raw animal instinct. His right hand pressed against my lower back, and he held my right hand with his left. I rested my other hand high on his chest. He felt so good that close to me. He smelled like heaven. I could only imagine what he would taste like. I was getting distracted by my rogue thoughts and worried about falling on my face.

"Ben, I can't dance."

"Shhh, dancing is not something you think about. Let your body do the thinking, and you will be fine."

I nodded and did my best to do what he said. The song we swayed to was *Trust In Me* by Etta James. Ben was right. Once I stopped thinking and allowed my body to do what felt natural, I melted into him, and together we melted into the sweet, soulful song. I wrapped my free hand around his neck and rested my cheek on his chest. Ben held me tighter to him, and I felt inexplicably at home in his arms. He encapsulated me, separated me from my surroundings. I wasn't worried about nosey onlookers, judgmental stares, work, my lost inner self, or the story telling ink on my back. Ben's thumb brushed softly back and forth across my lower back like he did at our table. I sighed with utter contentment. He brushed his chin against my temple, and I lifted my head from his chest to look at him. We locked eyes. Heated, fierce, smoldering blue green eyes bore into me, making me feel completely bare to him. I stared back, giving as good as I got. Ben lowered his head close to mine.

Oh God, he's really going to kiss me!

He placed his soft, full lips on mine and kissed me chastely. He ended the kiss before I wanted. It was so perfect, but so brief that it left me wanting. Longing. Yearning. Needing. The song ended, and we stood staring at each other for a moment before he led us back to our table. During dinner, he kept his hands on me at all times. His hand on my knee. His thumb lazily stroking my back. Holding my hand in his. I made an attempt to brush my hair away to hang down my back a few times, and every time Ben stopped my hand and narrowed his eyes disapprovingly.

I guess he does like the tattoo. He probably wouldn't if he knew what it was all about.

We danced many times throughout the night. Every dance was just as intense as the first one. We melted together during each song and I had the feeling that in Ben's arms was where I belonged. The thought scared me witless. But, God, how I wanted him. I wanted to feel his lips against mine again. I wanted to feel his lips all over my body. I wanted to put my lips all over his body, taste his skin, to feel the weight of him above me.

While taking a break between songs, Ben went to the open bar to get drinks. A handsome man approached me at our table.

I looked up at a sandy-blonde haired man with beautiful blue eyes and smiled nicely. "I was not going to approach you, but I knew I would be a complete fool to not introduce myself to such a beautiful woman."

Smooth, chief.

He shoved his hand in my direction. "I'm Stephen Mitchell and you are?" I hesitantly put my hand in his. There was something about Stephen that seemed fishy, but I couldn't quite discern what it was.

"Hi. I'm Kathleen Cooper."

A smile slid across his lips, and I was sure that my instincts were more right than wrong. "Can I talk you into a spin around the dance floor?" He did his best to look pleading.

"I don't think that's a good idea. My date will be back any second."

"Just one dance, Kathleen."

"Call me Kat, please."

"One little dance, Kat."

I groaned and gave in despite my better judgment screaming that this guy was bad news. "Oh, fine. One dance." I rose from my seat and placed my hand back in his when he offered it. Stephen pulled me to him when the music picked up. I felt someone staring at me while we danced, and my gut told me it was Ben.

I hope he isn't pissed. Wait. So what if he is pissed? He has no claim over me. I am not his girlfriend. I'm his employee, for Christ sake! I can dance with whomever I choose to. It's just one lousy dance.

Stephen interrupted my rebellious private rant. "You know, if you're here with Benjamin Chase, you're bound to be disappointed by him." Stephen shook his head at me with pity.

"I am in fact, here with Benjamin Chase, but why would I be disappointed in him?"

"Are you his girlfriend?"

"What business is it of yours?" I shot back a little too defensively.

"It isn't. I just figured that a beautiful woman like you should know that being involved the womanizing Benjamin Chase will only lead to heartache. Why waste your time with someone like him?"

Asshole!

"And I assume you would have me believe that your motivation for taking a jab at Benjamin Chase behind his back is solely because you have my best interests at heart? Me? A total stranger to you?"

"Are you a lawyer as well?"

Could've been. Should've been.

"No, I'm not a lawyer."

"Could have fooled me." He smirked at me patronizingly. I wanted the song to end already, so I could get away from this guy. He was irritating me. The last few notes of the song played after what felt like an eternity of dancing with him.

"Well, Kathleen, it was a pleasure." He slipped a business card into my hand. "And just in case you decide that you don't want to be caught up with a womanizing playboy, give me a call. I would love to take you out sometime."

Yeah, jackass, we'll go out on the tenth of never.

I nodded curtly and turned to walk away. When I faced our table, Ben was nowhere in sight. My heart sank.

Shit! I've pissed him off. What if he took off and left me here?

Suddenly, a hand wrapped around my elbow and forcefully whirled me around. I gasped and stumbled before Ben grabbed me by my waist and pulled me into his strong steady body.

"Care to dance again? Or did Stephen, a man whom I despise, tire you?"

I cringed inside. *Ah, shit! That guy was his enemy. No wonder.*

I directed my eyes toward the ground to avoid Ben's scrutinizing glare. "What did I tell you about looking me in the eyes, Kathleen?" He lifted my chin. I stared him in the eyes and could see he was pissed and... jealous?

"You're mad at me aren't you?"

He sighed. "I'm not mad at you. I'm mad at him. Please don't do that again. I have enemies, Kathleen, and they would like nothing more than to take a shot at me publicly. Stephen chose to dance with the woman I brought as my date who just so happens to be the most breathtaking woman in the room. He danced with you to get to me, and I am sure he badmouthed me. Right?" I looked away from him again out of shame. I should have known better. Ben was wealthy, powerful, and successful. He was bound to have enemies who waited around for an opportunity to pounce.

"Right," I mumbled. "I'm sorry. I didn't think... I didn't know."

"Forget it." His tone was clipped and harsh. "But I will remind you of one thing, Kathleen. You are here with me. Tonight you're mine," he said while pulling me closer. My stomach turned and ravenous sexual need filled me. His words sounded like a threat, a promise, and a statement all in one. He didn't ask what Stephen said about him, nor did he tell me that whatever Stephen said was bound to be lies.

Is he a womanizer? Does he admit to it? Google will shed some light.

After my dance with the enemy doused the mood, we chose to leave. I didn't want the night to end, but I was eager to get to the bottom of things with the help of Google. Before we left, Ben excused himself and approached the event coordinator that I recognized from earlier in the evening. He reached into the breast pocket of his jacket and pulled out what I could tell was an envelope.

Donating to the charity, I guess.

Ben shook hands with the man, then came back to my side. He placed his arm around my waist, and we left.

CHAPTER FOURTEEN

Consumed

The ride home from the ball was tense. Ben didn't say anything, and I had little to say since the dancing-with-the-enemy debacle. I didn't want the night to end, especially on a sour note. "Look, I'm sorry about Stephen. I didn't know. Tonight was wonderful, so don't let him, or me, ruin it for you." He kept his eyes askew, and his jaw was tense. We sat close but not touching and he barely looked in my direction.

"The night isn't over, Kathleen."

Not over? What?

"It's still early. We're going to have drinks."

Try asking next time!

"Um, okay, I guess. Where are we going?" Ben finally looked at me and smiled tightly.

"My place." I couldn't keep my reaction from showing. My eyebrows shot up, and I jerked my head back as if I had been slapped.

I can't go to his house. I'm not ready to go to a private place with him.

"That's nice of you to invite me, but I think it's best if I go home."

"Don't be ridiculous. You're dressed up and you look amazing; taking you home before you have had a decent night would be insulting." His words came out firm and gave me the feeling that he was not willing to negotiate on the subject.

Fine. Whatever.

I sighed and rolled my eyes while looking out the window at the passing scenery. "Okay, Ben."

He placed his hand on my knee and squeezed. A tremor of arousal shot through my body, and I shivered. "Cold?" Ben asked wearing an ostentatious smirk.

Before I could answer, he released my seat belt and wrapped his long, muscular arm around my waist and slid me across the leather seat. He pulled me into his warm body, and I nibbled on my lower lip nervously. The car drove through a set of massive wrought iron gates and up to a wide cobblestone circle drive. Ben's home was brilliant. Extravagant. Huge. It had a French architectural theme. There was a multitude of large unique windows and a stained glass window above the double door entry. We walked up the stairs to the doors, and Ben ushered me into the foyer.

"Ben, your home is... wow!"

He chuckled while arming his security system. "Thank you."

"Come with me. We'll have some wine, and I will give you the tour." I followed him into his kitchen, and he uncorked a chilled bottle of wine and poured two glasses. The tour left me dazzled. His home was filled with oversized luxurious furnishings. The living room had soaring ceilings with exposed wooden beams. I couldn't imagine a more lovely home if I tried. He took me throughout every room in the house except for one. We walked right by it, and the closed door stayed that way. He didn't acknowledge the space or explain. I wondered what was behind that door, but decided that my curiosity, for once, would have to wait.

His home was fit to be called a mansion, but it was warm and inviting at the same time. There was a captivating photograph above the fireplace. It was huge and framed, and it monopolized my attention the very moment I saw it. The photo depicted a grassy field with a tree line in the distance. Just beyond the tree line was the setting sun. The sky appeared to have angry looking clouds that seemed stormy at first glance, but upon looking closer, it was obvious that the storms were merely cast in shadow. It seemed as if the intensity of the sun was too much, so the clouds hid in the shadows cast by the first line of clouds that bore the brunt of the light. Where the rim of the dark clouds met the burst of golden orange from the sun was the focal point. The edges of the dark clouds were luminescent and glowing with the rays. It made the clouds look ablaze at the rim, like fiery heat licking at the edges to banish the darkness. I was awestruck by the beauty and the contradiction within the photo. It was dark and light all at the same time. I wanted to sink into a plush chair in the sitting room and stare at the photo all night. Ben reached for my hand and tapped a button on a remote. Soft music filled the space around us. The song was *Blue in Green* by Miles Davis. It had always been one of my favorites.

"Dance with me, Kathleen." Ben broke the trance that the photo had on me, and I glanced at him. He seemed to be staring at me like I had stared at the photo above his mantle. He had rid himself of his jacket and tie. His shirt was unbuttoned at the top showing just a glimpse of skin. I nodded my head, and his arms encased me. He pulled me close to his body and guided us into a slow, swaying dance. My breathing stalled when one of his hands left my bare back and he cupped my face and neck while he leaned toward me and rested his forehead against mine. His hold on me was purely intimate, and despite my apprehension, I dissolved under his willful touch. He closed his eyes and breathed deeply, and I followed suit. I shoved away my own personal fears and allowed the fire that burned between Ben and me to battle away the darkness that loomed over me for so long. We were a human, living, breathing version of the photo above his mantle that I was so taken with.

We danced slowly while the strains of soft jazz filled our ears, and the heat from our bodies pressed together expunged any lingering tension from the ball. I could hear only the music. I could smell only him. I could feel only him. I could see only him. The world fell away, and only he and I remained. We stilled. He leaned forward and cupped my face with his other hand and pressed his lips against mine, and this time it was not a brief, chaste kiss. I could feel his desire. His soft lips kissed me deeply, passionately. I moaned into his mouth as his tongue slipped across the threshold of my lips and deep into my mouth. Tasting, searching, longing for more. I flexed my fingers against his chest, squeezing his muscles.

"Ben," I mumbled against his lips.

"Kathleen," he rumbled back in a husky, lust-filled voice. He broke the kiss, and we both gasped to fill our lungs with precious air. I pressed my thighs together to mollify the aching need that pulsed there. Ben ran one of his hands down my arm and pulled my hand to his face. He pressed his lips to the palm of my hand and then guided my hand to rest on his cheek. He closed his eyes for a moment. The gesture was extremely intimate and made me want to run for the hills and stay forever all at the same time. He shifted my hand from his cheek, and his deep blue-green eyes burned holes through me as he placed a soft kiss on the inside of my wrist then on the inside of my forearm, near my elbow. He placed my arm back where it was resting on top of his broad shoulder, then resumed our desperate kiss. Frantic need overwhelmed the both of us.

"Ben. Please." I pleaded. He stopped and looked at me for a moment.

"My patience has run out, Kathleen. Are you ready to stop fighting against this?" I stared into those intense blue-green eyes, and with sincerity that surprised even me, I answered him.

"I don't want to fight anymore." My voice was small, but no less genuine. Hearing an answer that clearly pleased him, he grabbed my hand and made long strides to the grand staircase leading to the second floor. My heels clicked against the glossy wooden floor, and I was afraid I would fall.

"Ben. Wait." He turned back to me and swept me up into his arms with the utmost fluidity and climbed the stairs. He stopped in front of his bedroom door and kissed me again. He carried me into the room and stopped beside his enormous, cherry wood four poster bed. The walls were painted in a dark shade of cinnamon, and the lighting was muted. The entire atmosphere of the room was gentle, warm, and seductive. The moment I was carried into his room I felt like a sex kitten in some forbidden place lapping up the essence of all things erotic and sexy. The feeling was empowering, and I indulged in it. I slowly unbuttoned his shirt while doing my best to calm my shaking hands. I freed his arms from the shirt and released it to fall to the floor. His eyes stayed locked onto me. I could see something wild and passionate in those blue-green depths. I jerked the undershirt over his head, and it joined his other shirt on the floor. Ben's hands were all over me. One hand cupped my face while the other cupped my breast, and he tweaked my distended nipple between his thumb and forefinger through the delicate fabric of my dress. His bare chest had a dusting of dark hair across it that tickled my sensitive skin as he pressed me to him. His chest was hard, warm, and broad. Ben released my breast and both of his hands roamed to my hips.

He held me tightly and rocked his hips into mine. I felt his erection fighting to be freed from the clothing that separated us. I reached for his pants, but Ben caught my wrists and whirled me around so that my back was against his chest. Our breathing was fast and choppy. His fingers dug into my hips again as he pulled my ass against his erection and ground into me. The palm of his left hand left my hip and laid flat against my back as he pushed me forward to lie across his bed. He teased me more with hard grinding motions against my ass. I moaned as arousal enveloped me. Hot, wet, desire gathered at my center and drove me to moan and whimper, desperate for relief. I wanted nothing more than for Ben to be deep inside me, claiming my body with his. He leaned forward until his chest grazed against my back.

"I fucking love this, Kathleen." His fingers drifted over my inked skin and his kisses berated my spine from the nape of my neck down to the small of my back.

I shivered as chill bumps peppered my skin. He reached up,

unclasped the dress at my neck and pulled me to stand. The dress slinked down my frame and pooled at my feet. His grip steadied my trembling body while I stepped out of it. Ben turned me to face him again. I stood before him in my ecru lacy thong. He paused and his eyes glided over me. He kicked off his shoes and socks and swept me back onto his bed.

Oh God, this is really happening.

Ben hovered above me as I hesitated and became nervous thinking about how sex with him could screw everything up.

"Ben. This could mess up everything," I whispered. He closed his eyes slowly and shook his head.

"No Kathleen, it won't. You're killing me. I've wanted you since the moment I laid eyes on you. I know it's the same for you. There's no denying this anymore."

He wants me.

I had to agree with him. The connection between us had been disarming and profound since day one at the Book Ends. It had only intensified in the month and a half since we'd known each other. Ben nudged my thighs apart with his hand, and I opened myself to him without a second thought, spreading wide to accommodate him. He settled between my tremulous thighs and rolled his hips into me. I moaned and squirmed beneath him. He lowered his head and began kissing my jaw down to my collar bone. He licked, kissed, and nibbled as he made his way between my full breasts. His powerful hands kneaded my breast as he covered my taut nipple with his hot wet mouth. He licked and flicked my nipple in a teasing manner, then sucked hard, drawing my sensitive peak deeper into his mouth. I drew in air through gritted teeth. I twined his wavy chocolate brown locks in my fingers and held his head to my breast. I arched my back as my hips undulated beneath him, searching for more. His hands roamed freely over my curves while I lifted my leg and tucked a toe into the waist of his pants and tugged, urging them off. He unfastened his pants and kicked them away. He was glorious in just his charcoal gray boxer briefs. They hugged his form revealing just how exquisite his body was.

Ben licked a hot trail down my torso around the piercing in my belly button. He flicked the metal belly button ring with his tongue and lapped at my skin. His fingers slipped past my lacey thong and glided like silk through my wet opening. He smoothed my arousal over me with his deft fingers.

"Oh, Kathleen, you're ready and waiting for me." He let out a growl the moment his amazing mouth covered my slick wet opening. His tongue slid in and out of me and alternated between shallow quick flicks and deep lingering strokes. My breathing became erratic as Ben's mouth edged me closer and closer to climax. I could feel a tightening deep in my stomach, then Ben moved his tongue over my neglected clit and slowly slid one, then a second, long finger into my pulsing opening. His fingers lazily stroked my inner walls as his tongue rolled like a warm wave across my clit. Over and over. Back and forth. Up and down. In and out. I was ready to explode into pieces. I moaned loudly.

"Oh! Yes! Don't stop! I'm so close!" My pleas only made him continue with a fervor I hadn't yet seen from him. He worked me harder, faster, deeper. The dam broke, and I burst at the seams in an explosive, mind-altering orgasm. I cried out his name as the best climax of my life raged through my quaking body.

"Mmmmm, you're the best thing I've ever tasted, Kathleen."

As Ben spoke, his warm breath assailed my sensitive clit, and I trembled even more. My head fell back into plush down pillows. By the time I looked up to find Ben, he was kneeling between my legs, sheathing his thick, considerable length with a condom. I gasped at the sight of him. His body was the epitome of male perfection, and his chest rose and fell rapidly in anticipation. His cock was thick and long. Undoubtedly the most, well-endowed man I had ever seen, much less been intimate with.

Ben crushed his lips against mine, and his tongue dove into my mouth. I could taste my pleasure on his tongue, and it was erotic. I wanted him. I needed him. He settled his hips between my thighs. The crown of his rigid cock was poised at my opening. I was so eager to have him in me. He looked into my eyes. The weight of his stare was too much. I escaped behind my closed eyes.

"Open them. Look at me, Kathleen. I want to see your eyes when I take you."

Oh sweet Jesus! Can words make me come?

I stared into his fierce eyes, and with one swift, hard, thrust Ben was buried to an untouched depth within me. He let out the most erotic and slow groan I had ever heard come from a man. I gasped, startled by his size and power. His balls were flush against my ass, and his erection was completely sheathed by my quivering channel. He paused, allowing both of us a moment to adjust to the immense pleasure we were giving each other. I sighed as my eyes rolled back in my head.

"No. Open them," he demanded in a firm, raspy voice. My eyes snapped back open compliantly. He retracted his long shaft so that only the very tip remained at my opening, then thrust hard back into me, burying himself once again. My moan only drove him further. He ran his hand down my side and grabbed my thigh roughly, forced me to open wider and propped my legs high on his hips. This new angle allowed Ben to push deeper into me. He rested one forearm beside me, semi caging me in a sexy prison formed of defined muscle. His other hand remained on my thigh digging into my flesh to the point of pain. I had my arms wrapped underneath his and my nails clung to his back.

"Ah, you're so tight," Ben groaned as his hips rolled expertly, driving himself deeper still into me. His pace quickened, and my hips met his, thrust for thrust. His lips came to mine, and our tongues battled in a deep breathless kiss. My core began to tighten again, my channel clenched around his cock, and another mind-blowing orgasm tore through me while Ben kept the same pace, painfully drawing out my climax as he worked towards his own release.

Once I came down from my orgasm, Ben pulled out of me and in one swift graceful movement, flipped me so that I was face down, with my ass perched in the air for his taking. He ran his hands up my back and growled deeply before nudging me back open with the tip of his cock. His hand twisted into my hair, and he tugged my head backward slightly. He plunged into me from behind. I could barely breathe through the intensity of each thrust. I felt like I was drowning in the most exquisite sea of pleasure. He released his grip from my hair and both hands dug into my hips. Without warning, Ben's powerful hand came down hard across my ass and caused me to clench my muscles and gasp in shock. A twinge of pain shot through me, but was replaced with pleasure the instant he smoothed his hand over my reddened cheek.

"Are you going to fight me anymore?" His voice was raw and

demanding as he kept relentlessly pounding himself into me. "Who does it belong to, Kathleen?" Ben growled through gritted teeth. He was so rough and animalistic. It was exquisite. I wasn't sure what to say and couldn't think clearly anyway. I was barely able to breathe through each powerful, deep thrust, much less speak. I hesitated. Ben's hand came down harder and landed on my ass again with a loud smack. I clenched again. His hand instantly smoothed over my flesh. It was a delectable mix of pleasure and pain that I was unfamiliar with. This time, he leaned forward and whispered into my ear in a harsh voice. "Who's is it, Kathleen?"

"It's yours! It's all yours!" I cried out in a euphoric mix of pleasure and pain.

"Are you going to fight being mine anymore?" He repeated his question refusing to let me skate around it.

"I won't fight!" I said through my panting.

"Fucking right," he rumbled. His pace increased to an unforgiving speed, and I felt his cock grow even bigger and more rigid. I knew he was close.

"Oh, Ben! Fuck me harder," I demanded.

He plowed through me hard and fast, then abruptly stilled while buried to the root. His body rocked and shuddered as he detonated, spilling his seed deep within me. He stayed buried within me.

"Wow," I murmured breathlessly. Ben grunted and withdrew. I winced as a small sharp pain shot through me.

"You are..." he shook his head. "There are no words, Kathleen. No fucking words." Ben disposed of the used condom, and I smiled triumphantly as our languid bodies lay together on his bed. We stared at each other while we came down from the other-worldly sex we just had together. I shot up and darted from the bed.

"Shit! Shit! Shit!"

Ben sat up slowly and watched me scramble across his room for the door, stark naked.

"What's the problem?" I glanced back at him, still lying there like some sex god perched high on his four poster throne.

"Chey is going to kill me! I didn't text her. She's probably worried out of her mind." I left Ben in his room and shot down his stairs to locate the abandoned clutch with my phone inside. I returned to his room and dug out my cell.

"Six texts and one missed call. Shit!" Ben watched me closely.

'Hey. How is the ball going? -Chey'

'Kat? -Chey'

'You can respond any time now. -Chey'

'Dammit Kat! -Chey '

'I am a split second from calling you if you don't respond. -Chey'

'WTF, Kat?! You didn't answer. I swear I'm gonna send out search parties to find you! Please, I'm worried now. -Chey'

My thumbs moved like lightning over the keyboard to text Cheyenne.

"She can't be too worried, Kathleen. Surely she knows your safe with me. I would never let anything happen to you."

Nothing bad anyway. What just happened was definitely... *something. Something amazing!* I smiled coyly. Ben chuckled as if he heard my thoughts. I glanced over at him suspiciously.

Creeper.

"Yeah, it was pretty amazing, Kathleen."

Shit! I said that out loud!

My eyes bugged out of my head, and an embarrassed blush took over my skin.

Moving right along!

"Chey and I don't operate like that, Ben. We have a standing rule, and that is to check in with each other before, during, and after we go out somewhere alone or with someone else." I decided on a short and sweet text in hopes that she would show me some mercy and not give me the third degree.

'So, so, so sorry, Chey! I'm fine. With Ben. Be home later. –Kat'

I flopped back into the pillows and sighed dramatically. Ben was lying on his side, facing me. The sheet clung to his hips, just barely covering him. I stared at his nude form beside me and suddenly became very aware of my own nudity. I grabbed the sheet to conceal my bare body. A sexy smile crept across Bens features as he snatched the sheet from me. His arms snaked around my waist, and he slid me to him with one effortless, fluid movement. I giggled and turned into him.

No sheet to cover me? Fine. Ben's body will cover me just fine.

I snuggled into his chest knowing that our night together was one I wanted to repeat. Hopefully in the near future.

We stayed together for a long while just breathing each other in. I knew I needed to get home before I spent too much time in his private space and made both of us uncomfortable. "Thank you for a wonderful night, Ben, but I should get going."

He scowled at me as I retreated from his arms and began gathering my things. I had a difficult time looking at him in the eyes. The last thing I wanted was for either one of us to feel used, and the mood was quickly turning sour as the space between us became bigger.

"It's getting late. Why don't you just stay with me tonight?"

I shrugged. "I don't know. Technically, you are my boss, and we already spend so much time together. I don't want to smother you." Ben was now standing beside his bed with his underwear on and his arms crossed over his gorgeous chest.

"Listen, Kathleen, you and I met before you came to the firm, and our attraction to each other began at that book store. I know that I hired you after the fact, but you earned that position. You are a brilliant paralegal. I checked into your credentials, and they confirmed it. You are a valued asset. It was just dumb luck for me that the woman who kept me awake at night and the brilliant paralegal who applied to my firm were one in the same." My neurotic self only heard one part of Ben's spiel.

Checked out my credentials? How much does he know about me?

"Credentials?" I asked after slipping Ben's undershirt over

my head and pulling on my panties.

"Yes. You earned your degree at U of C, right?" I nodded in confirmation. "Well, a friend of my grandfather's is a professor there. I'm sure you know him. Does the name Bruce Kramer ring any bells?"

Professor Kramer.

"Yes, Professor Kramer. I took his Legal Reasoning and Writing course. I liked him. Like him."

"I can assure you that he likes you, too. He spoke very highly of you."

Oh crap! Kramer probably sang like a bird.

"Uh, okay," I said flatly in an effort to feign indifference.

"It doesn't take a rocket scientist to see that you are a complicated woman. I certainly don't pretend to know what goes on in that pretty head of yours, but I think I know more about you than you realize."

"You're right. Outside of work, you don't know me at all, Ben. But, please, do tell me what you do know." I had my arms folded in a show of rebellion. I couldn't believe he had information about me. Well, I suppose I could believe it. He was, after all, my boss and a lawyer no less. It was his job to know things. I was only irritated because I was uncomfortable with someone I was so attracted to potentially having private details about my past before I had the chance to tell him myself.

"What I know is that you don't give yourself enough credit." Ben began crossing the room in a predatory manner with his eyes locked on mine as he spoke in a low, intimidating voice. "I also know that you graduated from the University of Colorado with honors, and you were on the dean's list." I nodded. "I know you took the LSAT and scored a 177, which is worthy of any of the top ten law schools in the nation, public or private. I would know, seeing that I scored a 176 and went to Stanford."

My face paled, and my hands got clammy.

Don't you think I know this, asshole? Don't remind me!

My breathing became uneven, and I was sure I was moments away from going into a full-tilt hyperventilating fit. "I know that despite having academics that could gain you admission into a top school, you applied to the University of Denver Sturm College of Law."

"You got in, of course." Ben shrugged and stopped in front of me, mere inches from my face. "Then didn't go." He whispered the last part, and I winced. The room got smaller. Much smaller. And my anxiety grew exponentially. I had never explained myself to anyone about skipping out on law school.

Only Cheyenne knew the truth behind the whole disaster. I told Aidan I wasn't going, and he simply said "okay," and that was that. He never inquired why, and I never elaborated.

Ben ran his fingers across my cheek and smiled warmly. My eyes shot around the room nervously as my chest rose and fell erratically.

"Relax, Kathleen. I don't judge you for your past choices, but I would like to know why you sold yourself short. Kramer told me you were brilliant and had a promising future as an attorney. What happened?" I shook my head in refusal and shrugged my shoulders dismissively.

"No. I don't want to discuss it. It's no big deal," I lied. "It's simple really. I just didn't have the ambition to do another three years of law school. Besides, I realized that the responsibility was intimidating. I'm much better behind the scenes, assisting. I'm content," I lied again and was surprised at how convincing I sounded. Usually I would be stuttering and mumbling like a child. This time I looked him straight in the eye and lied like a professional. Like a lawyer.

Should've been a lawyer.

Ben's incredulous look told me that he wasn't buying my lies, although they might be convincing to most anyone. Ben was definitely not just anyone. He was a handsome, successful, altruistic legal genius, extraordinaire. Even my deluded, jaded mind recognized what a catch he was, and I held no misconceptions about just how much even I would enjoy being by his side. I had to admit to fantasizing about being exclusively his, but the same issues remained. My past was ugly, and I was in no shape to carry on a relationship with anyone. The only thing this man appeared to be lacking was perhaps a family of his own. At the age of thirty-two, one would expect him to be married and have a child, maybe two.

Maybe he doesn't want a wife and kids. Maybe he was a player, like Stephen said.

I realized that it was more likely than not that Ben was single by choice and was most likely, indeed, a womanizer. I couldn't blame the guy, though. His looks and success made him a huge target for gold-digging phonies looking for wealth and status.

Why shouldn't he play the field and enjoy himself?

I was sure that's precisely what Ben was doing. At least, that's what I told myself.

Playing the field and enjoying himself.

It was a comforting thought for me. If Ben was merely playing the field, then I had no reason to worry about a messy emotional breakup. That was yet another thing I convinced myself of ,all while ignoring the twinge of pain at the thought of being just another notch in Ben's expensive bedpost.

"Okay, Kathleen. I won't pressure you to talk about all of that right now, but only if you stay with me tonight." I huffed and rolled my eyes, even though I was turning flips on the inside.

"Fine." For yielding to him and agreeing to stay, I was rewarded with the most charming smile I had ever seen. It was payment enough.

CHAPTER FIFTEEN

Full disclosure

I sent Cheyenne a text, letting her know that I would be staying at Ben's house that night. She texted me back demanding details as soon as I came home. There would be no avoiding that conversation.

I slept surprisingly well in Ben's arms. I was able to sleep straight through the night with the exception of the late night sex that he woke me up for. My chiming phone woke me from a deep sleep. I peeled Ben's arm off me and scooped my phone up from his nightstand. It was a text message from Cheyenne.

'2 things, Kat. Dallas Herald, pg.3 and you need to check your FB page.'

I groaned dramatically. Ben sat up and kissed my shoulder. "What's wrong beautiful?"

Oh, beautiful, huh?

"Um, that was a text from Chey. She said to look at page three of the paper and to check my Facebook." I texted Cheyenne to say thanks, then swiped the browser on my smart phone and started typing in the web address for the newspaper.

"Did she say why?" Ben asked, sounding just as curious as I was.

"Nope. Just said to check out both. It could be anything, knowing Cheyenne." I went to the website for the Herald and began scanning the site for whatever Cheyenne could have been talking about. When I saw a photo of me in my gown alongside Ben in his tux, I nearly fainted.

"What the... There is a photo of us in the paper and an article. Jesus Christ!" The photo must have been taken right after we arrived to the ball the night before. We were standing outside the Rosewood below the twinkling lights, and Ben's arm was around my waist. He was leaned in close to my face, and I was smiling like a love-sick teenager. If the photo were not in a major newspaper, it would have made for a lovely photo. I had to admit, Ben and I looked great together. His tall frame, leaned in close to my much smaller form, seemed to fit with it nicely. My auburn hair with scattered shades of red contrasted perfectly against Ben's rich chocolate-brown shaggy waves.

Yeah, we looked great on each other.

"Dallas's high society turned out in force at the black-tie charity ball supporting M.A.I.Y (Mentors for the Advancement of Inner-city Youth). Contributors dug deep into their wallets and pocketbooks to make hefty donations to the cause. The president of the organization reports that the ball was a success. Raising well over one million dollars, Dallas's own legal Golden Boy, Benjamin Chase of Chase and Associates, pictured above, is reported to have made a significant donation on behalf of him and his grandfather, Theodore Chase. The event secured donations that will fund the expansion of projects for the program. The expansion will include a new facility for program participants to utilize. The facility is rumored to be double the size of the previous one and will include top-of-the-line computers, a full-sized gym, an indoor swimming pool, tennis courts, a library, and a business center that will aid young adults who seek help with employment and career preparation."

The caption below the photo caught my attention.

'Major contributor, Benjamin Chase sharing a moment with the lady in his life at the ball'

I read the article and caption aloud to Ben. He didn't say anything when he got up and left the room, leaving me in his bed wondering what the hell had just happened.

Special lady in his life? This freaked him out? Bet he is trying to figure out how to do damage control. God forbid the ladies think he is taken.

I smirked and laughed inwardly at my own sarcasm. Moments later, Ben reentered the room with his laptop in hand.

Yep. Doing damage control. Probably going to release a statement denying involvement with me.

"What are you doing?" I cautiously asked him as he flopped back into his bed and opened his laptop. He began typing. I resisted the urge to peak at his screen.

"I'm going to the website," he said nonchalantly.

"Oh. Going to release a formal statement denying the lady in your life?" I said facetiously and playfully elbow-jabbed him.

He looked pensive as he turned his attention from the computer screen to me, and I immediately felt regret for saying something that implied that he was a ladies-man concerned with salvaging his single status with the public. I sounded like a judgmental ass who believed that jerk Stephen. I had never told Ben what Stephen said. Nor did Ben ask, but based in his reaction to my snarky comment, I guessed that he likely knew the things Stephen said to me.

"I-I'm sorry. I didn't mean anything by it." There it was. I was stuttering again.

He turned his attention back to his screen while he spoke. "No Kathleen, I was doing no such thing." I decided to avoid asking any more questions or even acknowledging the article. I moved along to the second thing Chey told me to check despite my growing aversion to discovering anything else that would undoubtedly spoil my mood. I logged into my Facebook account, and my jaw dropped.

Holy notifications, Batman!

I had multiple messages from friends and family wondering what the occasion was that had me all done up.

The picture of me in the gown that I uploaded attracted lots of attention. The biggest shock came from Aidan. He posted a comment on the photo of me.

'Even more gorgeous than our wedding day, Kathleen.'

"Aaaaaaghhhhh!" I tossed my phone on the bed towards my feet and covered my face with my hands while I counted to ten. Aidan was being a possessive jerk incognito. He had never once mentioned how I looked on our wedding day, and the only reason he was doing it in such a public way was to lay claim to me.

Here is a novel thought Aidan: I don't belong to anyone!

I screamed inwardly. When I looked up from my short reprieve, Ben had my phone in his hand staring at the photo, and comment. My gut twisted the moment I saw the confusion on his face. He wore an expression that was unmistakable. I could tell he was shocked and displeased. He tossed the phone back onto the bed and went back to looking at his computer screen. I felt obligated to explain. He deserved to know at least a few things about my past, mainly my marriage and subsequent divorce from Aidan. A peek at my past was the very least I owed him.

"Ah... I um, I was married before. My divorce was final right after I moved here to Dallas." Ben seemed to listen to me objectively with an indifferent expression on his face.

He might not even give a shit about Aidan's comment. Why explain?

He gave me a tight nod of his head and sat silently staring at his computer screen and typing. He stopped and turned to me. "The divorce. His idea or yours?" I shrugged.

"Mine," I said nonchalantly.

"So where is..." He raised his brow, prompting me to fill in the blanks.

"Aidan. His name is Aidan, and he lived in El Paso, last I knew. Though I wouldn't know for sure. The last I spoke to him or saw him was the day you saw me bust my ass in the airport. He could have taken a job someplace else by now." Ben grinned while obviously reminiscing about the most embarrassing moment of my life.

Jerk! It wasn't funny. Well, okay, it was funny, but not that funny.

The moment passed, and his impassive look returned. "It would appear that he may not be over you." He pointed at my phone.

Okay, fine. Going to give him the whole story. Maybe just the summarized version.

I drew in a deep breath and readied myself before I opened the metaphorical can of worms. "It doesn't matter if he is hung up on me or not. We were married for seven years; yes, do the math. I was very young and dumb." I rolled my eyes and nodded my head dramatically. "We lived in a few different places. Always wherever he was offered a better position than the last. Texas, Illinois, Colorado, and then back to Texas. Aidan is in real estate development and travels a lot. I was left alone most of the time. Cheyenne has been my only lasting friend. She has been there for me through every affair, every lie, every woman who swore she was in love with my husband, everything."

Even through the car accident that took my baby.

I kept that detail to myself. For the time being. Ben winced.

"Ouch. You said every affair as in plural? How many?" I covered my face with my hands, utterly embarrassed. I didn't have an actual numeric answer for Ben, so I gave him the next best thing.

"Aidan cheated so often I lost count. Dozens of women. Anyway, it doesn't matter. I had to walk away and he decided to confess his undying love and regret when I was in El Paso finalizing everything. Too little, too late. So here I am." I flopped back into the pillows as Ben shut his laptop, set it aside, lay back, and rolled toward me. His intense blue-green eyes staring down at me lit my skin on fire and ignited something inside me.

"Indeed, Kathleen. Here. You. Are." He said pausing for chaste kisses between each word. I rolled onto my side to face him and peppered his chest with kisses. I was beginning to realize that nuzzled against Ben's chest was my new favorite place to be. He sighed as I indulged in my new favorite place.

Love this.

My thoughts about 'loving' being snuggled up against his chest should have been alarming to me. Normally, such a thought would be alarming, but in that moment in his arms, against his warm all masculine chest, I couldn't be further from alarmed. Being there felt good. It felt right. I allowed myself the moment free of all self-doubt and inner conflict. Ben must have lost patience with my teasing kisses because one minute I was in my new favorite place and the next I was once again on my back with Ben resting the full weight of his erection against my wanton body. His eyes bore into me.

"I meant what I said. No fighting this, Kathleen." His voice was nothing short of stern and the right amount of intimidating. I nodded my head.

"I won't," I whispered breathlessly. He came down on me and kissed me senseless. His lips worked their magic on me. I moaned into his mouth while his expert tongue slid back and forth against mine. He groaned when I slid my hands down his back to grip his perfect, firm ass in my hands. I squeezed his rear and snaked my legs around his waist. Despite my limited height, I was able to cross my ankles behind him. I was wrapped around Ben in a heated, sex-kitten death grip. He chuckled through our kiss when I wrapped myself around him like I'd never let go. His mouth left mine. I whimpered and pouted mockingly.

"Don't, worry baby, I'm not going anywhere, and neither are you."

I'm not?

Before I could give it much thought, Ben resumed his mouth plundering. He gripped my wrists and wrenched them high above my head. He held my wrists in one of his big hands easily to allow the other to wonder down my body. His free hand massaged my breast. He took my taut nipple into his mouth. I tilted my head back and moaned. He abruptly abandoned his ministrations on my breasts and his mouth came to m,y neck. He moaned appreciatively. He licked and sucked at my skin.

"I need you," he whispered, and I wondered if he even meant to say those words aloud. He leaned towards his nightstand and grabbed a condom. He covered his pulsing erection and poised the wide crown of his cock at my slick opening. We were both panting and frantic to consume each other. His lips crashed into mine as he sank into me slowly, sliding in inch by rigid inch. I was thankful for his tenderness with me. My body had not experienced a man in months, and taking Ben's thick length the night before had left me sore in the best kind of way. He paused once he was fully buried in me. I felt the tip of his cock against my womb, and the thought that he was touching me there filled my stomach with butterflies. He remained completely still in me.

"How long has it been?" He probed.

"A while," I whispered.

"How long is a while?" He demanded an answer.

"Not since Aidan. Eight months." My voice was full to the

brim with mortification and shame. I squirmed beneath him pleading for him to move. But he remained still, holding me by the wrists and looking me in the eyes.

"He the only man you've been with?" I was sure that my face had reached the pinnacle of deepest shades of red. "That's what I thought." Ben let my wrists go and wrapped my arms around him. "Doesn't matter. You're mine now, baby." He withdrew from me, leaving just the tip at my opening and slid back into me, stroking all the right places. I clung to him with my arms wrapped around his body. He took me deep and slow. Each deep stroke butted against the deepest parts of me and edged me closer to climax. I dug my nails into his back as I got closer to bliss.

My core tightened, and my center tingled. Ben grunted into my ear as he, too, drew closer to his own release. "Me and you, baby." Hearing his possessive words in my ear sent me flying over the edge into a glorious head-spinning orgasm. My body clenched around Ben's cock and milked him for every drop of his release. His full weight came down on me while we reveled in our post coital contentment. He brushed slow circles on the cap of my shoulder with his fingertips. We lay silent together. Ben's lips rested against my neck in the most comfortable way. I could have lain there for hours, days even. He finally withdrew himself from me, and I genuinely pouted. Ben disappeared into his bathroom and returned only a moment later. He slid into his bed and sidled up beside me. We were lying together, bare as could be. I smiled my completely sated, delirious smile. "Better?" he murmured with his lips pressed to my temple.

"Mhmm," I cooed back. Ben returned my smile with one of his own and slung his arm over my shoulder. His graceful fingers began drifting up and down my spine coaxing a shiver from me. He chuckled deep and low. The sound rolled through his chest and vibrated against my lips.

"What's with the tattoo, Kathleen?" My heart seized in my chest, and my mind raced. I felt like a fish out of water flipping and flopping all about in a frantic state of oxygen deprivation. I didn't have an excuse for it, only the truth. I went with the latter.

"It's a long story."

"We have all day, Kathleen."

Here goes.

"So after I moved here, I had it done. It's a representation of my past, of all my mistakes. Of someone I know and hope to forget. The bluebird represents freedom and beauty," I said rather flatly. Okay, so I may have edited the truth a bit, but I didn't have it in me to explain the lot of it or lay all of my cards on the table for Ben. He would run in the opposite direction if he had the slightest clue of how screwed up I was. I would need time to process this thing I had with Ben before I could reveal the details of my past. Ben looked disbelieving as he nodded his head and said

"Hmm." I could tell that he knew I was holding back. I felt crushed by the weight of unspoken truths and needed to get out of there quickly. I couldn't stand to look at him knowing that he deserved something I couldn't give at that moment: full disclosure.

CHAPTER SIXTEEN

Diddling

❦

I had finally convinced Ben to take me home after we shared the lunch he prepared in his fancy kitchen. He had held my hand and kissed me softly every chance he could. He smelled my hair and kept me within touching distance the entire time I was with him. He whispered sweet words of affirmation into my ear that sent chills up my spine. Neither one of us confronted the boss-employee dilemma. I had assumed we would just muddle through the awkward mess later. Or not at all.

When I arrived home, Cheyenne was her tenacious self, asking a million and one questions. "So, was he, is it..." she said with arched eyebrows and prompting nods.

I sighed dramatically. "You have zero shame; you know that, right?" She shrugged and smiled proudly. "Yes, Chey. He is definitely, um, blessed, in that department." Cheyenne squealed like a stuck pig and hopped from one foot to another.

"I knew he would be! He is too hot to not be blessed all over. Details, Kat! I want details!"

I knew she wouldn't give up easily, so I conceded to her curiosity and recounted the entire night with Ben. Cheyenne listened to my blow-by-blow account of my night with dreamy eyes.

"So are you two going to date now or what?"

I shook my head vehemently. "No way! The last thing I need right now is a man to report to. I am in no position to commit. You know that."

Cheyenne nodded knowingly. "Well, I think that guy Stephen, or whatever his name is, is full of it. Clearly Ben has a thing for you. I think he wants you!" I shook my head and rolled my eyes.

"Doesn't matter what he wants. I can't and shouldn't date anyone, especially not Ben. Besides, last time I checked, diddling the boss is never a good idea! Probably won't happen again." I told a lie. I hoped that it wasn't a fluke and that Ben would be a repeat offender. We both giggled.

"Kat, what y'all are doing to each other is hardly diddling. Y'all are flat out bangin' each other stupid, honey!" Cheyenne mused in her southern drawl with her hands firmly planted on her sweat-pant-clad hips. She only employed that southern-belle accent when she was being dramatic, pissed off, facetious, or was in her mother's company. According to her, I was the same way, although I don't notice it in myself.

"Come on; its workout time, Kat," Cheyenne said as she skipped out of the room singing "Kat and Ben kissing in the tree..."

I shook my head and traipsed off to my room to change into

gym clothes. Truthfully, I was already plenty sore from the night before with Ben, but working out was a staple in our daily routines. Sweating out my stress and nervous energy at the gym sounded great at that moment despite my aching, over-sexed body.

We worked out until we were both physically spent and in dire need of sustenance. We went for Chinese take-out and an evening in front of the TV watching sappy romantic movies. A Saturday evening well spent, in my opinion. I left my phone at home while we were at the gym and hadn't checked it since I got home. I went to get it thinking that maybe my mom would be calling like she always does on the weekends. I smiled when I saw the designer clutch sitting on my dresser. My smile quickly faded when I dug out my phone and realized that the damn thing had died.

Shit! Mom is going to lecture me about this.

'Kat, you better answer when I call, or I will worry myself to death!'

My mother had a flare for the dramatic. Once I plugged in the phone to charge, I powered it back on. Immediately I received four text messages simultaneously and a bell chimed, alerting me to a new voicemail. I opened the text messages first. All but one from my mother. All consisting of the pretty run-of-the-mill chastisement for not making myself available to talk. I huffed and moved on to the last text message which was from none other than Ben.

'Hope you are having a nice day. I want to see you again this weekend. I will pick you up tomorrow at noon. Be ready. –Ben'

"What the hell?" I muttered quietly to myself as I sat on my bed staring at the cell phone tethered to the wall by its cord.

What does he mean he IS coming to pick me up? Demanding!

I remembered how demanding he was in bed the night before and my blank stare turned into a scandalous smile.

Fine. I don't care if he was being pushy via text as long as he got pushy with me in bed again. Oh, I will be ready Ben. You can count on that.

I ignored the niggling part of my brain telling me I should not be diddling my boss, that it would only lead to trouble, and texted Ben back with a sly grin on my face.

'I'll be ready Ben. Will you? –Kat'

Less than two minutes later he messaged me back.

'I'm always ready baby ;) –Ben'

My smile broadened.

Did he seriously just send me a winky face?

I shook my head and texted my mother to let her know that my phone had been dead, and I would call her the next day. I left my phone to charge in my room while Cheyenne and I enjoyed our movie night, interruption free.

The next morning I practically skipped through the apartment with excitement to see Ben soon, which only further irritated my laser-eyed Cheyenne. I ignored her glares as I glided around in the kitchen making her favorite breakfast: fresh hash browns, eggs, thick-cut smoked bacon, and grits with salt, butter and cheese. The world may never know how on earth the two of us managed to keep feminine figures, considering the food we ate. Our daily caloric intake was embarrassing, really. Cheyenne and I ate like queens. Thank God for good genes and gyms; otherwise we would have been overweight queens. She always did most of the cooking, but I would occasionally wander into her domain and whip up something great. I knew her favorite breakfast would pacify the grumpy leprechaun that had taken over her petite body.

"You know, Kat? If banging your boss makes you this damn chipper, then you need to keep on banging, oh excuse me, *diddling*."

I chuckled. "If your theory stands, then maybe you should *start* diddling your boss. Then maybe you wouldn't be possessed by some evil leprechaun every morning," I shot back with a smile and peeked over at her to see her fighting to contain a smile of her own.

"Yeah, well, that isn't really an option since my boss happens to be a stuffy older woman who I am convinced bullies small children for fun." We both laughed boisterously.

"Hey, maybe that is the problem!" I snapped my fingers and pointed one at her. "You kind of look like a small child." I cocked my head to the side, looking at her speculatively. "Yes, a small child minus the boobs, curvy hips, and round ass. She's confused is all." I saw Cheyenne reach for a linen napkin wrapped in a heavy decorative ring, and I ducked knowing that it would be sailing my way any moment.

"Shut up, you hooker! Are you saying I have a big butt?" I stood up, still laughing.

"No matter what kind of ass you have, it's obviously one that

Tuck loves!" She grinned and gave me a nod and a wink.

Oh. Tuck and Chey are diddling!

Cheyenne told me all about her and Tucker over breakfast. She gushed, dreamy-eyed about how wonderful he was to her, how his body was amazing, about how great his tattoos were, and about how successful his business was. Despite outward appearances, despite looking like a tattooed bad boy, Tucker was quite the entrepreneur. She told me all about the string of tattoo parlors across the state that he owned. She gushed some more about his Harley and his amazing house. It would appear that Cheyenne and I were both getting lucky in the successful-hot-man department. I went and ruined the mood by asking if she had been to the doctor in Dallas yet. She nearly bit my head off, and her mood went from happy to irritated, in two seconds flat.

"Chey, I'm not trying to pry, but that doctor you were seeing said that further tests could help figure out what the problem is."

She stood from the table abruptly, snatched our plates and stomped back into the kitchen. "I don't need or want to go back to any damn doctors. I won't ever have kids. Simple. Drop it."

I sighed and kicked myself for upsetting her. "Please, don't get upset. I just... I just know that you and Matt tried, and you wanted a baby so bad. That can't just disappear overnight right? What can it hurt to do more tests?" She turned to face me, pinning me to my seat with an icy glare.

"Kat, what hurts is getting my hopes up and having them dashed every time a new doctor confirms what the one before them told me. I'm infertile. It's next to impossible for me to conceive. So pardon me for not wanting to go through more emotionally exhausting appointments to some fertility doctor who can't do a damn thing to help me. Just leave it alone, please."

Beneath her glare I could see the anguish in her eyes. I relented and dropped the subject. Cheyenne retreated to her room, to lick her wounds no doubt. I felt like a huge heel for upsetting her. I didn't bother her before I left with Ben. I just left a note on the counter where I knew she would be able to see it.

"I'm sorry, babe. I'm an ass. Be back later. Love you. –Kat"

I decided to wait outside for Ben to show up. I needed out of the apartment. He drove up at noon right on the dot. He leaned over to the passenger side and with his long arm opened the passenger door for me. I slid across the cool leather in my simple sundress and gave him a tight smile.

"What's wrong, Kathleen?" He didn't try to disguise the concern in his voice. I looked down at my hands in my lap and sighed in defeat. "I upset Cheyenne." I said weakly.

He arched a quizzical eyebrow. "Ah. A roommate quarrel?"

"Hardly. No, I just asked her about something that happens to be a sensitive topic. I hit a nerve. Quite unintentionally, though." He nodded his head as he drove.

"So mind me asking what the sore topic is?" I narrowed my eyes on his profile as he looked ahead, keeping his eyes fixed on the road.

He is a lawyer, for crying out loud! The man knows how to keep secrets, Kat! Spill it, I yelled inwardly.

The idea of him being able to keep secrets so well didn't make me feel better at all. In fact, it made me rather uneasy. "Cheyenne and Matt, her ex-husband, tried to have children. When she didn't get pregnant after a year of trying, they went to see a fertility doctor. He ran tests and diagnosed her with 'unexplained infertility.' He tossed out some numbers that did nothing to console her. Said that one in five couples deal with this unexplained infertility and that she has a less than ten percent chance to conceive a child." I babbled on while Ben nodded and looked over at me occasionally. "She has been to a half a dozen specialists who have all said the same thing. But the last one she saw recommended that she do more conclusive tests to see if there was anything that could be done. I asked her if she had made an appointment to see a doctor here yet, and she kind of went ape-shit on me. I should have known better." I pursed my lips as I stared down at my knotted fingers. Ben's Escalade rolled to a stop in front of his house which was even more astonishing in broad daylight. He reached over and laid his large hand across my hands effectively stilling my fidgeting.

"Hey. Don't. Don't do that to yourself. You are an excellent friend. You asked because you obviously love her. You shouldn't beat yourself up. Understand?" I sat silent in my seat. He trapped my chin between his thumb and index finger and tilted my head up to meet his eyes. "Do you understand, Kathleen?" I suddenly felt consumed with emotion and did my best to swallow it down.

"Yes, I understand, Ben."

"Good." He said before he jumped out and walked around to open my door. Ben had not said what he had planned for me, so I was confused as to why we were walking up the front steps to his house, yet again. As soon as we entered and he shut the door behind us, I decided to find out what he had up his sleeve.

"What are we doing—" He stopped me before I could finish. He came at me full tilt and swept me up onto my tip toes in a passionate kiss. I was tucked in his arms close against his hard warm body as he kissed me like a man starved for affection. He groaned, and it sounded a lot like a sound of relief. As if I were pacifying a craving. He released my lips from his, and we both came up for air.

"I couldn't wait another moment," he said breathlessly as his forehead rested against mine.

"No need to explain. Not for that," I replied, my voice sounding breathy and seductive.

"You're very cute when you're sad. I couldn't resist that mouth of yours a second longer. I nearly stopped the car halfway here to kiss those pouty sad lips of yours. I had planned on taking you out to lunch, but I changed my mind. I want you in the privacy of my home right now." A devilish smirk worked on the corners of his lips. My mouth hung open slightly, and the familiar tingle deep in my stomach returned. He turned me on so effortlessly. I was incapable of fighting against what came so naturally between us. I didn't want a relationship, and I knew I should not risk so much by being intimately involved with the man who I worked for, but the pull between us dominated my every thought.

Maybe just a physical relationship. An agreement to have just sex between two consenting adults. That would be fine. Will he agree to that?

I thought to myself while the true Kathleen laughed at me condescendingly. I ignored it. I told myself that I had to find a time and a way to discuss this thing between us with him. I stepped into his space and placed my hands on his chest while I kept my eyes locked onto his. I slowly slid my hands from his chest to his toned, defined stomach. He sucked in a breath, and feral desire overtook him. He audibly growled and wrapped his arms around my hips, then pulled me forcefully into his body. I was shocked and turned on at how rough he could be. It only made me want him more. I wanted him to push me to my limits. I wanted to know how far Ben and I could push each other. I didn't care about anything else, only hot, rough, heavenly sex with him. I wanted as much as he would give me. I was shamelessly greedy. His hand fisted into my hair, and he jerked my head back, giving him access. His mouth went directly to my neck and nipped my skin, then he soothed the love bite with his gentle rolling tongue.

"Ben," I whispered as my eyes rolled back. His hands slipped down to the hem of my sundress, then underneath the fabric to cup my ass. With grace and little effort, his strong muscled body lifted me to wrap my legs around his waist. His growing erection pressed against the fabric between us. He kissed me madly for a minute, an eternity. I wasn't sure. Time escaped me while I was under the spell of Ben's seductive touch. One of his hands came between us as he held me up with the other. I felt him slip his fingers into the dainty lace triangle of my panties and rip them away from me. His hand quickly went to his pants. With a flick and a zip, he freed his erection and positioned himself at my center. I gasped.

"Ben! Wait. Condom" His eyes grew wide, and his features softened marginally from heated and possessive to embarrassed. I smiled at him encouragingly.

"Oh shit, sorry," he said.

I giggled like a school girl, and he chuckled too as he carried me with ease up the stairs to his room. He laid me across his bed and quickly covered his twitching cock with a condom. The moment he was ready, he scooped me back up into his arms, and I once again wrapped my legs around his waist. He backed me toward the wall beside his colossal bed. My back hit the wall with a thud as he impaled me, and all the breath left my lungs. I gasped to draw in air.

"God, I love this tight pussy of yours," he growled through gritted teeth. He was not gentle or sweet. He drove into me relentlessly. He grunted and groaned as he pulled my hair and plundered my neck and mouth. He took me over as if I belonged to him and what we were doing was as natural as breathing. I was enjoying every damned second of it. He kept me pinned to the wall as one hand reached between our connected bodies and began rubbing small enticing circles around my clit. My body begged for release, and the moment that recognizable tightening gripped my insides, he eased back on my clit allowing my impending climax to slip away. He kept up his pace and thrust hard into me while building my climax and letting it slip away every time. I was getting emotional in my desperation for release.

"Go ahead. Get mad." He whispered breathlessly in my ear.

"Damn it, Ben!" I whimpered.

"Is that all you got, baby?" he questioned in a low husky taunting voice. Tears threatened to form in my eyes.

"Fuck you!" I felt his mouth turn up into a grin.

"No, baby, I'm fucking you," he growled in my ear. His thrusts became even harder and deeper, and I almost instantly came apart between his hard body and the wall. Blood rushed to my head leaving me with colorful spotty vision as my body rode an epic wave of climactic pleasure. The moment my orgasm caused the walls of my channel to clench around his cock, he shuddered over and over and spilled into me. He brought us to his bed and laid me back slowly as he drew himself out of me. He lay across me while he worked at catching his breath. He lifted his head to look at me through heavy, sated eyes.

"Come on. Bath."

I shook my head. "I can't. I don't have any other clothes. My panties are trash thanks to you."

He laughed. "You have clothes." I was confused.

What? I didn't bring a bag.

He read the look on my face before I could speak. "I took the liberty of getting you a few things. I anticipated you refusing to bring a bag to my house, so I remedied the problem. I told you no fighting this, Kathleen," he warned.

Did you now, Mr. Controlling, bossy sex god?

He pulled me to stand and held me by the shoulders until I was steady on my feet. He led me to the master bathroom which was elegant and fit for a king. It was all marble, granite, and brushed nickel. The walls were a cool blue with a tray ceiling trimmed in white to punctuate the design. The focal point of the open concept bathroom was absolutely the largest white claw-foot bathtub I had ever laid eyes on. I was unaware that they were even made that large. The whole room had a very Victorian feel to it. All the palest of blue with white trim, the fixtures included a double vanity with oversized water basins, gorgeous light fixtures, an enormous mirror, and a standalone shower big enough to accommodate at least six adults. There was also a bidet, of all things. I was quick to casually place my fingers to my mouth to stifle my growing amusement at the mental visual of Ben straddling a bidet to tidy himself.

My private musings came to a halt when Ben tugged me to the monstrous claw tub and began adjusting the water temperature. Water poured from a uniquely designed faucet that rose from the floor right in front of the tub, reminding me of a water fountain. There were two handles for hot and cold water and there was a polished shower head attached by a hose to the fixture. It sat in a holster-type stand and had a valve to operate it at the junction where the hose met the main spigot. Ben held my fingers lightly while he sat on the edge of the tub adjusting the water and pouring in bath oil that filled my nose with the smell of something I was unable to name. It was slightly minty and lightly floral.

"What's that scent?"

Ben stood and pulled me close to him. He ran hands down my back. "It's jasmine and mint oil. Do you like it?"

My breathing became shallow as his hands roamed freely over my body.

"Yes," I murmured, barely loud enough for him to hear. He gripped the hem of my dress and swiftly pulled it over my head, then made quick work of stripping me from my bra, tattered panties, and shoes. I stood before him wearing only a light blush across my skin. He removed his own clothing while I looked on, getting more aroused by the second. He firmly gripped my hand while I stepped into the comforting warm water. He followed me in and sat across from me.

"Ahh." My eyes closed. I eased back, allowing the intoxicating scent of the oil to envelope me as I sank lower into the huge tub.

"Feel good, baby?"

"Mhmm," I moaned when his hands found one of my feet and he began massaging. I was relaxed in Ben's bathtub with his hands massaging my feet and calves. I felt so at ease there with him. It was an odd thing, considering how much he rattled me on a daily basis. My emotions were always all over the place when it came to Ben.

But in that moment, in his bathtub with him massaging me, I was tranquil. All thoughts of inadequacy, regret, sadness, anger, and anxiety left me. It was only the two of us and the extreme magnetism that pulled us together. There was no escaping whatever it was that was between us, and in that moment with him, I didn't want to escape it. I didn't want to deny it. I didn't want to deny him.

In reality, I wanted nothing more than to be his. I felt safe with him. My eyes fluttered open when I felt Ben shift in the water. He spread my legs and pulled me to him so I was straddling him on his side of the bathtub.

He placed a soft kiss on my lips and gazed at me. "Tell me what you are thinking, Kathleen." His voice was a soft whisper against my lips.

"I was just thinking that I could get used to long hot baths complete with massages after hot sex with the handsome, successful, charming Benjamin Chase." My sweet smile turned slightly devilish.

"A man can hope," he muttered, speaking mostly to himself, I surmised. Little alarm bells started sounding loudly inside me. My body stiffened fractionally in his arms, and just like that, the flip was switched back to closed off from open and tranquil. The emotional rollercoaster was exhausting.

"I, um, why don't we get out now? The water is cooling, and I'm all pruned." I held my hand in front of his face so he could see the wrinkles on my finger tips. He held my hand in his and kissed each finger tip softly while keeping his eyes on mine. I could tell that he saw through me. He knew I was allowing my past to get the best of me as always.

"You have nothing to worry about."

I snickered sarcastically. "No, Ben. I have plenty to worry about in my life."

"That's not what I mean, and you know it," he said firmly.

I nodded and looked down at my hands swirling in the water absentmindedly. "Well, then what is it you meant?"

He nudged my chin upward with his gentle touch. "Look at me. You know what I mean, Kathleen. You are so damn scared of feeling this thing between us. You're scared, but you don't have to be. Not with me."

No, I'm positive I have good reason to be scared with you. We could rip each other apart. His voice was velvety smooth in my ear. I wanted to believe that he and I could somehow go with the natural flow of things between us, but I knew better. I had too much baggage. Too many scars. Seven long, unforgiving years' worth.

"Ben, listen, I don't know what this is between us, but I can't give more than I am already giving. This thing needs to stay physical. I can't afford any emotional connection between us. Besides, getting emotionally involved with you is almost certainly going to cost me my job."

"Fine, we will do this your way. For now."

His words sent a chill down my spine. I couldn't be sure if they were a threat, a promise or both. Either way, one thing was certain: Ben had me in his grip, and I was in for the most exciting, heartbreaking, amazing, turbulent ride of my life. I just didn't know it yet.

CHAPTER SEVENTEEN

Under duress

"Come with me." Ben said warily. He enfolded my hand in his and led me through his house to the one mysterious door that he skipped over during the tour of his home. He paused at the door and looked to me. I smiled marginally in an attempt to ease his obvious anxiety.

Benjamin Chase nervous? This could be bad.

He turned the door knob and led me into the dimly lit room. I stifled my gasp the best I could. "Ben, this... this is amazing," I whispered to him as he squeezed my hand in his. "Photography, huh?" I looked to him, and he shrugged bashfully.

"I was hoping that if I open myself to you, you'll return the favor." There was a hidden plea in his voice, and my heart melted into a gooey puddle in my chest.

Oh, Ben.

"My grandfather bought me a camera when I was a kid, and I fell in love with all things photography."

"I can see that." I grazed through the large cool space. The room was filled with all things photography. It was clear that this was his hobby. His passion. There were shelves scattered throughout the space that displayed cameras of all types. Old and new. I imagined that some of the older ones were antique and likely worth quite a bit. The walls were riddled with photos of all sizes. Some were in color. Some were in black and white. But all of them were landscapes. Every single one was some type of transient moment that Ben obviously knew how to capture. I was spellbound by his work.

He stood in the middle of the room silently watching me wander through the room that housed his passion, taking in his amazing work. I paused.

"The photo above your fireplace. You did that," I said with my back to him.

"Yes."

"It's enchanting. I wish I could have been there with you." Words fell from my lips, uninhibited by my fears. Ben crossed the room and pressed his front to my back as his arms coiled around me. He leaned in close to my ear.

"I wish you had been with me, too." I turned in his arms to face him.

"All of this is amazing Ben."

He smiled marginally and shrugged.

"Where were all of these taken?" I asked while motioning my arms outward.

"Mostly all over California. It's really all I did in my spare time while I was at Stanford. I use to drive all over until something drew me in. No one except Trev knows about it." His voice sounded a bit defeated, and I felt sorry for him.

"Why wouldn't you share this with everyone? You're talented. These photos are amazing. This room is amazing. It's a gallery in its own right."

"I just don't show my photos to anyone. I have enough to deal with. My family expects a lot of me, and I intend to live up to those expectations. Chasing some crazy dream of being a photographer is not in the cards for me." With that explanation, his arms fell from me, and he turned away. He was putting up a wall of defense to dissuade me from pushing the issue and perhaps warn me?

Fine, we will do this your way. For now.

There would be no way I could let this go. It was obvious that he loved photography, but refused to pursue it or even share with others because of his reputation and obligations. I had to find a way to convince him that he could fit in his hobby and his career, and no one would think less of him for being so artistic. He could have been a circus clown, and it would not change how much of a courtroom shark he was. I pulled him back to me by his forearm. He wrapped his arms around my waist.

"Well, thank you for sharing with me. I love it." My words were honest, and I hoped he took them to heart.

For the remainder of the day, we spent quiet time together, most of which was enjoyed in Ben's bed. He was a magnificent lover, and I simply could not get enough of him. His blue-green eyes blazed through my body any time they landed on me. His scent was intoxicating when he came near me, and his skin was warm and consuming when he touched me. I was fully and irrevocably addicted to all things Benjamin Chase.

Monday, July, 1st, 2013. Day Forty since I started at the firm.

I managed to convince Ben to take me home the night before. He didn't fight me much on the issue, largely due to the fact that I didn't ask. I flat out insisted on going home to smooth things over with Cheyenne. Allowing any issues between us to simmer didn't sit well with me. I came home to a grumpy best friend, but managed to cheer her up with an offering of cheesecake and her favorite wine. I apologized and promised not to push, pry, or meddle. She smiled with a mouth full of cheesecake, signaling the all clear; a truce was formed. I would have bought a case of those cheesecakes, stock in the wine, and apologized until I was blue in the face as long as I got to see the tension slip from her features and a bright smile take its place. All was well once again on the home front.

Ben made it a point to make things relaxed between us at work while remaining discreet. Throughout the morning he would shoot me a smile or wink when no one was looking. I had been worried about the newspaper article with our photo from the ball, but no one mentioned it. I dismissed the uneasy feeling that came over me the moment I got to work. I feared I was being watched. Had I paid closer attention, I would have realized that my fear was warranted. But I ignored my nerves, the photo, and my unease. At lunch that day as I sat beside Ben at our usual place in his office, I worked up the courage to ask a question that had been nagging at me. He seemed to be in a great mood.

Thanks to me.

I debated how to ask for a moment, then decided to just go for quick and blunt. "How are you so wealthy? Surely not all your wealth is from the firm."

Without looking at me, he quirked his eyebrows, then relaxed them again. He spoke without looking in my direction. I admired his handsome profile as he spoke. "High yield investments. I took risks. They have paid off generously, and in case you haven't noticed, I don't run some little firm." His lips twitched a bit at his own sarcasm.

Hmmm... smartass!

"What kind of investments?"

He finished his lunch and cleaned up his area. "The risky kind that either make a man a wealthy genius or a bankrupt fool. I'm the former."

No specifics. Of course.

He glanced down at his expensive watch and continued. "But at the moment, I am about to be a very lucky man for entirely different reasons that have nothing to do with money." He turned to me, and I knew I was in trouble.

"Oh, is that so?" I teased.

"Fact," he affirmed.

Then Ben took me on the couch in his office, hard and fast, but still not lacking one bit of pure passion. I was so addicted. That evening, just as I was preparing to leave work, I wandered into Ben's office through his open door. All the staff had already left for the day, and I was finishing up some work. When I strolled into his office, he was standing near his windows with his back to me. He was on speaker phone with someone, though I had not the slightest idea whom.

"I'm not sure about him, hon. I thought I ought to let you look into it first. I've invested quite a bit, and I spoke to him about getting out. But, I ain't seen a hot red cent of my money from that man. That John Murray is up to no good. I can smell it." The voice of what was obviously an older woman with a southern drawl came through the speaker on Ben's desk, loud and clear. She may have sounded like an older woman, but was no more mild tempered than a cobra.

John Murray? Who is he? I thought to myself.

"I've met him before, Sheryl, and I have heard whispers of illegal dealings he has his hands in. I will see what I can confirm, though. Until then, keep things quiet, and don't mention this issue to anyone else. I mean it, Mrs. Stratton. Not a soul. I will call you once I have more information." Ben's tone was low and intimidating. Something had him on edge, I could tell. I wasn't sure who this John Murray was or what was going on with Sheryl Stratton, but I took mental notes of that phone call and decided to look into the issue, if for no more reason than to appease my curiosity.

Damn curiosity!

As they say, curiosity killed the cat. I later found out that sticking my nose into John Murray's business would put me into the position of the proverbial cat. The call ended, and Ben turned towards me. I decided to play out my bluff.

"New client?" I asked, knowing full-well that that phone call was not with a client. It was personal. Ben casually walked back to his desk.

"No. Family friend asking a favor."

"Oh. Okay. Need my help?"

Ben raised his head from the papers on his desk, and his

blue-green eyes took on a menacing look. "No. I won't need your help in his matter, and you will not get involved. Understand?"

"Uh, sure. Yeah. Well, anyway, I am headed home." I turned to exit Ben's office before he could burn a deeper hole into me with those eyes of his.

"Kathleen." I stopped and turned to face him.

"Yes?"

"Join me for dinner?"

Yes! I squealed inwardly.

"What did you have planned?" Inside I was excited to spend private time with Ben, but I managed to pull off a cool exterior. Ben's lips turned up into a grin.

"Dinner. I will pick you up in, say, an hour."

"Okay, Ben." I smiled shyly and strutted out of his office, then all but skipped like a schoolgirl to my car. I was thoroughly enjoying my new job, more specifically, my new boss and lover. Ben arrived at my house on time as always. The moment I opened the apartment door to him, he waltzed right past me.

"Uh, come on in Ben, please," I said with as much petulance as I could muster.

"Which room is yours?" His pointed question was his only response to my sarcasm.

"My room?" I asked as I sashayed past him heading towards my private space. Ben followed without answering my rhetorical question. Once he crossed the threshold of my bedroom, he surveyed my space quickly and immediately went to my closet.

"Hey!" I cried out standing by my bed. "What in the world are you doing?"

"Packing your bag." His voice was flat, and his eyes never came to mine. He was so handsome walking with authority in the clothes he wore to work. A navy blue suit that fit him flawlessly. Crisp white shirt with a deep red tie that he had since rid himself of. A few of the top buttons of his shirt were undone, showing a bit of skin that I instantly wanted to put my mouth on.

"Ben!" He kept moving through my room, throwing clothes and other random things into a small bag he found in my closet.

"You're staying the night with me."

"I am not! You didn't even bother asking me." I crossed my arms over my chest indignantly and scowled.

"Why bother asking? You would surely refuse even though I know you want to be in my bed as badly I want you there. So I went around the problem. I'm taking you home with me. My home."

Oh my.

"Damn you, Ben! You can't just... just do... that!" I flung my hand outward towards the whole of him. He stopped, and his heated eyes landed on me, lighting my body on fire. My stomach stirred down low, and my breathing stuttered. He dropped the bag in his hand and stalked toward me. He gripped my hips, turned my body, and pushed me flush against the wall. His lips were millimeters from mine. He gathered my hands in his, pulled them above my head, and pinned my wrists against the wall. His solid body held mine.

"I have to look at your sweet ass all day at work knowing exactly what's under those clothes. Hours of teasing. Every time you walk in or out of my office, you tease me. Your perfume teases me. All of you teases me. Devouring you all night is the only way to survive not having you all day. You're coming home with me," he growled seductively. My stomach flipped. "I take what's mine. I do what I want with what's mine and this..." He grasped my wrists with one of his large hands freeing up the other. His free hand went between my thighs and cupped my already aroused center. "...is mine. You said it yourself, Kathleen. Don't you remember? Or perhaps you need to be reminded."

"I-I... was under duress. That's not fair," I murmured breathlessly while his hand began making slow enticing movements between my thighs.

"I would hardly call multiple orgasms during exquisite sex duress, Kathleen." He smirked arrogantly.

"You want me in your bed? Badly?" I asked. Ben's only response was a subtle chuckle and a slight shake of his head. Then he released me. My arms fell to my side, and my legs wobbled slightly.

Damn, he's good!

I had to admit, if what he did to me was in fact, duress, I didn't mind being under duress. All. The. Time.

"You already have things at my house, and if you need anything else, I'll buy it. Let's go." His hand swept mine from my side and tugged my pliant body forward, towards the door. Just like that, I was off to Ben's house again.

CHAPTER EIGHTEEN

Lonely lover

❧⁓

"This is delicious!" I exclaimed dramatically while forking another bite of Ben's shrimp scampi into my mouth.

"I'm glad you like it."

"'Like' it is an understatement. This is great. Who knew Benjamin Chase, legal mind extraordinaire, sex god, and talented photographer was also a whiz in the kitchen?" I smiled and winked at Ben flirtatiously.

"Who knew?" He shrugged.

"So Ben, where do you see yourself in five years? I know, very original."

"Ah, well, I'd like to think that in five years, my love life won't be as void as it has been most of my adult life." He muttered the last bit.

Poor Ben. He's lonely.

"You're lonely," I stated quietly. "You have so much. You are so successful. Yet you are possibly the loneliest man I know," I thought aloud, sounding more quizzical than I anticipated.

"I suppose you are right." Ben's voice was melancholy and defeated. He sat across from me with his shoulders slightly slumped and his head down. He was the most lonely man I knew, and I wanted to kick myself for asking the question that led to the turn in his mood from lighthearted to sullen. My heart began aching more for him than for myself and all my loss and misery. My misery took a backseat to more readily accommodate the lonely man before me.

It was confirmed. Ben had more depth than I knew, and I had it bad for him. Far worse than I dared to admit. There was much more to this man than appearances let on. He was strong and demanding. Arrogant and sure of himself. He was also artistic and meditative, and to my dismay, he was a sad man. It couldn't be any clearer to me that Ben was a man with many sides. I slid my chair from the table and began to move towards my lonely lover, intent on changing that. Once I made it to his side, he pushed back from the table, and I slid into his lap. I grasped his muscular shoulder with one hand and lightly cupped his angular jaw with my other hand.

"You're lonely, Ben." I leaned in and kissed him gently then sat back to look at him. "But you won't be tonight. Tonight I'm yours. Take me to bed," I whispered against his cheek as the stubble on his jaw lightly scratched across my face. As graceful as could be, Ben slipped his arms beneath my knees and around my back before he lifted me easily and began striding towards his room. He set me on his plush bed and stood back. He stared at me for a moment for reasons unknown to me. He had a curious look on his face.

"Don't just stand there. Come here," I demanded. He

walked slowly over to me, propped on the side of his bed, feet dangling. I hooked my fingers into the belt loops of his pants and pulled him forward between my knees. He said nothing while allowing my hands to roam his body freely. I knew what I had in mind was far more intimate than I should have allowed, considering I needed things with Ben to remain physical despite my growing affection for him. But I couldn't not do it. I was compelled to help him. To fix him. To repair the broken bits of the lonely man I had met at the dinner table not ten minutes before.

Make it better. Fix him. Make him happy, I told myself. Then, I threw caution to the wind and exposed myself to Ben and not just physically. I let him in. Not for me, for him. There we were. The lonely and the damaged giving each other the best of what we had to give in hopes that it would be enough. Even if just barely, it would have to be enough.

"What are you doing to me, Kathleen?" he muttered.

"Probably the same thing you do to me," I whispered back. I looked into his beautiful eyes and wished I could lose myself in them every second of every day. Before I knew it, I had rid Ben of his clothing and begun working on my own. He stood there, motionless, allowing me to take charge. I moved further back onto his bed and pulled his hand to join me. Once he was lying on his back, waiting for me, I straddled him and lowered my mouth to his. I led the kiss. I made sure to do my best to convey my feelings through the kiss I was sharing with him.

Not alone. It was the only thought that went through my head as I kissed him with everything I had. I wasn't sure whom I was reassuring, Ben or me. He wasn't alone. Neither was I. Together, we had each other, and I realized in that moment in his bed, above him, it was more than enough. I gripped his erection in my hand and looked him in the eyes.

"Trust me?" I asked breathily. He nodded.

"Trust me?" He countered, and without further thought I answered his question by sheathing his bare erection with my body rather than a condom. I took him into my body, and we were as close as two people could get. I sucked in air as the feeling of Ben's bare flesh filled me so completely. His eyes rolled to the back of his head, and his fingers dug into my hips pulling me down harder, to bury himself further. I lay forward, resting my bare chest against his and began to rock my hips gently over his, building pleasure for the both of us with each slow stroke. One of Ben's hands left my hip and tangled into my hair.

"I've never... Kathleen, you feel so good."

"I'm all yours tonight, baby. Feel me," I said into his ear. Ben groaned.

"Say you'll stay." The desperation that was so obvious in his voice pulled at my heart, and I could not imagine ever leaving him alone.

"I'll stay."

"You're mine," he reiterated. He curled into me, pushing me back upright then flipped me so he was on top. His body and personality so easily dominated mine, and I was beginning to love it. I was beginning to love **him**, and it petrified me. I wrapped my legs high on his waist, and he thrust back into me, hard. His erection drove deep into me and stole the breath from my lungs. The weight of his body pressed me into the mattress. Sweat misted his skin. I drank him in through every pore, through every cell in my body. We filled each other with wild, raw, unrestrained passion. We both drank from each other hungrily, greedily. We were determined to battle away our respective demons. His lips went to my neck and nipped, kissed, and sucked at my skin. A tightening began to grow deep in my core. I knew I would soon fall to pieces beneath my lonely lover.

"Ah, Ben!"

"That's it baby, right there." Not another ten seconds passed before I did more than fall to pieces. I dissolved beneath him. Blood rushed through my veins as Ben wrung me out. My body shook. My eyes rolled back. My breathing stalled. My back arched into him. My center pulsed and clenched tightly around Ben's impressive length, and he too, fell apart not a moment after me. We took time to calm our strained breathing before Ben withdrew from me. He kissed me... lovingly? What I got from that kiss was likely exactly what he was attempting to express. Gratitude. Gratitude for fighting away the loneliness and giving myself to him, for the night. *Just for the night.* Or so I thought. Ben lay beside me, stomach down, slightly crooked to allow his head to lay on my chest. His ear was to my heart, and I lazily stroked his hair and waited for him to give in to sleep. Less than ten minutes. That's how long it took me to coax my lonely lover off to slumber. His eyes were shut, his weight became heavier against me, his muscles relaxed, his breathing became steady and deep.

"Sleep now," I whispered while stick stroking his soft wavy locks. The sight of his eyes closed in peaceful sleep, knowing I had given him that, warmed my heart. I watched him sleep for what had to be about an hour before I tried to ease him off of me. The moment I tried peeling his leaden arm from across my waist, it tightened reflexively, and drew me nearer.

Oh my Ben, I'm not leaving.

I stretched to the point of pain to reach my cell phone that sat on Ben's nightstand. I reached it and righted myself again. I opened the browser on my smart phone and got to work.

Okay. Time to find out who this John guy is and if Ben has anything to do with him.

I typed his name, John Murray, into the search engine. Multiple results popped up. Mostly news articles. It would seem that Mr. Murray was having difficulty staying out of the news recently. I tapped my thumb on the first article I saw.

'John Murray, prominent investment firm executive, was brought in for further questioning this week. Police gave a brief statement informing the press that the death of William Kemp, Mr. Murray's business partner, was considered 'suspicious.' Police say that further investigation into the death of Mr. Kemp is underway and no official persons of interest have been named in association with his death. The autopsy declared the cause of death to be an accidental overdose. Mr. Kemp's widow also released a statement to the press insisting that Mr. Kemp's death was not an accident and that she had reason to believe there was foul play involved...'

"Whoa," I muttered quietly, careful not to disturb Ben. I didn't want to wake him from a peaceful sleep, but I mostly didn't want him to see that I took it upon myself to snoop into something he specifically told me to stay out of. I was sure I didn't want to see Ben angry. The article was dated two months ago. I searched his name again. This time I added a search for properties affiliated with his name. Multiple results came up. I decided I would drive by those properties and see what I could find. I wasn't quite sure why, but I felt the need to dig deeper into this John Murray character. Research had always been one of my strengths. I could locate and dig up information on just about anyone. Specifically information that a person would prefer kept buried. I researched all I could on my phone that night until the battery finally died. The next morning, my stomach woke me from a deep restful sleep to an empty bed.

"Love this bed," my hoarse morning voice croaked out. I slipped on Ben's shirt that was discarded on the floor from the night before. I smiled while fondly remembering the previous night's escapades. My nose led to the kitchen where I saw my shirtless lover whisking a sauce of some sort that looked simply decadent.

"Yum." Ben lifted his head from what he was doing and smiled broadly at me.

Oh shit! I probably look terrible.

"Good morning. Come here." I rounded the counter and came to a stop in front of him. His bare muscular arms encased me. He leaned forward and pressed his lips to mine. I ran my hands through his damp, tussled hair.

Must've showered already.

"Thank you for staying."

"You practically kidnapped me. I can't say I minded much, though." I winked, and he released me.

"I made you my signature crepes with rum caramel sauce and fresh strawberries." Ben plated my food and slid it in front of me at the breakfast nook.

"Oh. My. God. Marry me! This looks and smells out of this world. You are spoiling me now. I love crepes." I laughed.

Ben said nothing. I glanced up to him as I put the first fork full into my mouth. I froze. He stood leaning against the counter watching me closely. The look on his face was one I couldn't name exactly, but I knew it had everything to do with my teasing 'marry me' comment. I realized my mistake and averted my eyes back to my plate immediately and did my best not to clam up.

"Why aren't you eating?"

"I already ate after I worked out this morning."

"Oh. Shoot, Ben, you have to take me back to my place. You didn't pack any of my work clothes last night. I have nothing to wear!" I began to eat hurriedly.

"Relax, baby. I have something for you."

"How?" I asked incredulously.

He smiled slyly. "I bought you some things to keep here remember?"

"Oh. Yeah. Okay. But why would you do that?"

He shrugged. "I guess I don't want you to have a reason to go home. I'm happy when you're here."

I am too. I stared at him, not knowing how to respond to his honest words.

"Take your time, Kathleen. I'm the boss, remember?"

"I can't ride with you to work. People will notice."

"Doesn't matter. Besides, I am pretty sure a few people have an idea that we are... involved."

Involved?

"Fine," I conceded to him. I cleaned my plate in record time and we both ascended the stairs to get ready for work. I showered and then dressed in a great black two piece suit that he had bought for me. The pencil skirt fit like a glove, of course, as did the lilac blouse, suit jacket and heels.

"Ben, honestly, you can't spend money on me like this. My tab with you is growing exponentially. Geez! This stuff is pricey." I huffed at my reflection in the mirror.

"The price is irrelevant. You don't owe me anything, but if you insist on repaying me, promise to stay at my house this week. I have to go out of town this afternoon. I won't be back until Thursday morning. I'm sure Cheyenne won't mind."

Absolutely! Perfect. Time to snoop.

I did a better job of showing reluctance on the outside.

"I don't know, although I doubt Cheyenne will care. She spends every free moment with Tucker. She practically lives with him now," I muttered grumpily thinking about my AWOL best friend.

"If she won't be at your apartment, you are definitely staying here. I don't want you alone while I'm gone." As if he read my mind and knew I would love nothing more than to stay at his house, he smiled devilishly. "I'll get you a spare key and give you the information for the security system. Cleaning staff will be here tomorrow morning. They won't bother you. I will leave a message with the agency to let them know that I have a house guest."

Before we left Ben's home for work, he attached a spare key to his home to my key ring and gave me a slip of paper with the security code information on it. He quickly gave me a tutorial on how to operate the system. Once he was satisfied that I had it down, we left for work.

CHAPTER NINETEEN

I spent the morning waiting patiently on Ben to leave for the airport. I felt guilty pretending to be disappointed to be without him for a couple of days, but I had snooping to do. Having Ben out of town would allow me to dig into John Murray, undisturbed.

Talk about screwed up priorities.

"So fucked up, Kat," I muttered to myself in my little office. Just before lunch, Ben called me over intercom and asked that I take him to the airport. I doubted he needed me to take him. It was obvious to me that he wanted a moment or two alone with me. I didn't mind in the slightest.

"Ready?" I asked Ben.

"As I'll ever be. Let's go." As we walked through the parking lot to Ben's SUV, we passed Janis, Trevor's secretary. Ben didn't look in her direction, but I did. She looked at me with absolute disdain.

No love lost there.

In response to her dirty look, I smiled brightly at her and waved as if we were the best of friends. Her expression never faltered. I had no idea why that woman made my skin crawl, but she did. It was obvious that she was fixated on Ben, but I had a nasty feeling that told me that there was more to the story. This woman may have had a crush, but she also seemed to hate me on a very personal level despite the fact that she didn't even know me. Never mind the fact that it wasn't like I was making my involvement with Ben very obvious. We had both agreed to be discreet, and as far as I was concerned, we were indeed being pretty discreet. I wasn't making out with him in front of anyone, holding his hand or calling him by a pet name. Definitely pretty discreet given the reality of our situation which was two people who were undeniably attracted to each other and had amazing physical chemistry.

Ben glanced over to me in the passenger seat, smiled warmly and gave my thigh, just above my knee, a squeeze. His SUV glided to a stop in the passenger drop-off zone at the airport entrance.

"One more thing," he said as he pressed a button on his dash. The sound of a ringing phone filled the space around us.

"Trevor Whitmore's office. This is Janis."

Witch!

"Janis, this is Mr. Chase, please inform Trev that Kathleen Cooper will be staying at my home while I'm away on business, and I need him to make sure that if she needs anything, he sees to it."

Dammit. So much for discretion!

"Yes, sir." The line went dead, and I wasted not a moment. I was ready to pounce on him for tossing my privacy out of the window. I was sure to be the talk of the office thanks to him.

"What in the hell—" He leaned over the console, gripped the nape of my neck in his firm grasp, and pulled me to him. His mouth covered mine, effectively silencing me with a deep kiss. His tongue plundered my mouth, and his kiss effortlessly stole my breath. His lips broke away, but his forehead rested against mine.

"I'm going to miss you, Kathleen." My only response was the shallow uneven breathing that I did my best to reign in.

I pulled back from him a fraction. "Why in the hell did you do that?"

"You can't get mad at me for wanting to brag a little, that woman I'm crazy about is living under my roof."

I shook my head and wagged my finger at him. "No, no, no. This is only for a few days."

"See you Thursday morning, baby." Then he slid from the car, snatched up his bag, and made quick strides into the airport. I watched him until he was gone.

Baby. There it is again.

I walked around the car to get into the driver's seat and get back to the office. I made about a half a dozen adjustments to the seat before my feet finally reached the pedals, and I was off to work. Again. Before going back to work I stopped by my apartment and packed a bag for my stay at Ben's house, including comfy pajamas, my Kindle, a few toiletries, and my birth control. I would definitely need that since Ben and I were doing... whatever we were doing. I decided to drive past a few of the properties associated with John Murray on my way back to work. One was a rundown looking warehouse, a swanky home which I assumed to be his primary residence, and an office building.

Why in the world would he have a crappy warehouse in an industrial zone?

This property perplexed me. I couldn't see how this man would have any business owning such a property on the outskirts of Dallas. I found it odd to say the least. When I arrived back at work, I spent the remainder of my day digging deeper into the mystery of John Murray. I found contact information for the wife of his deceased partner, Mr. Kemp, and then I called her.

"Mrs. Kemp, I know this may sound odd, but I would like to ask a few questions about your husband and his involvement with Mr. John Murray. I am not with the police or press. I am just doing some research. I'm a freelance writer and... I uh, I'm doing research," I lied pathetically. The old widow either didn't care what my motivation was, or bought my poorly delivered lie.

"I'll do you a big favor right now and tell you if you don't already know. Sticking your nose into John Murray's business is a death sentence, sugar. I'd tell you to ask my husband, but he's dead. So you figure it out."

Oh, Crap!

"Um, yes ma'am, I know. I am sorry for your loss..."

"No loss to it. He was taken from me by that snake, Murray. They were in business together for years, and my husband wouldn't tell me what was going on; but I knew my man well. He found out somethin' about Murray that rattled him, good. I 'spect he was going to blow the whistle on the bastard," she said. "He ended up six feet under 'fore he could do just that. I told all the police and every reporter that has come callin' the same thing, but nothin' has come of it. Seems no one cares. He was the love of my life, and not a damn person cares." The sadness in her voice was palpable. She was sure someone had a hand in her husband's death, but no one had been held responsible for it yet.

"Ma'am, Mrs. Kemp, I'm so sorry. I promise if I find out anything helpful, you will be the first to know. Can we set up a time to meet? I'd love to ask you a few questions in person."

"I'm at home now. If you'd wanna swing by, you're more than welcome, sugar, but I meant what I said. You mess with Murray, and you're askin' for trouble. That man won't bat an eye at doin' you harm. You had better watch out for yourself."

"Yes, ma'am." We exchanged information, and I once again left work to visit with Mrs. Kemp in person. When I arrived at her home, she had no qualms about providing me with every bit of information she had available. She warned me over and over about Murray. I ignored her warnings. I told myself I was capable of dabbling into the sordid mess just enough to appease my curiosity and then withdraw myself just as quickly. I was foolish and wrong yet again, but I didn't know that then. Mrs. Kemp gave me an external hard drive and said she had no idea what was on it, but that she had recently found it in her husband's belongings. A note was in the plastic sandwich bag that the external drive was in. Scribbled in terrible handwriting was the name, 'Nate.' Along with the name was an address. Without further thought, I drove to the address straight from Mrs. Kemp's house. The address was a techie store. The front of the small store said, 'We repair your PC or its free.' I parked and strode into the store.

Not much business, huh? I thought to myself as I stood in

the quiet shop. Not one person was there. I heard shuffling from behind the counter.

"Ahem!"

A small-framed man about my age popped up from behind the counter. "Oh, ah, can I help you?"

I walked towards him. "You Nate?"

"Who's asking?" He backed away from the counter.

"My name is Kat Cooper." I extended my hand towards him. He took my hand in his sweaty hand briefly and introduced himself.

"Yeah, I'm Nate," he sputtered out warily.

"Okay, Nate, what can you tell me about this?" I removed the plastic-bag-clad hard drive from my purse and slid it to him across the counter. That's when things got crazy. He snatched the hard drive and marched to the door of the shop, flipped the sign from 'open' to 'closed,' and stalked back to me.

"Who the hell are you? How'd you get this? Are you trying to get us both killed?!"

Stupid. Why the fuck do I even care what Ben is dealing with here?

I knew exactly why I cared so damn much. It wasn't just my curiosity that drove me to snoop. It was the fact that I had begun falling for Ben and that I needed to know what he was dealing with where John Murray was concerned.

"Relax, guy! Mrs. Kemp gave this to me. She said she found it recently in some of her husband's stuff. I'm no one. I work for a law firm; I am just looking into this for Mrs. Kemp," I lied and pointed my finger at the hard drive in his sweaty palm while trying to remain confident.

"Lady, something tells me you have no idea who you're

messing with here." Nate's eyes began darting nervously everywhere in the room except at me. "These guys are the type you stay away from. You... you're putting both of us in danger by even being here."

"So tell me what's on the hard drive and what your involvement is, and I will leave." I folded my arms across my chest to punctuate my demand. He swallowed hard.

"I did some work for Mr. Kemp. That's all. Work is over. He's dead. I am so out of that shit." I cocked my head to the side and scowled at the small framed, nervous Nate.

"No, you aren't, Nate. You either tell me what I want to know, or I drag you further into this mess," I lied. I would never do anything so malicious. He ran his shaking hands through his scruffy light brown hair and caved.

"Fine. Come with me."

That was easy. Good job, Kat. Add bullying techies to your resume.

My phone chirped as soon as Nate led us into a closet-sized space through a narrow hallway at the back of his shop. I had a text message from my lonely lover.

'Landed in Cali. Miss you already. -Ben' I smiled as I read his short but sweet text. I shot him a quick text back.

'Glad you made it. Miss you a little, too. ;) -Kat'

"Okay, you want to sign your own death certificate? Fine. Kemp asked me to work on some things for him. I helped him uncover some dirt on Murray. I wish I had known the shit storm I was getting myself into before I took that load of cash from

Kemp to do this work." Nate shook his head.

"Go on," I prompted.

"Anyway, he brought me these encrypted files that he stole from Murray. Turns out, Murray has scammed millions, I mean, loads of dough from investors. Some of the files had information and photos of people he is involved with and the investors he has conned. A list of his known associates are on this drive." He held up the small square black hard drive. "Most of which are the criminal type, which means, not only could Murray have the need to get rid of you, but any one of these guys on this list could want you gone if they find out you have this info." Nate shoved the hard drive into my chest as if it were searing his hands by simply holding it. He began pacing in the small space. "Somehow, Murray has managed to keep things under wraps by convincing investors to stay put, along with their money. Kemp knew he was into some bad stuff. He was going to out Murray. Murray found out about Kemp's plans before he was able to go to the authorities, and Murray offed Kemp. I would put money on it. Kemp gave me a letter just before his death and said if anything happened to him, to give it to the cops."

"Have you given it to the police?" A look of shame came over Nate, and he froze in place.

"No. I was scared. I still am scared." I held out my hand expectantly.

"Give it to me. I'll take care of it." He crouched to the floor and crawled under his desk. He ripped something from the underside of the desk and handed me the envelope.

A letter from the grave. Interesting.

"Anything else I should know?" I asked.

"No. That's all I got. Everything on this hard drive is all the dirt that Kemp collected on Murray. He worked on it for months. I hope you know what you are doing. You are messing with the wrong guy. He has these huge goons that handle people like you and me. I'm talkin', like muscle you see in the movies or something." I ignored his ranting.

"Can you copy these files for me?"

He nodded. "Yeah."

I handed him the hard drive again, and in no time, he had a duplicate for me, and I was on my way. I decided the best course of action would be to hide the duplicate hard drive somewhere safe. Just in case.

In case what? Geez! What the hell am I doing? Ben is going to flip if he finds out what I'm up to.

I put thoughts of Ben out of my head and plotted my next move. I drove to the postal annex near my apartment and signed myself up for one of those small mailboxes that they rent out. I made sure to sign for it under my maiden name, Kathleen Hensley. I wrote a quick letter to Mrs. Kemp explaining that I wanted her to have the second key to my new mail box, and that if for some reason something happened to me, she would need to turn the contents of my box over to the police and Benjamin Chase at Chase and Associates.

Once I addressed the envelope to Mrs. Kemp, I addressed another large envelope to be sent to the box I had just rented. I stuffed the duplicate hard drive and the original letter from the grave into it and paid the cashier for the postage on both parcels. Just like that, ground work was laid. Curiosity and a need to know what Ben was dealing with started my mission, but I found myself driven to help Mrs. Kemp find answers. I felt that Nate was right. Mr. Kemp met an untimely end at the hands of Murray because of what he uncovered. He didn't accidentally overdose like the autopsy had declared.

If I had to bet, I would go even further and say that Murray likely even threatened or paid off someone at the Medical Examiner's office to ensure that the cause of death was declared accidental. Nate and Mrs. Kemp were both right. It was obvious that Murray was not the type of man you crossed or threatened. I forced myself to be even more careful while gathering more information to give to Mrs. Kemp and the police. I couldn't help wondering why the police had not gotten very far in the investigation into the 'suspicious,' albeit declared accidental, death of Mr. Kemp.

Murray have some dirty cops under his thumb too? Shit. That could be bad for me. No one to trust.

CHAPTER TWENTY

No clue

By the time I returned to work, most of my coworkers were filing out of the doors while I squeezed past them. I went to my office and immediately began taking down hand written notes. Earlier in the day, I had texted Cheyenne to let her know that I was still alive and would be staying at Ben's house for the rest of the week. She said she would catch up with me over the coming weekend since she, too, wouldn't be home until Sunday sometime. I had not spoken to Ben aside from our earlier 'miss you' texting. I was for sure missing him. I ignored the tightening sensation in my chest.

So what, you miss him. No big deal. He is a great lover; what's not to miss?

I tried to rationalize the pang of genuine sadness that was squeezing my heart as sexual frustration, but it was far from sexual frustration that had my insides in knots. I was lying to myself, but lying to myself felt much better than admitting the reality. The reality was I was involved with an amazing man who was unbelievable in bed, handsome, successful, smart, caring, and generous. And he missed me. I missed him too. A lot. I was missing the scent of him, his touch on my skin, his soft, full lips, the way his hand seemed to always find the small of my back, the way that, even in his sleep, he kept a tight grip on me. I missed the whole of him.

Should just forget about it. No way that falling for Ben could be a good idea. He deserves more than a screwed up, emotionally damaged woman. He should find someone else to get involved with.

I cringed at my private thoughts of Ben with someone else. I didn't want him with someone else but I also didn't want him with me. It was clear that Ben wanted things between us to go further, but I simply wasn't in a position to give anything to anyone. I was still trying to right my own world. I couldn't fathom dragging anyone else into my screwed up life. I would only get my hopes up, and inevitably, disappointments would come crashing in to wipe out everything I had gained. With my private thoughts swirling out of control, I decided to take a break. I backed away from my desk and clicked my heels down the hall towards the ladies room. I stared at the woman in the mirror and tried hard to reason with myself about falling for Ben. I used the facilities, gathered my thoughts, and resigned myself to focusing on my meddling into John Murray and all his business dealings. I would have to deal with my feelings about Ben, later. When I made the turn into the corridor that led to my office, I saw something odd. There was a shadow cast onto the slick floor outside my open office door. Whoever this shadow belonged to was in my office, standing beneath the buzzing fluorescent lighting that annoyed me on a daily basis. I charged forward towards my office making sure to click my heels against the floor loudly.

"Excuse me! What the hell are you doing in my office?" The person standing at my desk startled and jerked her head upward, righting her gaze from the scattered papers on my desk.

"Oh, I'm sorry," Janis blurt out while scurrying from my work space.

"I thought maybe you left your office open. I was just going to close it for you and shut off the lights. I'm sorry. I didn't know you were here." I stood with my arms bent at the elbow and my hands perched haughtily on my hips. I was completely unmoved by her apology and excuse. I wasn't buying it. She was snooping around me just as much as I was snooping around John Murray. I just knew it. I could feel it in my gut.

"Yes, because the light switch to this office is on top of my desk." I made a noise under my breath, laced with cantankerous undertones that I was sure would communicate my disbelief and abhorrence for her actions. "Well, do me a favor Janis. In the future, don't do me any favors. Okay?"

She said nothing in response to my snarky remarks and made hurried strides away from my office. I worked for an hour or so longer after my run-in with the nosey Janis. My ringing cell phone pulled my attention from snooping. Ben was calling.

"Hello?"

"I miss you too much," he said low into the receiver. I couldn't help but smile as I leaned back in my chair. I closed my eyes and tried my best to imagine that he was in the room with me, not two time zones away on the west coast.

"I miss you, too," I murmured into the phone. I heard him

breathe deeply as if wanted me missing him.

"It's driving me crazy thinking of you sleeping in my bed without me. Makes me want to come home now."

"You'll be back soon enough," I reminded him.

"Not soon enough for me."

"Ben, I have to go, someone is calling."

"Okay, Kathleen. I will talk to you tomorrow. I miss you. I mean it."

"I mean it, too. Bye." I did mean it. I ignored the niggling tug in my chest again while I answered the incoming call on my cell phone. It was Cheyenne, and she was shouting and talking to what sounded like more than one person.

"Chey! What the hell is going on?"

"Kat, you better get your butt over to the apartment now! Someone broke in and trashed the place. The police are here."

"Oh my God! Are you okay?"

"Yeah, I am fine. I wasn't here. Tuck just brought me back to the apartment to get some of my things to stay at his house, and we walked into a trashed apartment!"

"I'm on my way!" I hung up the phone before she could respond and began gathering my things. I quickly made copies of the photos and notes that I had gathered about John Murray and sped to my apartment and my very shaken best friend. When I walked into the apartment, I could barely believe that the sight before me was the apartment where Cheyenne and I lived. It looked like a tornado tore through the place, destroying everything in its path. I stepped over broken picture frames and around turned over furniture to get to Cheyenne. She was standing with Tucker. His big arm was draped over her petite frame protectively. A police officer was speaking with them.

"What in the hell happened?" Cheyenne whirled around to see me surveying the state of our place. I was sure the color had drained from my face. I was irate. I could barely believe that someone had broken into our apartment and vandalized the place.

"Kat! See what they did?" Cheyenne screeched and flung out both arms.

"Uh, yeah, I see what the hell happened. Can't exactly miss it, Chey," I shot back, disgruntled.

"Hey! Don't you dare snap at me, Kathleen Cooper! That's not fair!" Cheyenne ordered with her hands planted on her hips and her cheeks slightly red as they always were when she was getting upset.

"Sorry," I muttered.

"How did this happen? We always lock the doors, and since the front door and lock are both still intact, I'm assuming that the door was either unlocked or someone picked it," I stated, looking towards the officer in front of Cheyenne.

"No forced entry, ma'am. So the door could have been unlocked or picked. Difficult to say either way. We are dusting for prints now." I nodded my head in understanding.

"So what was stolen?"

"Nothing, it seems." The officer shrugged then looked around himself.

"Nothing?" I asked him incredulously.

"Not one thing." The officer reaffirmed.

Oh, shit. Definitely Murray.

Realization and guilt crashed down on me like lead. I knew if someone broke in and didn't take anything, his motives for breaking in could be far worse than theft. He didn't take any of our jewelry, electronics, the expensive silver that belonged to Cheyenne's great-grandmother, or either one of the two small safes we kept in our rooms. This brought chills to my skin and caused me to visibly shiver.

"Fuck. Not good," I mumbled as I turned away from the group and surveyed the state of disarray that our apartment was in.

The wheels in my head began turning. The fact that I had been warned about digging into John Murray's business more than once earlier in the day did not escape me.

If this has to do with John, then word must travel damned fast.

I instantly felt guilty as well as outraged and worried at the thought of this being the result of my snooping where I shouldn't have.

So if this is a warning, I will stop digging. That's it. Just stop. What about Mrs. Kemp? *What about finishing what you've started?*

I placed my fingers to my temples and began rubbing in a circular motion to ease the firestorm going on in my head. "Any ideas on who may have done this ma'am?" The officer asked. I turned to face the group again.

Yep, and it's all my fault Murray had our apartment trashed. Brilliant, Kat. Really just fantastic.

I glanced at Cheyenne who was once again in Tuck's protective embrace. I swallowed down the urge to tell all.

"No clue," I said with a shrug. It was good thing that Cheyenne was turned into Tucker's chest because she missed the lie I tossed out. One look at my face, and she would call me on it. I couldn't tell the police anything they didn't already know about

John Murray and quite simply, I wasn't sure if the police were under his thumb. If John Murray had the police in his pocket, it made anyone in uniform suspect and therefore a useless resource to me. I decided to push forward, gather what I could as quickly as possible, then go to someone I trusted. Ben. I knew he would be furious with me for digging into something he specifically told me to stay out of, but he would be the only person I could trust to take the information and make things happen. If John Murray did in fact have anything to do with the death of Mrs. Kemp's husband, then I would gladly take my punishment from Ben if it meant bringing her some peace and some justice.

Neither Mr. or Mrs. Kemp deserved what they had gotten. Mr. Kemp was dead, and Mrs. Kemp was left thinking no one cared enough to look into the circumstances under which the love of her life had died. Mr. Kemp knew that Murray was a criminal who was stealing obscene amounts of money from people. He was trying to do the right thing, and it appeared that doing the right thing had gotten him killed. I hoped that the same fate didn't await me. I spoke with Cheyenne and Tucker a bit more after the police left and reassured them that I was fine staying at Ben's house alone. Tucker offered to call Ben and let him know about the break in, but I promised to call him myself once I got back to his place.

I lied again. Tucker took my weary best friend home, and I gathered up the broken bits of my home and tossed them into the trash after taking plenty of photos for the insurance company. I secured the place again and set my car in the direction of Ben's home. I didn't call or text him again that night. I wouldn't know what to say, and I was beginning to think that my lover was honing his ability to see through me, even on the phone. I couldn't afford for him to find out about my activities. He would be on the first flight back, and my information-gathering efforts would be halted.

CHAPTER TWENTY-ONE

Have to try

I stayed awake for much of the night thinking about everything I had discovered throughout the day. I also couldn't quite shake the creepy feeling about Janis that shadowed my thoughts. I couldn't put my finger on it, but that woman's behavior was strange. Her glares and evil vibe went far past the average catty female behavior. She stirred an uneasy feeling within me that I found impossible to ignore. I decided that I would dig into Janis Harper's life next. I finally drifted to sleep.

My chest feels heavy. Very heavy. I'm heaving in and out, trying to catch my breath. *Who's there?* I can hear voices, but I can't see anything. I beg my eyes to open and they do, but there must be cloth over my eyes because I still can't see a thing. The cloth is scratchy across my eyes like burlap, and I realize that the same type of cloth is stuffed into my mouth. I can't breathe through my nose, and the fact that I can't catch my breath with just the use of my nose is scaring me. I'm covered in a cold sweat. My heart is pounding really hard. I can feel that my wrists are bound, but my hands still shake viciously. A fear-induced whimper escapes my lips. I'm so scared. *Calm down, Kat. Breathe in. Breathe out. I must be having a panic attack.* I am so frightened, I feel like I might be sick, but I push the nausea down deep.

My mouth is stuffed with cloth that tastes like dust, so getting sick is not an option. I strain to hear the faint voices around me. I hear men. Three, maybe four, different male voices. I hear footsteps approaching me, and I let out a muffled, blood-curdling scream from behind the dusty cloth shoved in my mouth. A hard thud rings through my ears and vibrates through my skull. Despite my hindered vision, I see brightly colored spots that remind me of highlighter pens. Something warm is on my face. My hands instinctively fight against the bonds that hold them so that I can touch the assaulted area. The warmth is spreading downward. Down to my cheek. Now my jaw. Now my neck. My face feels like it has a heartbeat. *I'm bleeding.* The warm feeling is blood. There must be a lot of it. I can feel it rolling down the right side of my face and down my neck. I'm crying now. I'm sobbing hard. I can barely breathe. *I want Ben. Where's Ben? He will save me.* I think he loves me like I have come to realize that I love him. *Where is he? I need him. Please, God. I don't want to die!* I hear the male voices come nearer. I begin hyperventilating.

What are they doing? I am so scared.

The adrenaline coursing through my veins urges me to fight,

to run if given the chance. I know that's what I'll do. I will run if I can. I let out another scream from behind the dusty cloth gag. I'm asking for help, but the cloth makes my plea indecipherable. Another thud, but I don't feel anything except more warmth running down my face. I'm thankful for the adrenaline racing through my veins. It's pushing me forward. It's the only thing keeping me going right now, other than my need to see Ben again. I want Ben. A grumbly voice fills my throbbing left ear and all at once, I can smell cigarettes, liquor, and generally foul breath. It smells awful. I want to vomit again, but I remind myself to choke the nausea down. No getting sick with a gag crammed in my mouth.

"Quit trying to scream or it's going to hurt worse!" the man threatens.

This makes me cry more desperately. *Please. Please. Please, don't hurt me. I am begging them from behind the dusty cloth. Please, let me go*

"Don't you fucking scream!" he warns me, and I nod.

"I'm going to take off you blindfold."

I force myself to calm down. I have to figure out where I am and how to get away. The foul-breathed man jerks the cloth from my eyes, and I blink rapidly to clear my vision. Blood has seeped into my right eye, blurring my vision in that eye, but my left eye has cleared. I can see. I am in a dark space that has an echo, and a bright light beams down on just me. *Must be a large room. A garage maybe.* I quickly scan the room, but can't see beyond the light that is beaming down on me like a spotlight. I look down at my feet. It's a smooth concrete floor that my fee limply rest against. The large man that I can now see steps off to the side, and darkness envelops him.

The male voices whisper as they stand just beyond the light that would make them visible to me. They are all cloaked. *Cowards.* I'm getting more angry than scared now. It's the adrenaline, I'm sure, but I don't care. I don't think I am going to get out of here. They are going to kill me. I can feel it. Yet the cowards won't show their faces. They are hiding beyond the shadows that concealed them so well.

"Cowards!" I scream from behind my dusty gag. They laugh at me. *Laughing! Sick, disgusting, cowards!* I hear the clicking of what must be dress shoes. One set. Wait, two sets of clicking dress shoes against the concrete slab floor. I see the shape of a very tall man come into focus. He walks toward me, and I can see his face clearly now. I want to scream, cry, gasp and get sick all at once, but can't. I have stopped breathing, and the only thing that jars me from my shocked gaze is the pain squeezing my lungs, demanding oxygen. *Breathe!* I draw in air through flared nostrils. "Aidan!" I scream at him, but he says nothing to me. His lips turn up into a grin and I am sure that he is enjoying seeing me bound and bleeding.

Aidan wants me dead. The scenario in front of me makes my blood run cold. The other set of dress shoes peeping out into the circle of light around me walk forward to stand beside Aidan. I blink rapidly again. I can't believe my eyes. *Ben. It's Ben. My Ben. Why isn't he rushing to my side to save me?* He is whispering to Aidan and smiling. They are shaking hands as if they are friends. "Ben!" I scream at him, but he does little more than stair at me with a narcissistic expression on his face. He makes no move to help me. *He doesn't love me.* The realization hits me harder than the man with the harsh breath, and I am not sure which reality hurts the most. The idea of Ben not being in love with me, or the fact that for some reason, the only two people that I have ever fallen for are both standing in a room, facilitating my demise. *Why?* I am screaming for him, but he won't help me. Pain sears my heart. I am sobbing so hard. I can't breathe. Ben is walking to me. He has crouched to my side. His lips are against my ear. "Told you to stay out of it, Kathleen." His voice sounds so cold and evil.

"Please, I'm sorry!" I'm screaming. I can't breathe at all now. I am choking. I feel something clawing at my chest. I feel close to the end. Everything has gone black.

I jumped from Ben's bed and realized that it was my own hands that were clawing at my chest. I rolled from his bed and fell to the floor disoriented and gasping for air.

Just a nightmare, Kat. Just a nightmare. Just a nightmare. Just a nightmare.

I chanted in my head. Sitting on the floor beside Ben's bed, I wrapped my arms around my bent knees and pulled them tight into my chest. I was so shaken by the nightmare. It felt so real. Tears were slipping down my face, and I hadn't even realized I was crying. I focused on my breathing instead of thoughts of my lover and ex-husband trying to kill me. My dream was completely irrational. I knew that, but I couldn't help but wonder why I would dream of such an awful thing. I glanced at the clock on the nightstand. I had not been asleep for more than two hours, and it was already time to get up for the day. My irritating alarm began sounding loudly, and I startled.

"Damn," I groaned. I slid back into Ben's bed to linger a bit longer before I had to get ready for work. I buried my face into his pillows and inhaled my favorite scent: Ben. I ached for him in that moment. I needed nothing more than the feel of his arms around me and his comforting presence to shake away the awful visions from my nightmare. I lay in Ben's bed for a long moment and reveled in the fact that I was falling for him. I wanted him. I needed him. But most importantly, I wanted to be who he wanted and needed, too. I was scared to get hurt again or to hurt Ben; that was the last thing I wanted. In fact, I would never forgive myself if I hurt my lonely lover in any way. I would just have to find a way to be enough for him. I would have to find a way to let go of my past so that I could give him my future. I had no guarantees for Ben, but I would offer him what I could, nonetheless. I knew I wasn't even close to being able to satisfy another person's appetite for love, support, and trust, but I was compelled to try. I had to try for Ben. I had to try for both of us.

Gotta talk to him when he gets home. Just come clean about things. Tell him you've fallen in love with him and that you're scared, but that you can't not try. Tomorrow morning.

I ignored the fact that I looked like the walking dead. Death warmed over looked better than I did. My eyes had bags under them thanks to lack of sleep. My nose was bright red and stuffy from crying after my awful dream. My eyes were red-rimmed and puffy. My cheeks looked pale and void of life in contrast to my bright red nose and eyes. My hair was less than its best mostly due to lack of effort on my part. I doubted that I had the energy to endure another day of digging into John Murray's life while juggling my normal workload, but I had no option. I needed to get as much done with Ben away in California as I could. Once he returned, I would be unable to snoop so freely. I dragged my sluggish ass into work and was shocked to see a huge bouquet of red roses sitting right outside my locked office. Aw! Ben.

CHAPTER TWENTY-TWO

Grave digger

I bent down and picked up the large bouquet while unlocking my office door. I set the arrangement down on my desk and grabbed the envelope that was taped to the vase. It was a full- sized envelope with just my name scrawled across the front. I slid my finger across the seam and pulled out the greeting card inside. I opened the card and dirt scattered onto my desk.

"What in the world?" I muttered to myself. I opened the card to see a typed message to me.

'Digging your own grave, Kathleen Cooper.'

I went numb for a moment as I read the frightening message. The roses obviously were not from Ben.

Who sent these?

I scurried from my office straight to Joyce at the front desk.

"Have you seen anyone delivering flowers this morning?" I asked while my hands shook slightly.

Joyce's brows furrowed, and she shook her head slowly side to side. "No, Kat. I've not seen any delivery people this mornin'." I made no effort to respond or even to explain. I scrambled to a half a dozen other coworkers and asked them if they had seen anything, and no one admitted to anything.

Janis!

I strode angrily to Janis's desk. "What do you know about the flowers on my desk right now?"

"Flowers? I don't know about any flowers," she said without making eye contact with me. I glared down at the creepy woman who nosed through my office the night before and made it a point to make her uncomfortable like she made me uncomfortable. I was sleep-deprived, scared, and missed Ben. I was a complete bitch.

"No clue huh?"

Fucking bitch!

I could hear a bit of the old me seeping through my words, and it bolstered my confidence to deal with the creepy, nosey, Janis. I leaned forward and placed the palms of both my hands flat on the surface of her desk.

"That's a good thing," I whispered snottily.

Janis glanced up at me, and the pure hatred she so obviously carried for me was pouring from her. She gave me what I assumed was her best evil eye just before I whirled around in my heels and marched back to my office. I flopped down at my desk and stared at the roses.

Think, Kat.

I tapped my fingers on my desk as I began thinking of the

awful predicament I had put myself in.

What do I do now? Call Ben? Call the police? No. I can't tell anyone what I know yet. It's not safe now. Dammit, Kat.

I slapped my hand on my desk and decided that I would have to work within the safety of my office for the day. I couldn't drive all over town snooping into things with John Murray clearly keeping a threatening eye on me. I relocated the roses and the card to the top of a filing cabinet in the corner of my office and did my best to ignore the foreboding bouquet. I managed to work right through lunch. By some divine miracle, I successfully juggled my normal work and the not-so-little project that had, so far, earned me a vandalized apartment and threatening messages at work.

I rolled my eyes thinking about how I was either incredibly brave or incredibly stupid. I was likely both. I dug through my purse for the apple I tossed in it on my way from Ben's house that morning. I found the poor excuse for my lunch and began devouring it despite its bruises. With one hand clutching my lunch, I used my free hand to peck out keys on my keyboard for an internet search regarding one Janis Harper. I hit the 'enter' button and watched as multiple results filled my computer screen. I tossed my lousy lunch into the garbage, wiped my hands and glided the cursor over the search results and began clicking away. There were several results linking Janis Harper to someone by the name of Laura Keys. There was also a related search result with a string of links including changing identities, starting over, delete yourself from the web in twelve easy steps, along with a long list of other options. I had never heard the name Laura Keys before, but I knew typing it into a search engine would give me something. I typed in 'Laura Keys, Texas' into the search box and gingerly tapped the enter button with my pinky.

"Pay dirt," I mumbled to myself. I clicked on images first. When the first thumbnail was opened to full size, I stopped breathing. It was of a woman. The woman in the photo was named Laura Keys, but I knew the woman in the photo as Janis Harper, my jealous, nosey coworker who had a crush on the man I had fallen for.

"Oh. My. God," I whispered as I studied the photo of Janis, Laura, whatever her real name was. I clicked back to articles and opened the first one I saw.

'Investigators are still working at the scene of a fatal car crash that occurred on county road 332, early Saturday evening. The only vehicle involved was reportedly in flames when first responders arrived at the scene. The driver and passenger of the vehicle have been identified as Michael Keys, 28, and his son, Neil, age 4. The two victims were deceased at the scene. The driver, Michael Keys leaves behind his wife and the mother of his son, Laura Keys, age 25.'

I covered my mouth with my hand.

Poor Janis. Her husband and her son had died.

The newspaper that printed to article was 'The Buckston Tribune'. I knew Buckston to be a small town in west Texas with little or nothing to see or do. It was certainly not a town that was on anyone's bucket list. I clicked on a photo of Michael Keys and once again stopped breathing. Janis's husband, Michael was easily my Ben's twin. The two men looked so alike you would swear they were somehow related, even though I knew that was not possible since Ben admitted he only had one sibling. Samuel, who was only two years younger than Ben, and lived in Dallas as well, though we had yet to meet. In fact, Ben had spoken about his family, but I had yet to be properly introduced to his parents, grandparents, and younger brother.

"Holy hell! No wonder Janis has a thing for Ben. He is like a carbon copy of her dead husband. She's obsessed. Psycho," I said barely loud enough to be considered audible.

How did she end up in Dallas all the way from Podunk Buckston?

My brows were furrowed, and I was in deep thought when my desk phone rang. I quickly extracted myself from my thoughts and scooped the phone from its cradle.

"Kathleen Cooper," I stated professionally.

"Mmm, I have forgotten how much I love hearing your voice." Ben's voice flowed from the phone and instantly wrapped me in the seductive tone that came through the long distance phone call.

"Ah, I see." I leaned back in my chair and took a moment to enjoy the distraction that talking to Ben offered.

"So, you miss me and love hearing my voice, and here I am thinking maybe you enjoyed more than just my voice," I teased playfully. Ben chuckled low into the phone, and I smiled, utterly proud of myself for coaxing a chuckle from my lonely lover.

"Yes. Well, I happen to love hearing your voice, but there is plenty more that I love about you."

Oh.

Before I had a chance to say a word, Ben went on.

"How did you sleep last night?"

"I had this awful nightmare this morning. I wished you were

in bed with me. I was pretty shaken up."

"What was it about?"

"Oh. I don't remember the nightmare. I just know I woke up scared and pretty freaked out," I lied.

"Mhmm." Ben sounded like he was skeptical of my story, but wasn't going to press the issue. "I'll be back in the morning, so tomorrow night, you shouldn't have to worry about missing me should any bad dreams arise. As long as you agree to stay with me tomorrow night, I will be beside you."

"As if I can resist staying in your bed."

"I will see you in the morning, Kathleen."

"In the morning, Ben." I reiterated then returned my desk phone to its cradle. Not ten seconds later my phone rang again. I picked it up once again from its cradle with a smile on my face.

"Miss my voice again already?" There was no answer, but I could hear heavy breathing on the other end of the line.

"Hello? Who is this?" I demanded.

"Still digging, Kathleen Cooper?"

"WHO IS THIS?" I shouted as I jumped from my office chair. The electronically distorted voice didn't say anything else, and the line clicked dead.

This is way out of control. This is crazy! It's okay, Ben will be back in the morning, and it will be time to come clean about snooping around and how I really feel about him. He will know what to do.

I glanced at the clock in the corner of my computer screen and was glad to see that the day had zipped by, and it was close to the end of the day. I began gathering my things and thinking about the distorted voice on the phone and Ben saying he loved many things about me. But most of all, I was confused about

Janis's past. I found out rather easily that she had suffered a terrible tragedy five years before, and she had obviously changed her name, but I couldn't quite piece together the rest.

Why would she want to leave everyone and everything she knew, move across the state, change her name, and live alone and apparently miserable?

It made no sense to me.

There has to be a reason she came to Dallas. She would have to have good motive for legally changing her name. People don't just change their names and uproot their entire lives for no reason.

I milled around my small office gathering my things and my research as I struggled to make sense of Janis's choice to abandon her past. I, of all people, could understand wanting to start over someplace new, but Janis took it to a new level. The information I gathered throughout the day only led me to more questions. I made copies of everything I had printed out and written and hid the copies in a falsely labeled folder in the filing cabinet in my office. I was smart enough to make copies, to hide things, to send messages to people who would know what to do in the event that something happened to me, but I was not smart enough to procure a can of pepper spray, a folding knife or even a well sharpened pencil to carry in my purse in the event that I would need to defend myself.

I sat in Ben's remarkably comfortable bed that evening with notes and photos scattered like confetti all around me. I made more notes and took stock of John Murray's felonious activities and associates. I knew that if by some miracle I was able to finish what I had started, John Murray was going to go the prison for a long time if someone with a score to settle didn't get to him first. I hoped, not for his sake, but for the sake of justice, that he was alive and well enough to stand trial and answer for his crimes. As far as I was able to tell, he likely murdered Mr. Kemp; he had also stolen more money than I knew how to sum up in words and had committed a host of other felonies that merited jail time. I wasn't sure how to get the truth out about Mr. Kemps death other than getting John Murray to admit to it, which I was certain would never happen.

"If the police get hold of the information I have, maybe they can squeeze some of people in John's inner circle. Someone is bound to sing like a bird if there's a deal on the table," I rambled aloud, talking to only myself and my research. I am not sure what time I fell asleep since I don't exactly recall falling asleep. I woke up feeling refreshed and caught up from the previous night's lack of rest. I made quick work of showering and getting dressed, taking extra care while applying makeup to accentuate my green eyes. I let my auburn hair flow instead of restraining it in my usual clinical bun. Ben preferred my hair loose, and I knew I would need to please him and kiss a little gorgeous lawyer ass before confessing to my activities during his trip to California. I sprayed my best perfume a couple of times over my favorite sleeveless shift dress and headed out the door with my things clutched in my arms. I came to a halt right outside the driver's side door of Ben's Cadillac while I dug for the key fob through my purse that could double for a small sized replica of a landfill. Random contents hid the keys to Ben's luxury SUV at the bottom of my cheap purse that was filled with plastic and paper wrappers, elastic hair ties, cords and chargers for my cell phone, tablet and one dead iPod, a multitude of pens and pencils, lip gloss, and a misplaced half eaten cracker that I had zero memory of ever seeing.

"Ah, what the hell, Kat?" I scoffed at myself and tossed the extremely stale cracker into the grass and went back to searching for Ben's keys. I knew I needed to hurry, or I would be late picking up my lover from the airport. I heard the sound of shoes shifting across concrete, and with no warning, I felt a sharp prick of pain in my neck. A few seconds later, I was slumped over in a large meaty man's arms, and he was dragging my limp body into the back of Ben's SUV. I heard muffled talking between men as everything went dark.

CHAPTER TWENTY-THREE

Coming back to life

This is another nightmare. This can't be real. I'm sleeping. Wake up, Kat! I screamed at myself, but still nothing. No light spilled into my eyes, and my body seemed to not be my own. Oh, God, please wake up. I felt so sleepy. What little grip on awareness that I had was slipping. I was being pulled into someplace dark, and I couldn't fight it.

"Is this bitch ever going to wake up?" I heard a faceless voice say with pure ugliness in his voice.

My body. Move! Open your eyes!

"I don't know, you idiot. How much did you give her?"

Give me what? What did he give me? Drugs? What kind?

"Enough to get the job done."

Two voices. Two people.

"Yeah, enough to knock her buck and a quarter ass out for over eight damn hours! He's going to be pissed when he calls, and we ain't got nothin' to tell him."

Him? Who him? John Murray? You two are Murray's muscle?

"Fine. I'll wake er' ass up right now!"

Shit! Don't hurt me, please!

"Wake up!" A big hand tangled into my hair and wrenched my head back from its slumped position with my chin resting on my chest. Another big hand came down hard across my cheek. Then again and again. I whimpered, and the man who was still pulling my hair stopped for a moment. My face began throbbing, and my skin lit on fire from his calloused hand slapping my face with brute force. I could feel welts surfacing on my cheek. My eyes cracked open slightly, but everything was fuzzy and unclear. Tears welled in my half-open eyes.

"See, she's awake now." The meaty man who was slapping me turned his head and craned his neck to look over his shoulder at a man whom I assumed was his partner.

"Good. Quicker we get this shit over with, the quicker we get outta here. I'm starvin'"

Get what over with?

"Please," I whimpered in a tone that scarcely resembled my normal voice. One of the men laughed boisterously. The other guffawed loudly sending chills down my spine. "Please let me go. I'll do whatever. Just... please," I sputtered out in desperation.

"Bitch, I got news for ya: Pissin' off the wrong man wasn't a bright idea. He wants the info you dug up. Now."

"I, all I know is what I had with me. In my bag..." The meaty man released my head, and I righted my posture as best as I could. But being bound to a plastic lawn chair made sitting comfortably impossible. I could see the two men once my vision became clearer. They were both large. One was muscular and built much like a wrestler, while the other was simply overweight, but big nevertheless. The muscular man bent at the waist and quickly swept up my messenger bag and purse from the floor. He brought them to me and turned both bags upside down to dump the contents in front of me. It was then that I looked around at where the men had taken me. I realized that the building we were in was the sketchy-looking warehouse I had been so confused about John Murray owning. Obviously, the building was used for illicit activity. Both men pilfered through my belongings and gathered up my copied research papers.

"You tellin' me this is all you got? Everything you know?" The overweight man stepped forward towards me and waved papers in my face as he bit out his question in a caustic tone.

Don't hurt me. Don't hurt me. Please! Ben. My Ben.

I wanted Ben more than anything in that moment, and I began sobbing as I nodded my head feverishly trying to convince them that I had no other information about John Murray. At least, not with me. I had set a plan in place that was playing out as I sat bound to the cheap plastic chair. I doubted the men knew about my rented mail box, the copied letter from the grave, the duplicated hard drive, or the letter I sent to Mrs. Kemp. They were all things I had to believe no one knew about. If the men and John Murray somehow knew about my plan, they would foil my attempts at securing the information that Mr. Kemp had lost his life digging up. His death and my abduction would all be for nothing. Not to mention the fact that in the event of my death, the information in my rented mailbox would be in Ben's and Mrs. Kemp's hands. I would be putting both of them in danger if it came to that. I had to make sure it never got to that point.

"I s-swear. I am just a paralegal. I was just curious. Please just take my stuff, but let me go." I was trembling so fiercely that my bones shuddered and ached. The heavy-set man looked at me skeptically and then moved forward. He bent down, grasped the front two legs of the seat I was bound to, and flipped me backward. As I went crashing backward to slam into the floor, I sealed my eyes and held my breath, waiting for the pain.

Oh God!

Despite stiffening my neck, my head cracked against the floor. I knew the man was screaming at me, but my eyes rolled around in my skull aimlessly, and my ears rang loudly.

"Don't lie to me girl! I'll cut the tongue outta that pretty mouth of yours!" he roared. I gathered as much air into my lungs as I could and screamed back at the man.

"That's all I know!" A painful sob tore through my scream, and my shoulders began to rock with my heavy weeping. "Please. That's all I have. All I know," I croaked out weakly still lying bound to the chair that lay back on the cold floor. The utility tape that wound around my ribs and over my thighs held me easily to the chair. My wrists were bound in front of me and the men fashioned a loop of sorts out of tape to fasten my bound wrists to the wide strips of tape across my thighs. It was all very rudimentary, but nonetheless effective. My wriggling, tugging, and pulling did nothing to free me from the chair I was strapped to. The heavy-set man tilted his chin towards the other man as he stepped away from me to take an incoming call on his cell phone. The muscular man righted my seat from the floor with one hand and watched me closely while waiting for the other man to rejoin my interrogation.

"Please," I whispered. The man was unmoved by my plea. I scrambled to pull my thoughts together.

Think, Kat. Think!

"Gotcha," the other man muttered into the phone and shook his head up and down. He hung up his phone, and I watched warily as he approached me. He said nothing just before he cocked back his balled fist and brought it down forcefully, connecting perfectly with my jaw. I sputtered and spit blood everywhere. It dripped freely down my chin since my jaw hung slackened.

"Seems you've made a bigger mess of things. Some lawyer is makin' a bunch of noise over you. Now we gotta go do damage control."

Ben! Ben knows I'm gone. Of course he knows I'm gone. He will find me. What if they get to Ben? What if they hurt my Ben?

The muscular man fastened a blindfold around my head, and I heard the distinct rip of utility tape. He secured the tape over my mouth and lightly slapped my face. More panic and worry consumed me as I listened closely to both of my captors walking in what I could hear was an easy stride out of the warehouse. Sobbing overcame me. I cried for some time, and my body rocked and shuddered as I resigned myself to these circumstances. My head hurt like never before. I was groggy. I had dried blood all over my face. I felt the skin across my jaw tighten as swelling grew from the spot where the overweight man's fist had landed. I was nauseated and unbelievably thirsty. I had no way to be sure, but it felt like a considerable amount of time had passed since the men shoved me into the back of Ben's

SUV. I remembered hearing the men talk about not having any dinner and how I had been knocked out for a long while after they drugged me with whatever was in the needle that I'd been stabbed with. At some point during their absence, I must have passed out or simply fallen asleep, but either way I was out cold when the men came waltzing back into the warehouse. I lifted my head weakly and listened to their approach. The two were speaking casually about common things as if they were neighbors or friends, and there I sat, kidnapped and beaten at the demand of John Murray. The men came directly to me, and in an instant, the tape was ripped from my mouth stealing the breath from my lungs. I gasped to calm my thumping heart and aching lungs. The blindfold was next. It was jerked from my head, and my entire brain and face was consumed with extreme pain anew. My stomach roiled and threatened as I fought to gain my bearings through the anguish that was tormenting me physically and mentally.

Don't vomit, I admonished myself as I swallowed down the powerful urge to be sick. *Focus, Kat! Find out what is going on.*

"Alright, girl. You sure you got nothin' you need to tell us?" The soft man asked me tauntingly as if he were enjoying my torture. The intonation in his voice made it clear that he was using me for entertainment more than information gathering. I knew that was bad news for me. No longer being of importance meant I was all the more disposable, and I knew I would be disposed of soon. I didn't bother responding to the man. I only hung my head with exhaustion and defeat. I couldn't give them the information I had without endangering Mrs. Kemp, Nate, and most importantly to me, my Ben. I accepted my fate in that moment strapped to that chair with comforting thoughts of Ben,

Cheyenne, and my family raiding my fuzzy brain, chasing away the hell hounds. I lifted my chin to stare at the thugs who worked for the even bigger criminal who started all of this.

"Fuck. You." The insult skated off my tongue with ease and left a tingle of exuberance in its wake. Just like that, the old me waltzed into that warehouse and I held tightly to the part of me I knew. It was the part of me that had left so long ago. It was the part that I longed for. It was the part of me that came to life in the moments just before what I was sure would be my death. I was glad to have the old me back all the same.

That felt good.

I inwardly relished my rebellious mouth. The pudgy man's head snapped back marginally as if I spit in his face, and his eyes widened.

That's right asshole. I said it.

I savored my moment and prepared for the pain I knew was about to crash over me. The man corrected his face, his nostrils flared, his jaw tightened and twitched, then he drew back and punched me like a heavyweight champ fighting for his title. My head popped back, then listed to the side as the metallic taste of blood flooded my mouth again, and I spit my life source out by the mouthful. I bit back the tears that fought to run freely. I controlled my emotion. I refused to give this man any more enjoyment at my expense. I knew he was going to kill me anyway. They no longer needed me; he made that much obvious when they came back to the warehouse. I was already dead as far as I was concerned. I clung to the thoughts and memories of the people I loved to strengthen me, to bring me peace.

"Wanna try that again?" the man screamed into my face. The smell of his breath sent my stomach into an uproar, and I could no longer choke down the nausea. I vomited violently, narrowly missing him. I groaned as my stomach lurched and stilled repeatedly. I pressed forward. I was ready to get this over with.

Sooner I'm dead, the sooner the info I copied gets to the cops.

I was in more physical pain than I had ever known and was ready to get it over with. Sure, I wanted to run. I wanted to live, and if given the chance, I would do just that. I would run. I would try to make it. But as it was, I was dead, and I knew it.

"I said. Fuck. You. Asshole." I bit out with as much venom in my voice as I could conjure. Blood dripped and sputtered out of my wrecked mouth. The muscular man gripped the other man's arm and pulled him back before he could bludgeon me and make a huge mess that I was sure they would be responsible for having to tidy up. He pulled him into a private huddle, and the men whispered to each other for a moment. The heavy-set man was animated. He tossed his arms outward and spoke with his hands.

Pissed him off.

I watched the men and wondered if dying would hurt. I hoped not. I was already in so much physical pain I hoped that death would bring... release. I simply waited for the end. I couldn't cry any more. I had no more tears. I had no hope to be set free unless my freedom came in the form of death. I prayed as I lost myself in memories of my loved ones. It was all I had to console me. After the men had a brief, yet heated discussion, they walked with purpose throughout the warehouse and gathered things into a pile before me.

Two shovels, a sheet, rope...

I sighed and looked away from the pile before me. I retreated back into my thoughts and memories while I waited for the end. A short time after they gathered their things, the muscular man began cutting through the tape that held me to the chair. He freed me from my bonds except for the tape that bound my wrists tightly together. The man stepped away from me, and out of nowhere, the overweight pig who enjoyed beating me stepped into view with a bat in hand. I could barely blink just before he aimed for the fences and swung. I heard a loud crack, and more pain ricocheted through my body lighting nerve endings on fire as it went.

"Arghhhhhh!" I screamed out.

"That's for that sassy mouth of yours, bitch! Now we know you can't run when we take you to your grave." The man spit on me while I instinctively leaned forward and clutched my shattered leg. I groaned and whimpered as pain clawed at my resolve.

"FUCK YOU!" I screamed at the savage man. The muscular man muttered something under his breath and ripped another piece of utility tape from the roll and stuck it across my mouth.

"You try to take this off, I will make sure your death drags out for days. Now shut up," he warned.

"Let's go. You drive the bitch in that Caddy. We gotta torch it," the bat wielding asshole declared, and I was once again slumped into the muscular man's arms and shoved into the back of Ben's SUV. The jerk with the Louisville slugger drove another vehicle ahead of us, and within twenty minutes, we were parked in a small opening in a field that was flanked heavily with trees. We were thoroughly hidden as far as I could see, and there was a pre-dug grave in front of the SUV lit by the headlights that pierced the darkness. I managed to piece together that I had been with the men for a day and a half.

Must be Friday night, I thought to myself.

Both men stepped out of their vehicles and stood together talking in front of the cars and my makeshift grave. Impulse and adrenaline possessed me, and I saw my opportunity shining in front of me like a miracle from the heavens. My eyes peered over the front seat and confirmed what I suspected.

Keys! He left the keys.

My muscular chauffeur left the keys in the ignition, and since I was no longer bound to a chair, I decided to go for it. I ripped the tape from my mouth and leaped over the seats despite the pain in my leg, head, and face. I slid easily into the leather seat, leaned forward, and turned the key with both hands. The engine roared to life, and I threw the gearshift into reverse. The men noticed the movement through the windshield and immediately began scrambling to the doors. Thankfully the auto lock feature on Ben's SUV engaged as I put the vehicle in gear. The doors were locked, and the men couldn't open them. As I sped backward, the men pulled guns out and began shooting. I ducked behind the wheel, and for once, thanked God for my generally short stature. I was able to sink low enough in the seat to avoid the bullets that zipped through my escape vessel. I cut the wheel hard and searched for a way out of the field. I put the car in drive and tore out of there, flinging dirt and grass everywhere behind me. I looked for the men in my mirror, and sure enough, they were chasing me in the other vehicle.

Shit! Shit! Find help. Go to people. Find some people.

My eyes scanned my surroundings, and I recognized nothing in the dark. I drove with renewed determination, and the adrenaline pumping through me made my injuries nonexistent for the moment. The men gained on me quickly and rammed into the back of the SUV. I fought against the steering wheel with my bound wrists, to maintain control. The men kept shooting at me. Bullets rained down on Ben's gorgeous Cadillac. The men kept at their efforts of setting me into a tail spin by ramming and nudging the Cadillac repeatedly. Each time I fought to keep control and prayed more fervently for a store, a gas station, a diner, anything.

"People. Please, let there be people," I chanted to myself. I saw an illuminated marquee in the distance and kept my eyes directed at what I hoped would be my salvation.

"People. Please. People." I rounded a corner entirely too fast and nearly crashed. I regained control and tore down the quiet street that I had turned onto. I knew I had to be somewhere outside of Dallas. We had only driven for about twenty minutes when we left the abandoned industrial district. I reminded myself that I would come up on the city if I could just hold on a bit longer. I saw an intersection near the illuminated sign that towered high enough for drivers to see from far off. I pressed down harder on the gas and barreled into the parking lot like a maniac. Much to my relief, I saw big rig trucks parked neatly, one beside the other next to what was clearly a truck stop-diner. I saw a state trooper's car parked right in front of the diner doors, and without further hesitation, I squeezed my eyes closed, braced myself and floored it. I crashed into the rear, quarter of the State Trooper's car. The trooper's vehicle skid sideways and took out a handicapped parking sign in the process. I wanted to cause a scene, and, well, I made one. Troopers and truckers alike poured out of the diner. I swung the door open with my bound hands, and stumbled out of the Cadillac deliriously on my broken leg. My eyes instinctively turned to locate my captors. They were gone.

Gone.

It was the last thought that tumbled through my tormented brain before everything went silent and dark.

CHAPTER TWENTY-FOUR

Staking a claim

✲

"As I told you last night, she has what is a called a simple fracture, which basically means it was a clean break. Her leg will heal in about six to eight weeks."

Who was that?

"As for the contusions to her face, we have cleaned them and treated them with topical antibiotic ointment. She has a hair line fracture in her sinus cavity, but there is nothing we need to do to treat it. It will heal naturally in a few weeks. The bruising will fade in about the same time. The thing we need to watch closely is the bleeding in her brain. Thus far, there has been minimal swelling. It has not increased, but it hasn't decreased either. She may wake up soon. So you may want to stay close."

"I'm not going anywhere. Thank you, Dr. Graham."

Ben! My Ben!

A phone rang causing me to cringe.

"Yeah?" Ben's voice was impatient, strained. "No. She isn't

awake yet, but I just spoke with the doc, and he says she may wake up, soon. How's Cheyenne?"

Chey! Oh, God, Chey! Did they get Chey?

My brain jarred and awakened a bit from slumber as fear for my best friend's safety ignited my awareness. "Ben." I found my voice, but it sounded foreign to my own ears. I sounded like someone else entirely.

"Gotta go," he snapped into his phone. I pried my heavy eyes open only a fraction.

"Oh, Jesus, baby," he breathed out. A sliver of light burned my weary eyes, and they reflexively watered.

"'s bright," I whispered and sealed my eyes closed again.

"Hold on a sec." Ben closed the drapes, turned off the overhead lights, and left on the small nightlight above my bed. I could tell through my eyelids that the room darkened, and I reopened my eyes. Ben came back to my bed and sat beside me on the edge. His strong warm hands swept my hands into his and squeezed.

"Ben," I croaked. Tears began spilling out of my sensitive eyes.

"Don't cry, baby. God, I'm so relieved to hear your voice." He shook his head then raised one of my hands to his lips to place a soft kiss first on the back of my hand, then on my bruised and raw wrist.

"I-I'm sorry," I sputtered and then began sobbing. Ben carefully scooped my battered body into his strong arms and held me close to his chest and comforted me.

"Shhh. Shhh. Don't cry. You're okay. We're okay. I'm here," he said softly against my ear. His chocolate-brown hair brushed against my cheek, and the scent of his skin filled my nose. Even in his presence, I longed for him as if he were not there with me. It was not enough to be in his arms. It could never be enough. I knew I would never get my fill of Benjamin Chase. I loved him. The stubble of his day-old beard grazed over my face as he brought his lips down on mine. His lips were soft and drew mine into the kiss as it deepened. We drank each other in for a long moment; then he released me but continued lightly cupping my face.

"I was so scared that I'd never see you again. They... they were going to kill me. The grave—" Ben laid me back into the bed and stroked my hair from my forehead. His deep blue green eyes grew stormy.

"I know, baby. You don't need to worry about them anymore. You're safe. Your things have been moved to my place. You live with me now, and don't you dare try to fight me on..." He held up his hand in preparation to argue with me about living with him. I cut him off before he could finish speaking.

"Thank you," I said quietly. Ben stopped and stared at me. His stormy eyes cleared and softened.

"I wouldn't have it any other way. I'm not letting you out of my sight."

"I know," I conceded.

"You don't have to do it until you feel you can, but at some point you need to tell me everything from the beginning." He spoke sternly and stood from my bed to pace the room. "I can hardly believe you put yourself into this situation. It was a monumentally careless and dangerous thing to do."

I sighed, knowing all too well that he was right. "I know," I conceded to him again. Despite my aching body, I began telling Ben the entire story from beginning to end. He made no comments or interjections. He only listened attentively and nodded his head on occasion. He listened to my story objectively until I began telling him what happened to me in the warehouse. I held nothing back. I recounted everything, including what I was thinking and feeling. The only thing I skipped was the many times I thought about how much I loved him. When I retold the parts with the baseball bat, the crippling blows to the face, and the rest of the physical assault, Ben's jaw clenched and the muscle there ticked.

"When can I go home?" His expression relaxed at my reference to 'home,' and he leaned in to kiss me again.

"I'll take you home as soon as the doctors discharge you."

I rolled out my bottom lip and pretended to pout like a willful, petulant child.

"Sorry, that won't convince me to break my severely injured girlfriend out of the hospital before she is deemed fit for release."

Girlfriend? He just staked his claim.

I beamed inwardly, knowing that I wanted nothing more than for Ben to stake his claim on me as his girlfriend.

"Girlfriend?"

"Yes, that's right. Girlfriend," he said flatly, then smiled a heart-stopping boyish smile. I did my best to mirror his sweet smile, even though I knew my face was anything but sweet at the moment. I moved on to the next person who was dominating my thoughts.

"I want to see Cheyenne," I declared while Ben poured water into a plastic cup and placed it carefully in my hand.

"I already texted her and Tuck. He's bringing her now."

"Thank you."

A half an hour or so later, Cheyenne stormed into my room like her perky ass was on fire. The moment she saw me somewhat sitting up in my bed with my eyes open, she burst into tears, and a string of inaudible words tumbled from her trembling mouth. I cried, too. She threw herself at me, and I was sure I was doing more comforting of her than she was of me. I scared my best friend. She shook as I hugged her to me and waited for her sobbing to subside.

"I'm sorry, Chey." She hiccupped and battled to compose herself. I braced myself for the lecture I was about to get. Tucker and Ben stood across the room and watched in silence as Cheyenne chastised me, cried, and chastised more. I only apologized repeatedly and nodded my head in agreement with my best friend's tirade. I couldn't imagine what I put her through, nor did I ever want to know for myself; but at the same time, she had no idea what I endured, and I was beginning to lose patience.

"I'll never forgive you for making me think the worst. You acted so selfishly, Kat!"

"Yeah, I did Chey. I was way fucking selfish for getting drugged, kidnapped, beaten, getting my leg snapped in two when one of them swung for the fences, and then personally seeing my would-be grave..." Ben stepped forward.

"That's enough. Both of you stop. Now isn't the time."

"I said I was sorry," I muttered. Cheyenne nodded, but I could see that she didn't let go of her anger.

Better buy some cheesecake and wine, I mused.

"Oh one more thing before we leave. Your mom and dad are on their way here, so heads up."

"Thank you." She hugged me again, but I knew our discussion was far from over. Tucker wrapped his arms around her as he always did and guided her out of my room. The reunion with my parents went as I expected. I was a child again. My mom was her usual dramatic self. My father was his typical quiet and foreboding self. I begged my dad to drag my mom back home as soon as I was settled in at Ben's house. Lord knows, I was glad to see my mom, but I couldn't survive her dramatics over every move I made.

Ben was already hovering over me and seeing to everything I could need or want. Thankfully, my dad agreed that I needed my space to heal and forget the whole experience.

The next day was Saturday, July 6th, 2013, day 45 since I began working at the firm. I was still in the hospital and feeling the full brunt of my injuries. I ached all over. My head was in a constant state of pain even though the doctors had been generous with the pain medications. As Ben promised, he never left me. Not even once, and I loved him even more for staying with me. I knew I was safe, but still felt out of sorts and generally just edgy.

"When did you know something was wrong?" I asked.

"When you never showed at the airport. I called Trev, and he said no one had seen you, and I just knew something wasn't right. I saw your earring lying in the driveway, and it was like the world was ripped from beneath my feet." He shook his head, and there was no denying how haunted he looked while recounting the morning of my abduction. He sat beside me on my hospital bed and pure torment marred his handsome features. "I thought I lost you. I don't-I mean I can't..." His chin dimpled and quivered as he fought against his emotions.

My thumb brushed circles over the backside of one of his hands. I leaned towards him and brushed my knuckles against his jaw. "I am so sorry, baby. I would never want to hurt you."

He swept my weak body into his and buried his face in my neck. "Never leave me again. You'll destroy me if you do. Without you I'm a ghost of a man, Kathleen."

He had taken a taxi from the airport and Trevor, Tucker, and Cheyenne were waiting for him at his home when he arrived. Ben was the one who found my hoop earring abandoned in the drive, alerting him that something had gone awry. Tucker and Cheyenne began combing the city; Trevor and Ben went to the office to see what they could find in my office. When Ben turned my office upside down, he found the bouquet of roses with the threatening message in the card. He dumped every file I had and also discovered my falsely labeled file with all of the copies I had made of the photos and information about John Murray and, incidentally, Janis. That's when Ben knew what I had done. They called the police who explained that a missing person's report could not yet be filed since forty-eight hours had not elapsed since I was last seen. Ben, being Ben, my take charge, bossy man called the press.

He pulled some strings and managed to get every news crew he could round up to come do a story on my mysterious disappearance. The story about the disappearance of the girlfriend of Dallas's most eligible bachelor aired that evening on the six o'clock news, and Mrs. Kemp had watched in shock as my photo appeared on the television screen. She called the number for the tip line that Ben had established. The first person she spoke to connected her to Ben directly once she claimed to know who had me. She had relayed to him all of the information that she had, and he began hunting for me with an even more narrowed list of suspects. Ben returned to the office after speaking with Mrs. Kemp personally and kept piecing together the mystery of my disappearance. Ben had kept both his and Trevor's secretaries late to assist in the search and was lucky enough to catch Janis talking on the phone with one bat wielding, overweight kidnapper. She had been tipping them off about Ben stirring the pot and getting close to finding out who had taken me and where I was. Ben startled her once she saw him, and she flew out of the building like a bat out of hell.

I remembered the call that the man had received on his phone. I assumed it had been Murray, but apparently it had been Janis. The men left me for the rest of the night, and I assume they had gone to dig my grave ahead of time so that dumping me would be that much quicker, therefore making them less likely to get caught. I stopped Ben during his recap of what happened.

"You know what happened to Janis, right?"

He nodded. "Yes. I saw everything you had in that file."

"Yes, but you understand that she is fixated on you right? You look like her dead husband; that's why she hated me so much. She was jealous."

"She's gone now, but she should be tracked down."

"Ya think?" I shouted. "The crazy bitch turned me over to Murray's guys on a silver platter, all because I'm with the man she is obsessed with!"

Ouch!

I held my head in my hands since my shouting did me no favors in the pain department. Ben dismissed my outburst and held me close to him, and it was hard to tell who was comforting whom.

By the time Ben had convinced the police that there was foul play involved and that Murray's properties needed to be searched, I was in that warehouse getting my leg broken. Ben explained that the red tape he had to cut through consumed valuable time, and he was close to finding Murray himself and holding a gun to his head until he made the call that would secure my release. When I escaped and crashed into the State Trooper's cruiser, I collapsed and was unconscious until I heard Ben talking to Dr. Graham about my injuries. As I lay in the hospital, the police were working on locating John Murray and his hired help who had allegedly fled the state in a hurry. The police were also looking into Janis's involvement. She, too, was in the wind. It disappointed me that John Murray had thus far managed to evade the police, but Ben assured me that he was going to be caught. I wanted to believe him. I spent five days in the hospital and was more than ready to get to my new home, Ben's home.

CHAPTER TWENTY-FIVE

Change everything

᠅

By the time I was discharged from the hospital on Wednesday, July 10th, day 49, I was ready to raid the nearest liquor store and drink away my irritation at being stuck in a hospital with both Ben and my mother smothering me. Cheyenne's frequent visits didn't help the situation either. She was no less pissed off at me than the first time she reamed me for being 'selfish'.

We arrived at Ben's house and there were a half a dozen cars parked in his drive. "Ughhh." Ben groaned, clearly annoyed.

"Um, did I miss something?" I arched my bruised brow and waited for an answer.

"It's everyone."

Everyone? Who's everyone?

My eyes darted from side to side, and I pursed my lips. "Everyone?"

"Tucker's truck is there." Ben's finger began pointing out the parked vehicles to identify the people who were clearly inside his house. "My mom and dad own that Lexus. That sweet E-Class belongs to my Gramps and Grandmother. My brother's Caddy is there. There's Trevor's ancient Honda."

"Hey! Don't say anything about those cars. They last forever," I stated defensively.

Ben rolled his eyes and sighed then came around to my side of his fancy BMW 750i. His hand found the small of my back like it always did, and he lifted me effortlessly and then climbed the steps to the front door with me in his arms. He paused in front of the door and gently put me back on my one foot while my broken leg hovered above the ground. His hands never left me. It was yet another thing I loved about Ben. If his hands were on me, they usually stayed that way for as long as possible.

"Baby, if you aren't up to meeting my family right now, I understand. I'll tell them to leave."

Baby. I love that.

For the first time in a while, I beamed on the inside, and my outside matched. I smiled wide and wrapped my arms around his waist. "It's okay. At least I will win sympathy points with my boyfriend's family. Have you seen my face?" I joked, and he furrowed his brows disapprovingly.

"That's not funny at all. They didn't come here to check out your injuries, Kathleen. I told my mom not to worry about things, but she insisted on everyone helping us settle in and making dinner." He shrugged, and I could tell that Ben's mom was likely just as bad as my own with her smothering love and affection. I could think of worse things to deal with.

We entered the house, and Ben helped me hobble along at my request, but tired of my show of independence quickly and scooped me right back into his amazing arms again. I didn't bother trying to fight him over it. I just sighed in resignation and let Ben carry me in his protective arms. I was utterly embarrassed, but my bossy boyfriend was unaffected by the curious gazes that watched us closely. Ben carried me to the sofa and set me down gently, then kissed my forehead and brushed his thumb over my bottom lip before running off to gather my medication and something to drink. While Ben scurried off to the kitchen, I surveyed the room and smiled coyly at all the faces that were turned in my direction. The only familiar faces belonged to Tucker, Cheyenne, and Trevor. Tucker and Cheyenne had left to retrieve our bags from the car. Trevor went to the kitchen with Ben. The remaining people in the room smiled back at me and appeared to study me with curiosity.

Awkward.

"Hi, I'm Kat," I said nervously. The first person to approach me was the only other woman in the room. The woman seated herself beside me on Ben's sofa. Her sympathetic eyes were a familiar shade of blue-green. Her hair was a mass of chocolaty brown that was cut into a bob. She took my hands in hers and looked at me as if she were prepared to jump for joy and cry all at the same time. I was extremely uncomfortable, to say the least.

"Kat, honey, I'm Cindy, Benjamin's mom. I have heard so much about you. I am so sorry about what you and Benjamin have gone through." She shook her head and clicked her tongue.

"It's all okay now." My response was automatic and simply not believable.

"Kat, meet my husband, Jeff." Ben's mom began introducing her family members to me, and one by one, they approached the couch to greet me properly. "This is our youngest son, Samuel, Jeff's mom and dad, Barb and Theo." Cindy grinned proudly once she introduced everyone. Ben was built precisely like his father, Jeff, but inherited mostly his mother's features. Samuel, Ben's younger brother, was a clone of Jeff.

Strong genes. I thought to myself as I observed and compared who favored whom. When I looked up, I noticed Cheyenne waiting patiently for her introduction. My friend was many things, but shy was not one of them. I saw the opportunity to distract attention from myself and leaped at it. "Everyone, this is my best friend and roommate, Cheyenne Reed and her boyfriend, Tucker Barrett." The Chase clan flocked to Cheyenne and Tucker. When I felt Ben's eyes on me, I scanned the room. I found him staring at me, his eyes fiery.

Oh. I know that look. YES, PLEASE!

He walked over to me slowly and sat beside me. "You amaze me," he breathed into my ear.

"How so?" He baited me, and I took it. I was officially fishing for compliments from my kinda-sorta-boyfriend. He didn't elaborate, and I knew he would likely go into detail later when we were alone. At least, that's what I was hoping for.

"Here, take these."

I tossed the pills he put in my palm into my mouth and washed them down. Sometime later I fell asleep on the couch, in part due to the comfy cushions, but it was mostly due to the pain killers I had taken. I felt Ben once again scoop me into his chest, and I instinctively snuggled in and inhaled my favorite scent.

I love you, I thought drearily as I nuzzled my face into Ben's firm chest. He stopped moving and set me down in his... our bed. He slid into the bed behind me, and held me close to him.

His arm always fit perfectly across the dip of my waist that my hips only exaggerated. He buried his face in my hair and inhaled.

"You belong here. I'll never let you go again." His promise should have alarmed me, but I felt quite the opposite. I felt so utterly complete in that moment in my Ben's arms, in his home. Arousal stirred low in my stomach, and my heart clenched from the complete contentment that engulfed me. I turned onto my side to face him. To face my Ben, the man I knew I had fallen for. I raised my hand and traced a finger down his bare chest. He shivered just barely. I licked my lips and leaned in to kiss his neck. He took in a deep breath and moved his hand to brush back my hair.

"I need you Ben." I knew he wanted me, too, but he was scared. I could tell that my bumps and bruises spooked him. He was obviously nervous about hurting me. I tried to convince him that my bruises looked far worse than they actually felt, but he was not buying it. It had been hands off. It had been over a week since the last time we had been together, and I was desperate for him.

"I need you too, baby." I got the distinct feeling that Ben wasn't only talking about sex. He leaned down and took my mouth with his. I squeezed the muscles in his back while we took each other in greedily. He groaned into my mouth and shifted so that he was above me. He was so careful not to rest any of his weight on me. He kept his eyes locked on mine, and I didn't try closing mine once because I knew he would only insist that I open them.

Ben made love to me for the first time that night, and neither of us had to say a word to relay to the other exactly how we felt. I knew he loved me just as much as I loved him. It would just be a matter of time before one of us spoke the three little words that would change everything. I wanted so badly to tell him, but I just couldn't will the words to come out.

The first week of living with Ben went wonderfully. We were both really getting used to being so close to one another. I felt safe, and the night terrors that had begun immediately following my abduction were soothed by Ben in bed next to me.

We worked well as a couple living together. Occasionally I allowed my mind to run away with me, and I thought about a potential future with him. I couldn't imagine a better one. The only thing that seemed to be a sore subject between the two of us was my desire to see if I could dig around on the internet for information about Janis Harper and John Murray's whereabouts. Ben adamantly disagreed with me on that topic. He insisted that I forget the whole thing and allow myself to move on. I found the prospect next to impossible when torturous nightmares were what awaited me when I closed my eyes every night. It was slightly ironic that being around Ben mostly cured my insomnia and caused my dreams to come right back, yet the sleep and dreams that I wanted so badly were now part of my fears. I dreaded sleep because I knew those nightmares, those visions of spurting blood and shallow graves, would come barging into my head the moment I was fully asleep. I held the rationale that I couldn't let go until I knew where these people were and that the police were arresting them for what they had done to me. I wanted justice, peace, and maybe even revenge.

CHAPTER TWENTY-SIX

Everything to lose

When I relocated to Dallas, it had been with a goal in mind. To find myself. I had always wondered if something major would happen to me that would jolt life back into me, awakening the long lost parts that I longed to have back. I wondered if it would be something huge. Something drastic. Something defining. I had wondered and hoped. It was Wednesday, July 17th, 2013. Day 56 at the firm. Then, there, in front of Ben, I realized that something major did happen. The series of events that had occurred collectively played a role in pulling the old Kathleen back from the world of forgotten souls and crushed dreams. My divorce, my move, my tattoo, working for Ben, being involved with Ben, my investigation, my abduction, and now my verbal quarrel with my boss/boyfriend all served as a defibrillator that shocked the old me back into existence.

"Give it back," I demanded in an annoyed voice with my hand outstretched waiting for what had been taken.

"No," he said firmly without even looking at me.

"I'm not asking, Ben. You had no right to take my laptop with you to work simply because you don't want me doing what I need to do."

He shook his head.

"I'm not a child!" I shouted.

"Then don't behave like one. You need to let this go. It's stupid and dangerous, and the police are taking care of things." Ben wasn't at all affected by my steadily rising temper. I tossed my hands into the air.

"Oh, yes, Ben. The police. They handled things great before I got involved, and let's not forget how awesome they were when I had been abducted from your driveway!"

"Kathleen, I am warning you to let this go."

Warning me? Excitement and unbridled anger rushed through me. In that moment, the old Kathleen, the real me, annihilated the door to my cloaked world, rolled through it in a tank, and set up shop, occupying the geography of my tormented heart and soul. In short, I was back! In force. Unwavering, wounded and pissed-the-hell-off. I leaned over the front of Ben's desk, firmly planted my palms flush against the cool, heavily lacquered surface and let loose.

"Benjamin Chase." I shook my head slowly as a sardonic smirk played across my mouth, and my cavalier gaze landed on the poor victim of my impending verbal assault. He sat behind his desk in his executive leather chair and appeared confident, but I saw the glint of anxiety in his eyes. It was all the green light I needed.

"Listen up, chief." Ben's eyebrows shot up to nearly his hairline, and his mouth hung slightly ajar. "Are you the one with night terrors? Dreams so vivid and real that you can feel tape around your wrists still? So real that you can still taste the blood in your mouth?" I growled menacingly. Ben's face fell in defeat. "No. That would be me. So you see, you don't have the right to dictate who, what, why, when, or how I do things. You have a right to discuss things with me, but I and only I will do all the final decision making on this front."

I brought a hand off the desk to motion towards myself, then placed it back in position on his desk. Ben leaned back in his seat and crossed his chiseled arms over the wide expanse of his chest.

"As far as your concern for what's dangerous or careless in my life? You can leave that to me, too. I will be the judge, jury and coincidentally enough, the damn executioner on that. Trust me, Benjamin: I am quite skilled when it comes to judging and punishing myself. I think I proved that. No open positions in that department. All full up." I narrowed my eyes on him, and he didn't even flinch. His lawyer face was better than any poker face I'd ever seen. "I did not get stupid with my little investigation into John. Something went wrong. That something happened to be some deranged psychopath who is obsessed with my boyfriend! I fully intend on finding out where Janis is. She started this nightmare, and when I do find her, and I assure you I will, she will pray for the mercy that death brings! I will rip her life apart, enjoy every damned minute of it, and hopefully finally be able to sleep like a baby that night. Agree or disagree, Ben. Either way it doesn't really matter. I'm finishing this."

Ben began shaking his head again.

"Kathleen, you will do no such thing! I won't sit back and

watch my girlfriend play vigilante! It's dangerous." I clicked my tongue.

"Well, chief, the good news for you is that you don't have a say in the matter. Your hands are clean, and your conscience will be clear, I assure you. This is my fight. I started it; I'll finish it. I won't let this lie. I don't have any other choice."

My gaze never left his as he leapt to his feet sending his chair rolling backward to crash into a bookshelf. He stood behind his desk and planted his hands on top, mirroring me. I had to hand it to Ben, when he got pissed, he looked and sounded quite intimidating. If I had been standing before him as the pitiful waif that I had been for so many years, I imagine I would have run from the room crying. There was no way in hell I would be doing that. I was determined to stand my ground, emotions be damned. Not even Benjamin Chase, the courtroom shark, love of my life, would be able to coax an emotional reaction out of me. Or so I thought.

"It's not my fucking conscience that I am worried about! You have everything to lose; you just refuse to see it." His jaw tightened, and he paused before continuing.

"You walk around thinking you have something to prove to everyone. You don't have to prove anything. Not to me. I know who you are. From the moment I saw you, I knew that I had to find out who you were. I knew that the person that the world sees is a million miles away from what's inside. I knew that from the start. That's why I lied my ass off and picked up that stupid book that day." My breathing stalled, and I stood up straight in front of his desk. Ben's eyes followed me like a predator preparing to go in for the kill.

"I don't know everything about your past, and I can't

understand why you can't let any of this shit go." I got that sick feeling deep in my gut telling me that I screwed up. Bad.

"Ben, I—"

"No!" He shouted. "I don't know what the hell happened to you, but I've been fighting against an undertow called your past. I have nowhere to go but under because you refuse to throw me a lifeline here. I fell for you as you are. I wish you could see that." He stood up straight and turned away from me as he walked slowly towards his scenic windows. "To see you fighting against this makes me very sorry for you, Kat. You're doing your best to keep me at arm's length, whether you realize it or not. This thing between us scares the shit out of me, too, but I recognized it for what it is, something rare and valuable, and I found the nerve within myself to set my fears aside and gamble on us. I wasn't a selfish coward! You..." Ben turned to me and jabbed a finger in my direction, making me flinch reflexively. "...are stuck in the past and walking around in the present with a fucking agenda, trying to prove something to everyone including yourself. You are either so damned blind to what's really in front of your face, or you're just too spineless to face it. To face me. I've begged you to see a therapist about the night terrors, and you dismiss my efforts every time. What else am I supposed to do? This woman..." He waved his hand at me. "...is not the woman I fell for. So even though this kills me, two things Kat: one, you will take a leave of absence until further notice. This office won't be used as a tool so that you can go on some vigilante suicide mission, nor will I watch you do it; and two, this thing between us is over. I won't be the only one willing to take a risk on us. If that is the case, then clearly I feel stronger about you than you feel for me. Maybe one day you will wake the hell up, leave the past where it belongs, and let this thing between us really happen."

My lip quivered, and tears filled my eyes. I stood there staring at him, but he wouldn't look me in the face. He was dismissing me, telling me to leave. He couldn't even look at me. I had let him down; I had let us down. I screwed up everything and didn't even realize what I was losing. Or if I did know it, I clearly ignored the hell out of it. I was so worried about going forward in a relationship. I was worried I would end up hurt. I worried about what I could lose. What I hadn't counted on was finding and falling for a man who was made for me. I had broken his heart. I had broken my heart. This pain was far worse than any I had imagined when deciding to avoid giving myself over to him completely.

"You said... You called me Kat." Ben kept his eyes directed away from me as if it pained him to even look at me. He stuffed his hands into his pockets, casually, and stood in front of the windows. He stood stock still and gazed out at the city.

"You should go."

"Ben, I—"

"Leave!"

I started at his demand, and tears spilled onto my cheek and rolled down my face. I brushed them away, hating what he made me feel. Sadness. Defeat. Regret. Guilt. Love. I sniffled and collected my things to leave. I made my way to his office door, and I felt his eyes on me. I turned just in time to catch a glimpse of him turning back to the windows. He didn't even want me to see him. I repulsed him. I was so consumed, fighting with ghosts from my past that I let Ben and possibly my future slip through my fingers. I knew I loved him more than anything on earth when he told me to leave his office. That pang of guilt and regret was something you only feel when the one person who holds your heart has been hurt. Ben was hurting. I was the one who was to blame, and I hated myself for that. I wanted nothing more than to make him better. To make me better, to make us better together. He couldn't stand the sight of me, and quite frankly, neither could I.

CHAPTER TWENTY-SEVEN

Left at the platform

❧

Seven weeks later...

Not possible. There's no way.

I was lost in my thoughts while I made my way, rather awkwardly, back to my car in the clinic parking lot. I was walking really strangely because my cast had just been taken off. It had been the only thing that remotely excited me in weeks. I was moments from taking nail clippers to that stupid cast. I didn't care that it would take me a year to get the damn thing off. I was sick and tired of having a troll club for a leg. My walk was off since I was used to hobbling around my apartment with the hard, bulky reminder of the ordeal I had gone through. I unlocked my Honda and waited for the initial wave of Texas heat to escape through my open door before daring to get in. I slid into the seat, started my car, flipped my AC to full blast, and stared off into space like some idiotic half-wit.

"How?" I asked myself.

What I thought would be a simple doctor's appointment to have my cast removed turned into a lifeo-altering event, and it all started with my agreeing to begin a prescription of antidepressants. I had been a basket case since Ben and I had broken up. I quit the firm instead of taking a leave of absence. Tossed aside my vendetta by handing over everything I had, including my personal notes to the lead detective assigned the Murray case which included the lovely neighborhood psycho, Janis. It wasn't so much that I was giving up, as it was I simply had physical and emotional wounds that needed licking and loads of junk food to eat. I had no more to give. No fight left in me. I had lost the man I knew I loved, and it was all my fault. He wanted and needed me, but I had been too consumed with myself. The 'Happily Ever After' train left the station with me standing on the platform.

After my kidnapping, I was informed by my doctor that if I felt a specific list of symptoms that I should consider taking an antidepressant. I declined the medication initially, but later realized that I was in a really bad place emotionally and promised myself and Cheyenne that I would tell the doc when I went back in to have my cast removed. I asked for the medication as I promised I would. That's when the doc informed me that I would be required to give a urine sample before they could prescribe the medication.

I would have liked to have had a photo taken of my face when the doctor returned to the exam room with the shocking news that I could not take the medication we discussed because it was not approved for pregnant women. I would have framed a photo of my face when he told me the news. I imagine it was priceless. I left the clinic in a daze with a referral to see an OBGYN. I drove home and thought about what my next move would be. For once, I was glad Cheyenne had moved out after Tucker had proposed. I missed her every day, of course, but I was thankful that she was not there at the apartment. If she had been there, she would have seen that something was wrong with me and pry until I caved in and told all. She had moved in with Tucker a couple of weeks before.

It took a lot of convincing her that I was happy for her, and I thought she should go for it. That was a raging-gargantuan-bold-faced-lie, of course, but I threw a fit and insisted she go. She finally conceded to my insisting and headed off into the metaphorical sunset with her new fiancé at her side. It made me sick. I was happy for her, but if I were being honest, I was swimming in jealousy. Although it was the innocent, normal type of jealousy and not the vindictive sort, it was still jealousy, which made me feel no better about my shitty love life. I had a man who had me move in with him before I went and trashed it all to hell. It was the only line of thinking that I managed to cling to all day, every day. When I made it back to my apartment, I lay on my couch for the bulk of the two days following the life-changing appointment. I watched mindless TV and stared off into space for nearly two entire days. It had to be a record.

The only thing that roused me from my mindless existence was the appointment with the OBGYN that I had been referred to. I knew I should tell Ben. He deserved to know that I was carrying his child, even if we weren't seeing each other or speaking. None of that should have mattered. Withholding the news about my pregnancy would be wrong. I couldn't bring myself to do that to the man I had fallen in love with so effortlessly. I had been so broken-hearted and depressed since we stopped speaking and seeing each other. I proved myself right. I had too much baggage. Too many scars. Too much past to overcome. Too many damned hang-ups. I could never be what Ben needed, what he deserved. I despised myself for that. I would have done anything for him, but I couldn't forget or let go of my past. Now that I was carrying a tiny little life inside me, I had so much to think about. The first thing I needed to do was to tell Ben that he was going to be a father.

Or I could just move away and raise this baby alone. I could do it. Women do the single mom thing every day and make it along just fine.

I shrugged, giving my thought free reign to wander through possibilities. Inside, I knew that I wanted Ben to know, and I wanted him involved. I could imagine him talking to my swollen belly, holding my hand during labor and delivery, holding our baby in his strong arms. My chest felt heavy, and I wanted to melt into my bed at my empty apartment and cry for days, weeks even. I forced myself to take a few cleansing breaths to force back the tears. The clock on the microwave said 12:27. I knew Ben would likely be having lunch right now. Tears threatened again as I remembered sharing my lunch hour with him. I missed him so. My hand absentmindedly caressed my belly as if touching the space that sheltered his child would somehow ease my longing for him. I carried a part of him within me. It only made me ache for him more. I took another cleansing breath and prepared myself to go to Ben's office. It took no time to get ready, and I pulled into a parking space at the firm at 12:58. I took the keys out of the ignition and gazed down at my belly. I couldn't believe I was there to tell Ben the news. I was still in shock mostly, but I knew I had to tell him. I drew in a deep breath while praying for strength. I slung my purse over my shoulder and began to get out. When I saw Ben's BMW glide into the parking lot, I froze to watch him. He gracefully walked around the fancy car after he parked. He opened the passenger door, and my heart sunk to my gut and tore into a million tiny pieces.

No! Please, no!

I screamed inwardly. The breath left my lungs, and I immediately felt ill. I continued watching as Ben opened the door for his passenger to exit. She slid out of the seat and smiled lovingly at Ben.

"Oh, God, no," I muttered to myself.

He has moved on. He has a girlfriend.

Ben smiled back at the leggy brunette. She was tall and slender, dressed nicely, and she looked sophisticated. Her makeup was nicely done. Her hair was cut into a choppy kind of style that rested at her shoulders and shined in the sunlight. It pained me to admit that she was attractive. In that moment, she looked like such a lovely lady, that I couldn't be angry at her. I couldn't be jealous. I couldn't find flaws in her. She was with Ben. He was gorgeous, successful, and so many other things that women look for in a man. This mess was my fault.

If I had just given us a shot; a real chance. If I hadn't been so damned consumed with myself and my past.

I continued watching as she placed a chaste kiss on his cheek, and they hugged. They both smiled and spoke for a moment; then she slunk across the parking lot to her own car and left. Ben waved at her and watched as she drove away, then went into the building. I sunk low into my seat and rested my head on the steering wheel. I was crushed. A familiar feeling swept over me. Consumed me. Engulfed me. It was the feeling that I had only once before felt. It was the same feeling when Aidan told me that I had lost our child in my car accident. It was heartbreak and devastation in its purest form. The feeling squeezed in around me and crushed my chest. I couldn't breathe. I couldn't think. I couldn't do anything but grip my hand to my chest as I struggled to remain conscious. My shoulders rocked and shuddered as I began to sob forcefully. It truly hurt. I wasn't sure how long I sat in my car sobbing. I forced myself to stop when I realized that my eyes were swollen and burning. My breathing was uneven as I wiped my face without concern for makeup and dug my keys out of my lap.

CHAPTER TWENTY-EIGHT

Gag-order

I somehow managed to drive home without killing myself or someone else. I curled up into my bed and turned off my phone, just before the heart wrenching sobs began again. I cried until exhaustion overwhelmed me, and I drifted off. I dreamed of a beautiful baby girl with blue-green eyes and chocolate brown hair swaddled in a pink blanket as Ben rocked her slowly back and forth in his loving arms. I woke from sleep to a banging noise. I rubbed my puffy eyes and rolled out of my bed. I swung my bedroom door open to a very irritated Cheyenne. "Just where the hell have you been? I have been trying to call you since yesterday. What the hell happened to your face, Kat? Jesus!"

"Hmph! Your humor and wit goes unmatched Cheyenne. Really amusing," I said flatly as I turned my back to her and crawled back into my bed.

"Stop being a smart ass. I'm serious; you look terrible. Is it Ben?"

"Don't," I demanded then pulled my quilt over my head to hide my face.

"It is Ben," she said sympathetically.

"Cheyenne, I don't really want to discuss it. Please don't push the issue." I admonished, and she sighed in resignation.

"Okay, but I'm here when you are ready to talk."

Don't hold your breath.

"Tucker brought me over so that we could get the rest of my things over to his house, well our house, I guess." She giggled like a teenager. I rolled my eyes beneath my quilt at her pleased laughter. It was wrong of me and extremely selfish, but I just couldn't conjure one ounce of happiness at that moment for my best friend who had found and gotten engaged to the man who truly was her soul mate. They were happy and eager to get married. He moved her into his lovely home and gave her anything that her heart desired. It stunk. It made my skin crawl. I was being shallow, I knew, but didn't have discipline to control the green-eyed monster. I wanted to run in the opposite direction from society as a whole and find some deserted island to inhabit. As lovely as the idea sounded, it was just a daydream. However, I did have plenty of money in my savings to live off of, and through my digging into the whole John the criminal situation, I became quite educated in the field of high yield investments.

Hmm, maybe I can play the stock market. Take a risk and hope for a hefty return.

I mused inwardly.

Something to focus on. I need to focus on something. I'll

play the investment game and figure out where the baby and I will live.

I was pleased with my plans, though I knew gambling on the investments was irresponsible with a child on the way. I wasn't sure if I would be staying in Dallas. I wasn't even sure if I would tell Ben about the baby after all. He was obviously dating someone else, and I simply refused to be the knocked-up ex who came calling and screwed up his new relationship. I wouldn't embarrass myself. The thought of telling him about the baby while knowing damned well that he had moved on made me feel sick to my stomach and completely cheap. I didn't know if I could bring myself to do it. I made the decision to make things work on my own for the time being. There would be no way in hell I would speak a word of the news to anyone until I was far enough along to be more sure that I was having a healthy pregnancy.

Three days later, I went to my second OB appointment. Monday, August 26th, 2013. Day 96 since my first day at the firm. I sat in the waiting room staring at the artistic paper mâché belly molds that hung on the walls. There were around a dozen of them scattered on the walls, hanging like paintings would. The multicolor molds varied in size and shape. Big round bellies, more pointy narrow bellies, wide bellies, small bellies, large bellies. Each mold was from the pelvic bone to the top of the breasts. I assumed that these had to be cast on the form of real pregnant women. Each one was so unique and real, I doubted anyone would be able to create them artificially.

A petite nurse interrupted my admiration of the art when she called me back to see the doctor. She was the same nurse that I met at my first appointment a few days prior. At the time,

I had only met with the nurse. She collected samples for lab tests to confirm my pregnancy, and I was given a brief rundown of what to expect at my first real appointment. This time, she had me undress, and I sat and waited nervously. A knock came from the door.

"Yes, come in," I said. The older female extended her hand to me, and I shook it.

She smiled warmly. "Hello, I am Dr. Lisa Miller; pleasure to meet you, Ms. Cooper."

"Please, call me Kat."

"Okay, Kat. Let's get started. We are going to do an ultrasound to determine how far along you are since you are unclear on when your last menstrual period was." She smiled again, and I suddenly felt like an irresponsible teenager.

How can I be so confused about my dates?

I kicked myself inwardly. I had been so distracted with Ben, the investigation, and our breakup that I didn't even pay attention to myself. I knew I must have gotten pregnant when I missed two pills while I was being held against my will by John's goons. I caught up on the two pills I missed as soon as I could. I read the information on the prescription, and it did say that catching up was possible, so that's what I did. I read further after I found out about the baby, and the rest of the paragraph informed me that while you can catch up after missing a pill or two, effectiveness would be decreased. In short, screw up and miss pills, you can take them, but you are taking a gamble. Dr. Miller rolled the ultrasound machine to my bedside. The nurse, who stood on the other side of the table, guided my feet into stirrups.

"You may feel a bit of pressure, but that is normal. Here we go." The screen next to me was all unclear and distorted. I had no clue what I was seeing.

"Mhmm," Dr. Miller mused. "Just there, Kat. See this?" She pointed to a shape on the screen that looked like a peanut. I gasped, and tears filled my eyes.

"Oh, I see it." I said softly, in complete awe of my tiny baby.

"These are the little buds that will develop into arms and legs. The head is here and that fluttering thing you see here is the heart," she said as she pressed a key on the machine and the sound of my baby's heartbeat filled my ears. It sounded so fast and strong. Tears spilled from my eyes, and thoughts of Ben came rushing over me.

Ben. Oh, Ben should be here. He should see and hear the baby. Our baby.

"Everything looks and sounds great, Kat. From the measurements, it looks like you are about eight weeks pregnant. The baby appears normal and healthy. Congratulations! Would you like pictures?"

"Oh, yes please!" After Dr. Miller briefed me on all things early pregnancy, she handed me the ultrasound photos and a prescription for prenatal vitamins. I scheduled my next appointment on my way out of the clinic. Once I was back in my apartment, I found myself staring at the photos of the baby. I was enchanted with my child already. I couldn't help but wonder if Cheyenne would ever get to experience what I did earlier that day.

"Oh shit! Cheyenne!" I squealed as I abandoned the bottle of prenatal vitamins and photos on the kitchen counter to retrieve my cell phone. After sending her a short text to let her know I was alive and well, I began to worry about her wedding.

Shit! Shit! Shit! The bridesmaid dress, will it fit? Will I show at all? SHIT!

I stopped pacing the floor of my living room and forced myself to take a deep breath. "Okay, just think, Kat." I said to an empty room.

I should only be about twelve weeks pregnant by the time the wedding rolls around. I shouldn't be showing, right? Lots of women are able to hide their condition well into the pregnancy. Yes. I will just have to be smart about it until I can find a way to tell Cheyenne.

Cheyenne's wedding was in just over four weeks on Saturday, September, 28th. According to a calendar that my doctor gave me, my baby was due on April ninth. At the time of Cheyenne's wedding, I would be twelve weeks pregnant, and conception was around the middle of July. My chain of thought ceased and wandered off, thinking about the timing of conception.

We broke up in the middle of July. A break-up baby. Oh God, that's awful.

My heart broke a little bit more with the realization that the little life I carried had been conceived right before we split up. Ben essentially dumped me, but gave me a gift in the process, even if he did it unknowingly. I still couldn't believe that I was going to have a baby. It had been weeks since Ben and I had last spoken, and I was no less devastated as the days passed. I still missed him desperately. Maybe even more as each day turned into the next. I felt so empty and alone in my apartment now that Ben was done with me, and Cheyenne was moving steadily into her very own happily ever after. Life went on without me. I was a painfully lonely, unemployed divorcee who got knocked up by a man that I had fallen hard for. I was utterly heartbroken and very conflicted about whether or not to tell Ben about my pregnancy. For the time being, I was resigned to a self-enforced gag order.

I ate half-stale cereal for dinner that night and watched an infomercial selling a fancy vacuum cleaner that I had zero interest in buying, but I watched numbly anyway.

CHAPTER TWENTY-NINE

Take it or leave it

I woke the next morning thanks to a powerful urge to vomit. I jumped from the couch and tripped over the cereal bowl from the previous night that lay on the floor. I barely made it to the bathroom in time.

Hello, morning sickness. Ugh!

After I rinsed my mouth and brushed my teeth, I returned to my spot on the couch to watch things I had recorded on my DVR. There was a loud knock on the door. My heartbeat sped up. I tiptoed to the door in my ratty clothes and looked out of the peephole, but the damn thing had been broken for a while; there was moisture trapped inside hindering a clear view of visitors. I groaned, reached for the baseball bat I kept around for safety, and swung the door open.

"Kathleen."

I nearly passed out.

What is he doing here?

I drew my own private conclusions while staring at him. "Do you mind if I come in for a minute?"

"No, not at all, come right on in," I said shaking my head while abandoning him at the wide open door to return the baseball bat to its position in the corner. "Have a seat," I said, motioning the loveseat opposite me. I flopped back down on the couch and pressed play on my remote, resuming my show and completely ignoring him. I didn't care that he was sitting in my apartment, nor did I care to know the reason for his visit. I was in far too dark a place to give a shit about anything. Least of all him.

"You look terrible, and so does your place," he said while surveying his surroundings. I joined in critiquing my home. Cereal bowl on the floor, empty water bottles scattered about, dirty laundry piled up in the corner, and there was a faint odor of vomit thanks to the morning sickness that had me racing to the bathroom just before he arrived.

"Gee, thanks Aidan, great to see you too," I stated with feigned sincerity.

"Kathleen, listen I heard about what happened to you last month. I can't believe you went through that. You should have called me."

"For what, Aidan? Honestly, we're divorced! I won't even ask how you got my address." I muttered the last bit shaking my head.

"I called your mom when I heard about what happened and told her I wanted to send you some flowers, and she gave it to me."

Of course she did.

"What's wrong with you? Are you sick?"

"I'm fine."

He guffawed loudly at my proclamation of being fine.

"You are anything but!"

I scoffed indignantly at my ex-husband and did my best to divert my attention to the TV screen.

"Fine, Aidan, whatever. You can leave now."

"I'm going nowhere. You obviously have something going on and could use some help around here."

"Stubborn and bossy as always," I said disapprovingly and added a tsk-tsk for good measure.

"Come out with it, Kathleen."

"Fine, I suppose it doesn't really matter. I'm pregnant!" His jaw dropped. "Yep, that's right Aidan. Pregnant. Knocked up. I fell in love with a guy, but I screwed it up by being... me. Then I found out about the pregnancy. He has since moved on with his life and now has a girlfriend. Cheyenne is engaged to prince fucking charming and has moved in with her soon-to-be husband. I'm unemployed and to top it all off, my ex-husband has just walked into my apartment and is currently staring at me like I have lost my freakin' mind, which drives me up the damn wall and makes me want to kick him in his balls!" I shouted the last bit, and his eyes grew wide and amused. "I don't see a damn thing funny here, Aidan!"

"No, you're right; it's not funny, but you are very cute when you're mad. Always have been."

"Just knock it off, Aidan."

"Okay, fine. Does the father know?"

"Nope, and I plan to keep it that way until further notice." He nodded subtly. I could see the wheels turning. "What?" I asked incredulously.

"I think you need me, and I know I need you. I can help."

"What are you going to do? Adopt my baby and raise it as your own or something?" I said jokingly. Aidan shrugged.

"I have done a lot of thinking and changing since you left me. I told you that the last time we saw each other. I told you I wouldn't give up. I meant it. We could try again. I could be the baby's father, your husband again."

"I was joking, Aidan! Jesus!" I shook my head almost too hard.

"Please, Kathleen, give me a chance. I'll show you. I can't stand not having you in my life." He pleaded as he moved over to me and squatted down in front of my seat on the couch. I sighed and rolled my eyes when he gathered my hands in his. I was far too emotional, thanks to the hormones raging through my body.

"Aidan, I can only offer to be friends. Just friends. That's a lot more than you deserve, so take it or leave it." He smiled his all-American-boy smile and nodded.

"I'll take it. I'll take it."

Aidan hung out with me for the rest of the day and into the evening. We watched television, and he went out to bring us some cheap takeout. My weakness. He knew me well. After throwing up way too much for it to be considered normal, he went out to the store to buy for me all the pregnant woman goodies. Saltine crackers, ginger ale, popsicles, and a wide assortment of foods for me to try. His rationale was that there had to be something I could keep down.

"Thanks Aidan. It's weird having you here, but I don't really have anyone else right now." I bowed my head as my brows furrowed and tears began gathering in my eyes.

"I told you: we may be divorced, but I support you, and if you are struggling right now, you can count on me."

"Yes, but you will be leaving soon, and I will be alone again."

"No. I transferred here to our Dallas office." My mouth hung agape.

"You what?" My voice came out high-pitched and sounded annoying, even to my own ears.

"I live here now. I requested the transfer."

I sighed. This complicated things. I honestly appreciated his being there as my friend supporting me, but if he stayed around me, things would certainly get awkward at some point.

What if he is my only male friend around once the baby comes? The baby might think that he is daddy.

"Hey, I could be your roomie," Aidan said jokingly.

"Don't even," I admonished.

"I know; I know. I'm only kidding. Listen, don't be so down, okay? Everything will work out." He swung an arm around my shoulder and squeezed me into his side. I was almost relieved to discover that there was zero spark between us when he embraced me. It was nothing like what I felt every time Ben touched me. I fell asleep on the couch while watching television with Aidan. When I woke up the next morning, I was comfortably tucked into my bed, and there was a glass of water on my nightstand with a note from Aidan.

'Kathleen, you fell asleep on the couch. I hope you don't mind that I moved you to your bed. I am going back to my hotel room at the Walshberg Hotel. Room number is 212. If you need to reach me, you can call me there. See you tomorrow. –A.'

I didn't mind Aidan being around to help me out. I was never able to trust him with my heart, but he always took care of things for me. He had always been a great caregiver, and in my state, I welcomed any help I could get. When I left my bedroom to get my cell phone from the living room, I was welcomed by a spotless apartment. I smiled at Aidan's thoughtfulness. It turned out that he was a bad husband, but a great friend. I decided to call Cheyenne that morning to let her know about Aidan before she found out on her own and thought the worst of it. Of course, when I told her the edited version of the story, she was more than skeptical and admonished me to stay away from Aidan. I eased her worry by making a few reassurances. I told her that Aidan was transferred here, that I had given him my contact information the last time I saw him, and that when he arrived in town, he called me to meet as friends, and I agreed. Lies, of course, but I was in no mood or position to tell the whole sordid story.

The next three weeks passed rather smoothly, and my friendship with Aidan remained just that. I opened up to him about Ben and explained the whole mess. He was understanding and supportive every time I lamented over the loss of Ben. He didn't have much to say, just gave the occasional nod and reassuring pat on the shoulder or leg. I was grateful for his friendship. I felt like something inside was coming together. Healing. Aidan helped me look into investment opportunities and start the daunting task of baby-product research. He and I were hanging out nearly every day and even went to dinner with Cheyenne and Tucker once. Cheyenne had texted me from across the table during dinner.

'He is so different. Weird!'

I texted her back. *'I told you! We are just friends. Things are different between us.'*

She nodded at me across the table in agreement. I was excited that Aidan was winning over Cheyenne as he had won me over. He had been nothing but a gentlemen since arriving at my apartment weeks before. He helped me with the dreadful morning sickness that would be better off renamed 'any-time sickness' because it struck at random. Cheyenne bought into the few white lies I had told her and even agreed that Aidan could come to the wedding with me. It appeared that things were as good as could be considering the circumstances. I could have been dead instead of shopping for baby gear and helping my best friend plan her wedding. That thought was never far away from the front of my brain. I was relieved that things were going semi-smoothly, even though most of it was based on a foundation of lies. It pained me to lie to Chey, but I could not ruin her pre-wedding bliss by waving my accidental pregnancy in her face, and to be completely honest, I found it tough to hang out with her for too long because of my own depression over losing Ben. Misery loves company, preferably someone who is equally as miserable as the other. I did my part as maid of honor, all while keeping my slowly expanding belly a secret. Cheyenne was distracted by the wedding and all things Tucker, so slipping under the radar was easier than anticipated.

CHAPTER THIRTY

Liar, liar panties on fire

Wednesday, September 25th, 2013. Day 126 since my first day at the firm.

Aidan agreed to come with me to my doctor's appointment. "Are you sure you don't mind my being here?"

"No, not at all. It's fine. I don't have anyone else to share the visit with. Besides, it's very exciting; wait till you hear the little heartbeat. It's amazing!" I said enthusiastically, clapping my hands. Aidan smiled warmly at me.

"Okay. I am excited; this is a new experience for me, too." His face fell slightly, and his gaze landed on the floor.

He's thinking about our baby.

"I know," I said as I patted his leg gently. He just shook his head and remained silent. Doctor Miller came into the room and ran through a series of questions about my diet, bothersome symptoms, and options for delivery. She gave me tips to help manage my morning sickness and pamphlets for birthing and parenting classes in the area.

"Shall we take a peek at your baby?" She looked to me, then to Aidan, and I could tell she assumed he was the father.

"I would love to," I squeaked. I was far enough along now that she pulled my top up and used an abdominal probe. The cool gel smeared across my skin as she glided the probe over my little baby bump. Aidan stood beside me staring at the monitor in amazement.

"Okay, Kat. See here, your baby has developed quite a bit since your last appointment. He or she now looks like a little person." The little baby in my belly was kicking and moving all about, even though I was still unable to feel the movements. I couldn't wait to feel my sweet baby kicking.

"I can see that."

"Let's listen to the heartbeat." She pressed a button, and the rapid swooshing sound filled the small exam room. I smiled from ear to ear and looked to Aidan. His brows rose, and he grinned.

"Wow, sounds like a strong little thing," he muttered.

"Yes. The baby has a great heartbeat. Measurements look normal and right on target. Want me to print the pictures?"

"Absolutely!" Aidan answered excitedly before I could. As we walked back to Aidan's car, he stared at the ultrasound photos in his hand. "Kathleen, this is the most incredible thing I have ever experienced. Thanks for sharing it with me." He slung his long arm around my shoulders as we walked. I peered up at him and saw how sincere he was.

"Thanks for coming with me, Aidan. You are still the only one who knows about the baby. It's been great having you around. I think I would be in a very bad way if I didn't have you to force me to get up every day and go on with my life," I admittedly almost shamefully.

"You're in love. Your heart is broken. I know, trust me, I know. But you have so much to look forward to now," he said while holding up the ultrasound pictures and waving them in front of my face.

"I know."

"I think you should tell Ben about the baby." I sat beside him in his car and looked at him bewildered.

"What? No!" I screeched.

"Come on Kathleen. What I just saw in that exam room was... there are no words for it. You shouldn't deny him or the baby a relationship with each other. New girlfriend or not," he said firmly.

"I understand what you are trying to say Aidan, but you just don't get it. He has moved on. He wanted more, he was clear on that, but I was too screwed up to give him, to give us, a proper chance."

"Just think about it is all I'm saying. You know that no matter what, I will be here for you." He took my hand in his and squeezed. I smiled at my ex-husband and new friend.

"I know. As bizarre as this relationship between us may be, I am so glad for it. You have been amazing. I mean it, Aidan, thank you. Feels like I finally let things go, you know?"

"I hope so, Kathleen. You deserve to be happy." His face grew sullen, and I hated that he was battling with his own demons and regret.

Saturday, September 28th, 2013. Day 129 since I started at the firm.

"Damn, Chey, I need help zipping." Cheyenne walked over to me in her silk bridal robe.

"Okay, suck it in girl!" I glanced over my shoulder at her.

"Hey! I'm not fat, dammit! It's my boobs; I can't get the zipper past these things, and I can't exactly suck in my boobs," I said with feigned indignation.

"Oh hush, I'm only joking. Okay, there you go."

"Ouch!" I involuntarily squeaked when she tugged the zipper up, tightly enclosing my tender breasts.

"Crap, did I get you?"

Oh shit!

"Oh, um nope. I'm good." Cheyenne spun me around by my shoulders to look at me.

"Wait a second. Liar, liar, lacey panties on freakin' fire! Kat, your boobs are huge!" She began surveying the full length of me with her blue eyes as wide as they would open.

Gig's up. Here it comes.

"Cheyenne, it's just this dress." She shook her head and wagged her manicured finger at me.

"No way missy! Your hair is super shiny. Your cheeks are flush. And this..." She pointed to my barely concealed baby bump.

"You're pregnant! Holy shit, Kat! Does Ben know?" She folded her arms over her chest and gave me the evil eye.

"Fine, yes, you caught me Chey. I'm pregnant. And no, Ben doesn't know." There was a long pause before a mischievous grin spread across her lips.

"Well, I guess that makes two of us," she said with a wink and a smile.

"What?" I asked utterly confused. All at once, realization hit me. "Oh my God, what? You, you're... oh my God. How? When?" Cheyenne beamed a to-die-for smile and shrugged.

"I don't know how except that by some miracle, that less than ten percent chance worked in my favor. I'm three and a half months Kat! The best part, the baby is healthy, and so am I. We wanted to wait to tell everyone after the wedding. That's why Tucker and I rushed the whole thing." I held my clammy palm over my mouth and stared at her in disbelief.

Oh. My. God.

"Oh, Cheyenne I'm so happy for you and Tuck. I'm sorry I have been hiding from you, but I was so scared to tell you. I didn't want to ruin anything for you two. This is a special time for you with the wedding and all, and I didn't want to be selfish. Only Aidan knew, and he has been so supportive."

"Hey, it's a special time for you, too!" She said as she rubbed my little belly. The water works started, and in our pregnant hormonal state, we wept for a bit while we hugged and congratulated each other. After getting Cheyenne dressed in her gorgeous gown, I helped her put on the finishing touches.

"You look stunning. Really, just... stunning." I wrapped my arms around her for a hug and kissed her on the cheek. "This dress is awesome, Chey. I can't even see your little belly."

"Yeah, well, I can, and let me tell you it's a good thing that this wedding is an intimate affair because I think I would pass out if I had more than a couple of dozen scrutinizing eyes on me at once." We both laughed. The wedding planner stepped into the bridal suite.

"We're ready for you Cheyenne." I winked at my best friend.

"You heard the lady, Chey. Let's go get you hitched." I moved to hand her the bouquet of viking-poms, white daisies, blue delphinium and solid aster wrapped in satin ribbon. Her hand stilled mine.

"Wait. Um, Kat, you should know that at the last minute, Tucker's brother couldn't make it to the wedding, some work related emergency or something. So, uh, Tucker called Ben to fill in," she said as her eyes stayed nervously askance.

"WHAT?" I shouted.

"Kat, please, they have been hanging out, and Tucker has become great friends with Ben. It was only natural for him to ask Ben to fill in, especially since he is the only friend of Tucker's who happens to have a designer tux or two just sitting around handy."

"Dammit. So he's out there right now," I stated more than questioned.

"Mhmm. He's out there." My fingers began rubbing in a circular motion on each of my temples involuntarily.

"The brother who was at the rehearsal last night just had to go?" I asked with closed eyes as my fingers kept working on my temples.

"That's what he said, so when we found out, we asked Ben, and he was happy to step in."

I groaned. "Is his girlfriend here too?" My voice became croaky and annoying, even to my own ears. My eyes were wide and filling with tears again.

HORMONES! I screamed inwardly, entirely fed up with crying all the time.

"I don't know if he brought anyone."

Game face on dammit! I took a deep breath while I kept my eyes closed to gather my resolve. "You know what? It doesn't matter. This is your day. I can manage all my personal drama." I gave my nervous friend a weak smile and snatched up my own bouquet. "Let's do this." When I entered the hallway outside the bridal suite, Ben was standing there looking pensive.

Oh, he is so handsome.

My heart melted at the sight of him in his perfectly tailored tux. He hadn't even noticed that I was in the hall. "Ahem." Ben's head shot up, and his eyes locked on mine. "Hello, Benjamin." His eyes passed over me from head to toe.

Please let him not notice anything different about me.

"Kathleen. Shall we?"

"Yep," I chirped far too excitedly to be convincing. I linked my arm through his, and we began walking to our mark. When our arms touched, my breathing hitched.

"Still there," I whispered barely loud enough for even me to hear. The spark and chemistry was definitely still between us. He was still so impossibly handsome. He still smelled like heaven. I still loved him with the entirety of my existence. Suffocating feelings of depression rushed through me, and it took all the strength within me to remain standing.

This incredible man beside me who happens to be the father of my unborn child will never be mine.

I swallowed hard and stifled my tears. I knew there would be plenty of time to fall apart later. I would have to wait. Aidan looked nice in his suit, and he smiled his signature all-American smile as Ben escorted me down the aisle to our marks beside the altar. Once Ben released me and we both took our places, his eyes found mine and didn't break away through the entire ceremony.

I silently begged him to let me be heartbroken in peace. My pleas went unanswered. The wedding was perfect. The way Tucker and Cheyenne looked together warmed my shattered heart. Ben watched tears of joy and sadness roll down my cheeks as Tucker kissed his bride. Once the ceremony was over, everyone commuted to Rosewood Mansion on Turtle Creek. It was a last resort venue. Cheyenne only agreed to book it because I insisted that it was fine with me. That it was irrelevant that the Rosewood was were the black tie ball was and that was the night that Ben and I had given in to the pull between us for the first time. I lied like the lawyer I should have been. It hurt like hell to be at the Rosewood with not one fleck lingering in the air of the closeness and magic that we had experienced that night. It bit at my heart. My soul ached the moment Cheyenne had even mentioned it to me.

It was a high-end place, and with their wedding being rushed, her options were very limited, so I insisted that she book it. The reception was outdoors. Cheyenne and Tucker's fifty person or so guest list made the magical, outdoor setting possible. There was no need for a sea of tables to be scattered everywhere. There were only two wide, long tables for guests, and a small intimate table for the bride and groom at the head of the two large tables. There was a fair-sized bamboo dance floor. The area was flanked by massive old oak trees. Outdoor lights were strung in a random pattern from tree tops on one side of the dance floor to the other trees, opposite the floor. The lights hung above the bamboo floor with a scattering of Japanese paper lanterns that appeared to be floating over everyone. The warm lighting was dim enough to give the reception a romantic cozy feeling. Flowers matching Cheyenne's bouquet were simply everywhere. There were so many flowers. It made the atmosphere smell divine. Of course, the sweet smell of the flowers only reminded me of my favorite scent and how his manly clean fragrance was far more attractive than any perky pink flower.

I settled into my seat next to Aidan and watched on as Cheyenne and Tucker had their first dance as man and wife. They melted together to the sweet notes of *Song Bird* by Eva Cassidy. Ben's eyes burned holes in me throughout the evening, and I did my very best to keep myself together. Thankfully, the night passed in a flash, and I went home, put on the coziest pajamas I could find and fell to pieces with thoughts of the love I'd lost and my favorite scent.

CHAPTER THIRTY-ONE

Allergies

❦

Cheyenne and Tucker opted out of an extravagant honeymoon for reasons I found out just before she walked down the aisle. Hers was considered a high-risk pregnancy, and she was discouraged from travelling. So, instead of flying off to some exotic island resort, they simply drove a couple of hours away from home to a really great lake cabin for a few days. Cheyenne couldn't be happier to be in some quiet cabin with the dream man that turned her life into a fairytale. The moment they returned from their mini-honeymoon, she dragged me out of my hole for some shopping and babbled on and on about how they fished on the lake for hours every day and cooked only what they caught and made love nonstop and blah-blah-blah. I nearly got ill a few times with what I was calling happiness-induced anaphylaxis. Because Cheyenne was my best friend, she allowed me my peeved scoffs and eye rolling while she recounted her honeymoon. It was yet another reason why she was irreplaceable to me. She understood that I was in love and heartbroken. Though she knew that the subject was a sore spot, she never forgot to ask me every damned day when and how I was going to tell Ben about the baby that was growing at a steady rate within me. I always discounted her meddling and told her she'd be the first to know what the plan was when I came up with one. I never came up with a plan.

Sunday, October 27th, 2013. Day 158 since my first day at the firm.

Nearly a month had passed since the wedding, and I had not seen or heard from Ben again. The only people I saw on a regular basis were Cheyenne, Tucker, and Aidan, of course. I had become a recluse, but my tiny circle of friends were all very understanding and patient with me. Or so I thought. I was still living off my savings and had yet to see any type of return from the stocks or moderate investments I'd made. I suppose if I had the emotion or mental capacity of a normal person, I would have become worried, but depression has quirky way of making all emotions other than utter sorrow disappear. The only thing I had found slightly comical in my state of melancholy was the fact that I single handedly kept up tradition by making sure my birthday the following month would be awful as always.

I managed to get the holy grail of all pregnancy books at Book Ends. Somehow I kept my emotions under control while I walked through the quaint little store that still smelled of new books, coffee, and complimentary cookies. I walked past the cook book section and my resolve to not cry slipped slightly, but I stifled the tears away and kept moving. I paid for my book, declined the bag that the cashier offered, and just stuffed my purchase into my landfill purse. I drove back to my desolate apartment, determined to forget about Ben for the remainder of the day. I was sprawled on my couch staring at the same smudge on the wall that had been the focus of my attention for weeks.

My phone rang, and I saw Cheyenne's picture flash across the screen. I groaned and swept my thumb over the ignore button. I had no desire to talk about the things Cheyenne wanted to talk about. She only had a few conversation topics to pick from lately. Newlywed life and how happy she was, her pregnancy and how ecstatic she was to be a mom, and then there was the third topic. Cheyenne's third favorite thing to discuss was my pregnancy and how once I told Ben about the baby, he and I should kiss and make up. Her words, not mine. My phone immediately began ringing again.

"Ugh. Dammit. Don't want to talk Chey," I mumbled while ignoring the call once again. The phone began ringing, yet again.

"Hello?" I clipped out.

"Kat! Listen. Are you at home?" Cheyenne sounded panicked, and it made my senses go on high alert. I sat up straight and located my keys with my eyes in preparation to go to my friend.

"Yes. What's wrong?" Cheyenne sniffled into the phone, and my heart sank.

Oh God. The baby.

"Chey," I prompted her to speak. She let out an exhausted sigh.

"It's Ben."

My Ben?

My voice began to tremble as I spoke. "What's wrong with Ben?" Cheyenne paused, giving away nothing. My heart constricted further, and my stomach churned queasily. "Cheyenne!" I demanded her to tell me the awful news I could feel coming.

"He—Ben's, I don't know if you know, but he never dropped the thing with Murray. He was attacked, Kat." My hand involuntarily went to my pregnant belly.

"Is he..." *Dead?* I whispered, unable to even say the awful word aloud.

"I don't know much more than that. I'm on my way to get you. We have to get to the hospital to find out if he is hurt badly." Cheyenne hung up while I sat on my couch looking catatonic as Cheyenne later described it. Her words sank in; my heart began beating wildly.

My stomach turned, and I was very close to being sick. I knew without a doubt that if Murray had arranged for someone to attack Ben, he would certainly be hurt badly. I recalled the injuries I endured, and I grimaced, imagining Ben with those types of injuries. I would be destroyed if I lost Ben. I knew I didn't have him physically, but emotionally? I had him. In my heart, Ben was mine, and I was his. I made the mistake of letting circumstances dictate my life and in the process, pushed away the man I loved, the father of my unborn child. With the time and space between us, I realized how much I was really capable of missing a person. I physically ached for him most days, and the nights were always far worse. I ached to feel him, to see him, to smell him, to hear him breathing beside me. Sometimes my chest felt so heavy with grief and loss that I thought that filling my lungs with air was an impossible task.

It hurt to breathe, to think, to exist without him. Distance and time always has a way of putting things into perspective for the misguided. Misguided was merely one way to describe me. When I was with him before, it was easy to get lost in the bad things. I was enraptured with those bad things. I was trapped in my past, and I allowed my irrational need for revenge to destroy the future that was practically kicking down the door to my heart. I was so occupied with the wrong things that I missed the signs that told me I didn't need to be my old self, and I didn't need to finish anything when it came to my abduction and the people involved. Ben had fallen for the current me.

He wanted the current me. Not the me I was before seven years of bad luck erased who I was. He made it clear that he saw glimpses of who I was before, and he wanted me just the way I was when we met at that book store. I wished every moment of every day that I could go back in time to change things instead of being disgusted with myself for ruining the very best thing that had ever happened to me. With Ben out of my life as if he were never really there, all the bad from my past that loomed over me got swallowed up by pure and absolute longing. I knew I'd rather long for him for the rest of my life and never have him again, than to have him and be stuck were I was with an agenda that only included what I thought I wanted, not what I needed.

I waited for Cheyenne to show up, and I prayed that when I arrived at the hospital to see the man I loved, the heart in his chest would still be beating. Cheyenne burst into the apartment that we use to share together.

"Let's go," she ordered. I stood from the couch on my shaky legs and numbly followed her. My mind raced, thinking of all the horrible scenarios that might await me at the hospital. I couldn't bear it if Ben died without my telling him exactly how sorry I was for being so dumb and how much I loved him. Cheyenne drove like a madwoman while I sat beside her, trying my best to pull myself together. I was so lost in my own head that I hadn't even noticed that we came to a stop in front of Ben's house and parked beside Tucker's truck. "We gotta run in and get Tucker; he's been working on something for Ben. I tried calling him, but his phone is off. Hurry," Cheyenne rambled. I grabbed my purse, leaped from Cheyenne's car without hesitation and trailed behind her to Ben's door. Without knocking she strode right in, and I followed. "Tuck?" she shouted through the foyer.

"In here," Tucker's deep voice boomed from the sitting room. We walked to the sitting room, and just before we entered, Cheyenne turned to face me. She grabbed me by my shoulders and looked me squarely in the eyes.

"I love you, Kat. You can be pissed but you'll thank me some day."

What?

Without further explanation, Cheyenne stepped behind me. She gripped me by the shoulders and steered me into the sitting room where I saw Tucker sitting across from the most beautiful sight I could have imagined.

CHAPTER THIRTY-TWO

Pieces

There he was. My Ben on his sofa with his head in his hands, and he looked like the most beautiful, disheveled, out-of-sorts man that I had ever laid eyes on. He was wearing pajama pants that I could see hung lazily off his hips. He wore a white undershirt that had seen better days. The stubble that had grown to a suitable beard appeared to be at least a week old. His hair was disorderly in the most delectable way. My fingers ached to run through his thick, wavy, chocolate brown locks. Ben dropped his hands from his head and looked up at me while I stood motionless, doing all I could to not faint.

"Not hurt," I mumbled.

"Sorry," Cheyenne and Tucker said in unison as they slipped from view. A second or two later, I heard the heavy front door open and shut. Ben and I stared at each other for what felt like ages. Finally he spoke.

"I had no idea they did this. Tuck just told me what they had done when you walked in the door." He put up his hands defensively. I continued staring in silence. "But you came," Ben stated looking somewhat puzzled.

"You're not hurt." My voice came out broken.

I'm gonna kill Chey!

Ben shrugged. "No, not physically." I winced at his implication. A tsunami of emotion crested and toppled over me. My composure crumbled, and my legs moved of their own volition, taking me to where he sat. I was sent crashing into Ben on the couch thanks to the momentum that drove me towards him. The familiar strong arms that I loved to be wrapped in encased my shuddering body.

"Hey. I'm okay." His warm breath caressed the shell of my ear. I began sobbing and hiccoughing, and if I had been in anyone else's presence, I would have been mortified at my emotional display.

"She, they, they said you were h-hurt. I thought maybe y-you were..." The words sputtered out of my mouth through sobs and sniffles. His arms held me tightly to his body.

"They shouldn't have done that to you. I know how you feel. Thinking the worst." His words and the memory of him telling me how he went out of his mind while I was missing caused my body to shudder and shake even harder. My Ben always did know how to read me like a book.

"Shh. It's okay," he cooed into my ear. "Come on. I'll get you some tissue and something to drink." He held me tightly to his side as he stood lifting us both from his couch. I was instantly reminded of my pregnant belly that was hidden discretely beneath the oversized hooded sweater I wore. When we stood together, my junky purse fell from my lap, and the contents went skittering across Ben's floor.

"I got it," I quickly volunteered then crouched down and began shoving things back into my bag with shaky hands. I finished picking up the mess, and Ben gripped his long fingers around my elbow and guided me into his kitchen.

"What would you like to drink? I think I still have a bottle of that wine you liked. A drink to relax might help," he mumbled while his eyes scanned the refrigerator in his luxurious kitchen.

"Um, no thanks. No wine."

Not since August 23rd when I found out about our baby, actually, I quipped inwardly.

"What would you like then?" he asked while looking through his refrigerator.

"Water is fine." Ben took out a bottle of water and slid it to me across his granite counter. I squirmed uncomfortably, not completely sure what I should say to him. "Thanks." That was all I could come up with. It was pathetic, and I knew it.

It was painfully obvious why Cheyenne had gone to such drastic, insane, awful, cruel, measures to get the two of us into the same room. She wanted me to tell Ben about the baby and confess to him how much I loved him. I just wasn't at all sure if I was ready to say those things. I hadn't planned on seeing him today. I had no idea how I should tell this man what I needed to say. He noticed my fidgeting as he watched me closely.

"Let's go back and sit down." I glanced up at him, and I knew that he knew something was up.

"Okay," I agreed weakly. His hand rested on the small of my back as I had come to expect him to do, but this time his touch made my body hum with pent-up emotion and physical desire. We sat down on the couch with plenty of space between us. He handed me a huge wad of tissues and kept watching me closely as he always did.

"Since you're here, I need some answers, Kathleen."

What? My brows furrowed.

"What? Why?"

He drew in a deep breath and sighed. "Because I need to know a few things so that I can have some closure."

Closure? Ouch!

I was sure that I winced at his mention of closure. So he has moved on. On the inside I slumped forward, gathered my head in my hands, and cried uncontrollably. But that was just on the inside. The outside was a different story. I sat as straight backed as I could and put on the bravest face I could pull together.

"Fine. Fire away, Ben." I huffed and blotted away the tears on my face.

"First and foremost, why did you quit the firm?"

Oh crap, here we go.

I inhaled deeply and set my water down on the coffee table. "You know why I quit, Ben." His jaw tightened.

"Are you fucking him? Are you back with Aidan?" My brows knitted together, and I felt my cheeks redden as my temper flared.

"Fuck you, Ben!" I shouted as I crossed and uncrossed my arms in frustration.

"You didn't answer the question." His tone was menacingly low, causing all my tears and sadness to temporarily ebb away, leaving only my steadily rising anger.

"Not that it's any business of yours, but no, I'm not fucking Aidan or anyone else for that matter. Aidan transferred here, and we are just friends, Ben. Which is more than I can say for you and me." He closed his eyes tightly for a moment at my verbal jab.

"Fine, why haven't I seen you anywhere? I have gone to the coffee shop we like nearly every day, and I have yet to see you there."

Doctor says caffeine is not good for the baby.

"Going there reminded me of you, so I found another coffee shop." I shrugged casually as I lied. I made sure to avoid Ben's skeptical stare since I knew how easily he could peer into my head.

"Okay. Why haven't you called me?" My head snapped back in shock.

"What?! Me contact you? I really don't think your lovely lady friend would appreciate your ex fuck buddy contacting you." He narrowed his eyes on me.

"Don't dare refer to yourself that way. You were far more than a fuck buddy as you so eloquently put it." He growled at me with a stern finger pointed in my direction, and I lost a measure of courage.

"Whatever." I rolled my eyes dismissively.

"You think I'm seeing someone?"

Please don't make me do this, I pleaded inwardly. I inhaled and shut my eyes trying to picture a relaxing scene, but only came up with the memory of the leggy brunette kissing Ben on the cheek. "I saw you," I whispered with my eyes still sealed shut. Ben slid across the cushions closer to me.

"You saw me doing what, might I ask?" His voice had softened, and I wanted nothing more than to melt into him.

"I came to see you in August, and I saw you drive up with a pretty brunette in your car. She kissed you on the cheek. She looked smitten with you." Tears began gathering again, so I turned away from Ben and fidgeted with nonexistent lint on my comfortable belly-accommodating yoga pants.

I shook my head and kept my focus fixed on my pants leg. I felt him slide even closer to me. He was so close to my side that I felt the warmth radiating from his body.

"What's going on with you, Kathleen?" he asked softly. I stilled my hands.

Tell him! My conscience screamed at me. I shook my head. "Nothing is going on with me, Ben. I'm fine." Even I heard the lack of conviction in my voice. I was far from fine. I was anything but fine. I was heartbroken, moderately depressed, pregnant with Ben's baby, unemployed, and a host of other things too innumerable to list. Ben backed away from me, and tears streamed down my conflicted face. I couldn't stave off my emotions anymore. Ben pushed me further.

"No, you are not! Tell me now, Kathleen," he demanded in a stern voice. "I won't accept any more bullshit from you! I deserve some answers, not this crap you've been handing me!"

Oh, fuck it!

I turned in my seat so that my shoulders were squared with his and let the flood gates open. Tears streamed freely like rivers down my face as I disintegrated before him. "What do want me to say Ben? What the hell do you want to hear? Huh? You want to hear that I am utterly broken? Depressed, miserable without you? Hmm? That you are all I think about? That I lie awake at night thinking about your skin against mine and that it makes my body ache? Literally fucking ache to feel your touch!" I widened my eyes and raised my brows dramatically. "Or maybe you want to hear the whole screwed up truth about my past and why I'm stuck there! Okay, fine! Let's see if this helps you get some closure!" His face went blank, and I overrode his attempt to interrupt.

"Kat—"

"Nope! You asked for it, Ben. You're getting it." I bombarded him with all the terrible truths about my past. I told him about neglecting my dreams and hating myself for having spent so much time with a man who betrayed me. When I told him about the baby I had lost, his shoulders slumped, and sympathy filled his eyes.

"Shit, Kat. I'm sorry. I'm so sorry you went through all of that." Tears kept pouring from my eyes as I exposed my past to Ben.

"I came here to Dallas to start over, Ben. I came here to get better. To find the part of me that I had lost years ago. That's what the tattoo is all about. I found you when I got here, and I tried hard to fight away my feelings for you. To lock away my emotions, but I failed miserably. Then you ripped my heart out when you sent me packing since I was too screwed up and stubborn. I wanted to try, Ben, but I didn't want to hurt either one of us! I wanted to try to get my crap together for you, for us and—" My gaze caught on something peeking from under the edge of the coffee table.

Shit! My book! I jumped to pick it up before Ben could see the pregnancy book I had bought. Ben's deep blue-green eyes that always had a way of reading my mind, followed my gaze to the floor. I glanced at him, and a confused crease marred the space between his brows. "I got it!" I said as I slid forward on the cushion to reach down for the book. I had my bag beside my feet so I thought if I could just slide the book from under the edge of the table and quickly get it into my bag, he would be none the wiser. I would have bought myself more time to figure out how to tell him about the baby. That's when our baby changed my plans again. When I leaned forward, something amazing happened. I felt something happen within me. A flutter then a very clear kick from my little baby. I froze and gasped. I righted my shoulders and my hand involuntarily slipped under my sweater to rest on my pregnant belly. Ben's eyes got wide.

"What's wrong?" he asked in a worried voice as he surveyed the look on my face, then my hand on my stomach. Before I could even work on conjuring any lousy excuses of cramps or food poisoning. He reached forward and fished out the book that barely peeked out from under his table. I watched him, completely frozen to my seat in amazement and hoping for more little moves from my baby. I watched his face pale and his chest rise and fall faster. "Wh-what's this?" He held up the book.

Now or never, I guess.

"What's it look like, Ben?" I asked quietly. He looked irritated. In a flash he was inches from me. He reached down and pulled my sweater up to beneath my breasts. "Hey!" I cried out. His mouth popped open.

"Y-You... You're pregnant?"

Guilty.

His eyes bulged, his voice was ragged, and he looked moments away from passing out. "You should sit back and relax. You don't look so good, Ben." His eyes were glazed over, and he looked upset.

"You're having a baby." He whispered with a clear undertone of disappointment.

Ouch. He doesn't want me or the baby. Great.

"Ben, I should leave." I made a move to stand, and he gripped me by the wrist with one hand while the other still held up my baggy sweater. He was just staring off into space.

"Who's the father?" he asked quietly. I scoffed and jerked my wrist from his grip. I was pissed at his implication and jerked my sweater from his other hand and allowed it to fall back into position.

"I'm no whore Ben! I'm over four months pregnant. You do the math, genius!" His eyes snapped back to me, and the glazed look was gone.

"Me?" he questioned.

"You got it, chief!"

"How? You were on the pill."

"I missed two pills when John had me. I tried catching up, but I didn't realize that doing that runs the risk of getting pregnant."

"I'm going to be a dad?"

"Um, yes. It would appear so." He became angry, so I dropped the smart mouth.

"Didn't feel the need to tell me? Shit, Kathleen! I've missed so much already." He pointed at my belly and it made me want to cower in the corner. "You are one selfish woman!"

"I'm sorry; I was licking my wounds when I found out about the baby and came to tell you, but saw you with the new woman in your life so I just kept the pregnancy to myself. This baby doesn't change the fact that we aren't together anymore, and you have moved on."

"Like hell! It changes everything, Kathleen, and the woman you saw was most definitely NOT my girlfriend or anything even close! She's my brother's girlfriend. I was looking over a contract for her."

Ah, shit.

Nausea bubbled up and began to consume me. I wasn't sure if it was due to my hormones or the fact that I hid from Ben because I was too much of a coward to talk to him since I assumed the brunette was his new woman.

"Oh God. I-uh-I don't feel so great." I pressed the palm of my hand to my forehead and leaned forward to rest my forehead on my knees.

"What's wrong? What do I do?" I could hear the worry in Ben's voice, and it was endearing, even through the powerful urge to be sick.

"I'll be alright, Ben; just give me a minute." He dismissed my assertion and tucked me into his side. We stood from the sofa again, and he guided me up the stairs to his room. The same room that I use to call mine for a brief time.

"You should lie down here. I'll get a damp washcloth. Stay here."

Don't think I could go anywhere right now.

A moment later, Ben returned with a glass of juice and a damp washcloth. "Here, sit up." I complied, and he lifted the sweater over my head and removed my shoes. I lay back to my left side while he folded the washcloth and pressed it to my neck. I began sobbing like the emotional, depressed, hormonal pregnant woman that I was.

"I'm so sorry. I'm so, so sorry, Ben." My voice cracked and wavered through my sobs.

"It's okay; don't think about any of that right now." Ben removed his shoes and slid into the bed behind me. His body spooned with mine and reminded me of how perfect we fit together. I lay in his bed in just my socks, yoga pants, and snug cotton tee. I sobbed harder thinking about how right Ben was and my shoulders rocked. "Shhh. Baby, don't cry."

Baby?

My heart and brain both stumbled on the words he whispered sweetly into my ear. I had been dying to be back in his arms. To be his baby again.

"You're right about me. I'm selfish," I whispered back through my tears. "You deserve so much more than me, Ben. I'll never forgive myself for screwing up everything."

"Don't. Just stop right there." His arms squeezed me tighter, and his voice grew stern. "I screwed up plenty, too. I never should have spoken to you like I did that day in my office. I shouldn't have been so I to think that if I pushed you away, gave you a taste of your own medicine, you'd wake up and realize that I wanted you. That I had fallen in love with you." My heart skipped a beat at his confession. He rolled me to my back and ran his thumb across my bottom lip the way that made my stomach flip. He leaned in and kissed me tenderly. I felt wanted, cherished, forgiven. His kiss intensified. His tongue slid like satin into my mouth caressing mine. I moaned softly, cupped his face and gave him everything I had. I wanted to show him how much I loved him. How much I needed him. He broke away from my lips and placed soft kisses on my cheek.

"Baby, I wish you would have just told me."

"I wanted to."

He resumed our kiss and pulled me closer to him. My hands roamed over his tight body. He rose above me, and I opened myself to him. He settled himself between my legs and pulled my shirt over my head. His hands swept down my chest to my belly. His eyes glistened.

"You're having my baby," he whispered. I smiled and nodded. His eyes came back to mine. His expression was wanting, pleading.

"Undress," I said. He stripped down to his boxer briefs while never letting his eyes leave mine. I had forgotten how perfect Ben's body was, and I suddenly felt very inadequate, but as if he were reading my mind, he said the perfect thing.

"I didn't think it was possible for you to be any more beautiful. I was wrong." His words were like a warm blanket wrapping me up. His eyes left mine and skated down my body to my belly.

"I felt the baby move for the first time on the couch." I shared the detail that changed the course our evening took. Ben's eyes widened.

"Really?" I nodded in affirmation. He looked like he was deep in thought at how to proceed, so I did it for him.

"Lie down." Without pause he moved from between my thighs and lay down beside me. I slid off my pants, then sat up and tossed one leg over his body to straddle him. I put my hands behind my back and unclipped my bra. I tossed it aside and watched Ben's eyes skate over my body. I had been slightly worried about how my body had changed, but he seemed to be appraising my curves just as he had done so many times before. Maybe even more.

"I think I like you pregnant more." He teased while cupping my enlarged, bare breasts in his hands. We both laughed at his teasing. I pulled his hungry hands from my breasts and slid them slowly down my ribs and brought them to a rest so that his hands were cupping my belly. His eyes were watching with an expression of wonder in them as my hands moved his hands to where his baby was growing within me. I reminded myself that all of this news was only minutes old to him, and I made sure to use kid gloves with him. I held his hands there for a moment, then let mine fall away to my sides. His large hands remained cupping my pregnant belly. His eyes were fixed there. I remained silent, allowing him to take everything in. He remained that way for a long time. He said nothing, only stared at his own hands resting on my stomach. Finally I interrupted his concentrated stare.

"Ben? Are you okay?" He only nodded while still staring silently. "Ben? What are you doing?" He finally looked up at me.

"Waiting." He said flatly.

"For?"

"For the baby to move again. I want to feel it." That's when I began laughing so hard I nearly peed myself, and my side began to cramp. I rolled off of Ben and clutched my aching side. "What? I think it's only fair for me to get to feel the baby kick, too." He admonished sounding only slightly pouty. I kept working at gathering my composure.

"Oh, Ben you can't sit and stare with your hands on my belly all day waiting on him or her to make a move." My laughing came back again full force, and the fluttering started again. I stopped laughing and grabbed Ben's hand. I let his palm rest against my stomach where I could feel our little baby squirming and kicking about. "I think my laughing woke up the baby. Doctor Miller says the babies do pretty much nothing but sleep non-stop." Ben shushed me. I mean actually shushed me like a parent would a child. Our baby moved, and Ben's face lit up.

"I felt it," he whispered. The slight movements faded away, and Ben looked like he was ready to pop open champagne to celebrate. He was so pleased that he got to feel our little baby fluttering around. "That was... incredible." His eyes were wide and intrigued.

"Yeah, it was." His eyes grew heated, and I knew that my man wanted to make our reunion official. I obliged.

"Are you mine?" His words were husky, filled with lust and passion.

"I always have been." With that he slipped off his boxer briefs, freeing his erection. He gently tugged my panties free from my hips and once again placed himself between my open, inviting thighs. I wrapped my legs around his waist and silently begged for him. I could see the apprehension written on his face. "It's fine. You aren't going to hurt me, Ben." His eyes read mine, and he positioned himself at my slick opening. He slid the crown of his erection into me, then the full length of him. I had forgotten how exquisite he felt filling my body with himself. He sank slowly into me, sheathing every pulsing, hard inch of himself with my ravenous body. He rested himself on his bent elbows, caging me and allowing for just enough space to look at each other. Once he was fully buried inside of me, his lips found mine, and they tangled in a kiss like none we had ever shared. His rugged facial hair tickled across my jaw as he moved back and forth planting seductive kisses on my lips, jaw, neck, and ears.

"Promise you'll stay with me, baby." He eased into a sensual rhythm, thrusting in and out of me and rolling his hips deliciously, stimulating every part of me.

"I'm staying right here." Ben sighed in relief and scattered kisses over my skin. The physical connection we were sharing mirrored the emotional connection that had been there even through the months we spent apart. I laced my fingers through his silky hair, and I kept my green eyes locked on the vivid blue-green depths. His breathing was labored just as mine was. We weren't having just sex. We were making love, and it felt as natural as drawing breath. Like it was a concept invented specifically for us. He slowly and sweetly built both of us to a delectable climax. His lips landed on mine, and I moaned into his mouth as a powerful orgasm raced through my body. My body clenched around Ben, and he erupted, spilling himself into me. We rode the wave of our orgasms together. Tears of joy and relief seeped from the corners of my eyes and rolled down my temples into my hair. Ben stayed planted in me while kissing me breathlessly again.

"I love you," I murmured against his lips. He kissed me for a moment longer before pulling his full lips from mine.

"I've been waiting so long to hear those words come out of your mouth so that I can say them back." He brushed his thumb across my trembling bottom lip. "I love you, too, baby." I took in his words and let them wash over me.

He loves me.

I let his words breathe fresh life into me and chase away the darkness that encompassed my every waking moment for months. I let those three words banish the terrible past and fill my heart with promise and hope for the future. A future that I prayed I'd share with Ben at my side. I fell to pieces beneath him and was put back together all at the same time. I was his. I was whole.

EPILOGUE

March 26th 2014

"C'mon, get up Chey! Seriously, no more dragging your swollen feet." I stifled a giggle at my snarky little jab. Cheyenne rolled away from me into the mountain of pillows around her and groaned a long string of inaudible words. "Nope, let's go." I demanded. I was anxious to get the show on the road. Cheyenne clearly wasn't.

"I just got comfortable enough to sleep, like, five freakin' minutes ago, Kat!" she whined. I laughed at my best friend's pathetic attempt at laser-eyeing me to death.

"I know how you feel. I sympathize; I really do. Now let's go. Doc said we have to be there by 7AM!" She huffed dramatically and rolled out of the bed she shared with Tucker. He stood at the open door and watched his very, very, pregnant wife shooting dirty looks in every direction. I was still immune to those laser eyes and lucky for Tucker, he was too.

Ouch! Ignore it. Not today, no way.

I thought about the tightening feeling in my swollen belly. I knew that even though I wasn't quite due, I could easily be in real labor. I had endured a few false alarms that set my world on its side because it was far too early for our sweet baby to make a debut. "Let's go already! I'm dying to dig out these cigars!" Ben's deep voice boomed from down the stairs. I shook my head knowing that he was serious about the cigars. He had waved the foul smelling things in my face when he brought them home. "Celebratory cigars" is what he said they wIre. i thought about how it was unfair that the men got to smoke cigars while the wives who just gave birth lie spent and exhausted in some uncomfortable hospital bed. I never voiced my opinion, of course. I just smiled sweetly and said "That's great, baby." We convoyed across town to the hospital and got Cheyenne all checked in, and the show began. Cheyenne was scheduled for a cesarean section that day since her little guy refused to cooperate and nestled himself into a cozy, albeit inconvenient, breech position. Doctors had no choice but to go forward with a cesarean section. Cheyenne was right on target at forty weeks pregnant, and we could not be happier that she was able to conceive and carry her miracle baby to full term. I was thirty-eight weeks pregnant and sat in the waiting room trying to decipher whether or not the contractions that I was feeling were the real deal or not.

Can't be in labor right now. It's Cheyenne's day. Oh, hold off just a little longer, would you? I begged inwardly, hoping that our baby could hear my pleas and sit tight just a day or two longer, but it would seem that Benjamin Chase's offspring inherited his strong genes because my begging went unanswered, and right there in the waiting room, my water broke.

"Uh-oh" I whispered.

"Uh-oh? What is uh-oh?" Ben jumped up from his seat, and his large frame went rigid when he looked down and saw the puddle of amniotic fluid on the floor. "Oh shit, baby, you, oh shit—" Ben began looking around and panicking.

"Ben!" His attention snapped to me. "Calm down. We're in a hospital. Remember? It's going to be okay. We need to tell a nurse that I'm in labor." I remained as calm as I could for my husband's benefit, but on the inside I was more nervous than the day we were married.

The day that Cheyenne and Tucker tricked me into going to Ben's house, we said we loved each other for the first time, and not a minute later after making love, Ben reached into his nightstand and withdrew the most breathtaking vintage diamond solitaire ring. He told me that his mom passed it down to him the day after she met me in his living room. It had been her mother's ring. She died years before, and the staggering big glistening diamond ring now belonged to Ben. She had told him that I was 'the one.'

He apparently agreed since he pulled out that ring, and with tears in both of our eyes, he asked me to spend the rest of my life as Mrs. Benjamin Chase. I said yes, of course, and Ben had me moved into the house with him the next day. We were married only two months later under tall oaks on Turtle Creek. Aidan was at our wedding and had been around, but not nearly as much as he was when he first moved to Dallas. I couldn't be sure, but I suspected there was a new lady in his life. He never volunteered any information, and I never meddled. Things were comfortable between us, and I planned on it staying that way.

Things at the firm settled down, though Janis' whereabouts were still a mystery. John Murray was apprehended in Mexico and extradited back to the United States where he was now awaiting trial on charges a mile long, including the murder of Mrs. Kemp's husband. Turns out, Murray's goons sang like I knew they would when they were caught at the Canadian border. They were offered a deal in exchange for their testimony against John Murray, and they took it. My night terrors still tormented me, but Ben was a healing presence at my side every night. I had long since dropped my snooping efforts, but Janis was never far from my mind. Not knowing where she was made me uneasy, and I knew being too complacent could cause disasters. I found that out the hard way at the hands of one bat wielding overweight guy and his muscle bound side-kick.

"Oh, that's strong," I said while trying my best to keep breathing. Ben held my hand dutifully through each contraction and coached me just as he had learned in the labor and delivery classes we attended. He was fantastic when it came time to deliver our little angel. I was and still am one lucky woman. We welcomed seven pound, two ounce, Serafina Esme Chase to the world. Our brown-haired, blue-eyed angel was born a mere four hours after our godson, Marshall Charles Barrett.

All of that brings me to the present where I sit comfortably in the living room of the home that Ben and I share. I was sorting through the hordes of congratulatory greeting cards that our friends, family, and Ben's associates had sent us. I slit the seam of yet another card open and looked up from my lap. I could think of no sight I loved more than the one before me. Our precious newborn, Serafina, swaddled in her pink blanket as my husband slowly swayed to and fro with her tucked safely in his arms. My seven years of bad luck brought me here, and here couldn't possibly feel any better than it already did. I flipped open the greeting card, and my blood turned to ice.

"No," I mumbled. I was looking at the birth announcement that I mailed out to everyone we know. The photo is of Ben and me cuddled up with our sweet baby girl. It was the perfect photo and choosing it from the lot of photos was an easy task. Except this one that had been sent back to me is not what I sent out to everyone. Not by a long shot. This was our photo alright, but someone has vigorously scratched out both Serafina's and my faces.

Who would have done this?

I was frightened and panicked now. Me being threatened is one thing, but our innocent, newborn child being threatened by someone who was hiding behind an anonymous envelope was a whole new world of fear, anxiety, and anger that I was being thrown into. I knew who the hell did this.

I held up the destroyed photo, and Ben's swaying stopped. He stood frozen in place, and his face has paled as he took in the disturbing picture. I looked him in the face. "Told you that psycho bitch needed to be stopped."

ACKNOWLEDGEMENTS

I have always believed that people are born with a predetermined calling. A teacher is born to one day teach. A singer is born to one day sing. A writer is born to one day write. I know that writing was what I was born to do. It is as natural and necessary to my existence as drawing breath. Along the line somewhere, I misplaced my pen and paper. I longed to have them back, but knew not where to look. Then one day, someone gave me back my pen and paper. To this person, I say, thank you. I am indebted.

To the countless friends who have supported me so vocally. Your encouragement and support were necessary tools in the writing of this book. Thank you.

To all my friends in the Indie author community: You all are an outstanding group of talented people who humble, inspire, encourage and entertain me everyday merely with your presence in my small world. Thank you for including me in yours.

To my family, a beautiful group of people with varying personalities without which I would live a dreadful, boring life: You are all invaluable to me. To my mother: You have been nothing but supportive in my endeavor to write. You have spent countless hours perched on a stool beside my desk listening to me read my work aloud. Your enthusiasm and encouragement have never wavered, and I thank you for that. It has been a gift beyond measure.

To Mandi: You are my Cheyenne. You are the muse to my writing and my life. You are a beacon of light through the dark when it threatens to cloak my world. It's you who I look to when I need a laugh, a shoulder, an ear, or a friend. Thank you for being you. Your friendship, support, understanding, honesty, and love enrich my life even further every day. I love you forever. Together, we take flight.

SEVEN YEARS of BAD LUCK

Playlist

⚜

"Anchored" by Tony Lucca
"Some Devil" by Dave Mathews
"Trust In Me" by Etta James
"Baby I Want You" by Amos Lee
"Shelter" by Ray LaMontagne
"Edge Of Desire" by John Mayer
"Bluebird" by Sara Bareilles
"Slow Like Honey" by Fiona Apple
"Give Me Love" by Ed Sheeran
"It Will Rain" by Bruno Mars
"Show You Love" by Cas Haley
"Falling Slowly" by Glen Handsard, Marketa Irglova
"I Want You" by Third Eye Blind
"Blue In Green" by Miles Davis

I'd like to thank all the artists that have been such an inspiration to listen to during the writing of Seven Years of Bad Luck. Many of the scenes in the book really came to life for me thanks to great music playing in my office. If you haven't heard any of the artists I've mentioned, by all means, go and purchase their music.

ABOUT THE AUTHOR

USA Today Best Selling Author, J.L. Mac is twenty-seven years old and currently resides in El Paso, Texas, where she enjoys living near her family. She was born and raised in Galveston, Texas. J.L. admittedly has had a long and sordid love affair with the written word and has loved every minute of it. She drinks too many glasses of wine on occasion, and says way too many swear words to be considered "lady-like." J.L. spends her free time reading, writing, and playing with her children

Twitter @JLMacbooks
Facebook- www.facebook.com/jlmacbooks
Blog http://jlmacbooks.blogspot.com/